NEARLY FOUND

NEARLY FOUND

ELLE COSIMANO

Kathy Dawson Books

an imprint of Penguin Group (USA) LLC

KATHY DAWSON BOOKS
Published by the Penguin Group
Penguin Group (USA) LLC
375 Hudson Street, New York, New York 10014

USA/Canada/UK/Ireland/Australia/New Zealand/India/South Africa/China
penguin.com
A Penguin Random House Company

Library of Congress Cataloging-in-Publication Data
Cosimano, Elle, author.
Nearly found / Elle Cosimano.
pages   cm
Summary: High school senior and science whiz Nearly Boswell, called Leigh,
is thrilled when she gets an internship in a forensic science lab, since it is a step
toward college and a way out of the trailer park—but soon she finds herself the target
of a serial killer, one who seems to know a lot about the residents of
Sunny View Trailer Park as well as her absent father's secrets.
ISBN 978-0-8037-3927-7 (hardcover)
1. Serial murderers—Juvenile fiction. 2. Murder—Juvenile fiction. 3. Criminal
investigation—Juvenile fiction. 4. Crime laboratories—Juvenile fiction. 5. Trailer
camps—Juvenile fiction. 6. High schools—Juvenile fiction. 7. Families—Juvenile
fiction. [1. Serial murderers—Fiction. 2. Criminal investigation—Fiction. 3. Crime
laboratories—Fiction. 4. Trailer camps—Fiction. 5. Internship programs—Fiction.
6. Mystery and detective stories.] I. Title.
PZ7.C8189Nd 2015   [Fic]—dc23   2014040313

Printed in the United States of America
1 3 5 7 9 10 8 6 4 2

Designed by Nancy R. Leo-Kelly
Text set in Dante

For my parents,
who helped me find myself

❖ ❖ ❖

"WHEREVER HE STEPS, whatever he touches, whatever he leaves, even unconsciously, will serve as a silent witness against him. Not only his fingerprints or his footprints, but his hair, the fibers from his clothes, the glass he breaks, the tool mark he leaves, the paint he scratches, the blood or semen he deposits or collects. All of these and more, bear mute witness against him. This is evidence that does not forget. It is not confused by the excitement of the moment. It is not absent because human witnesses are. It is factual evidence. Physical evidence cannot be wrong, it cannot perjure itself, it cannot be wholly absent. Only human failure to find it, study and understand it, can diminish its value."

—*Dr. Edmond Locard*

PROLOGUE

TJ WILES SAT BEHIND ME in chemistry class for nine months before I knew he was a killer. If I'd ever bothered to pay attention, I might have known sooner. I could have sensed the bitterness he felt for my father, my family, the rage boiling inside him. Maybe I would have felt what he was becoming, in time to save the people he killed.

But my occasional backward glance wasn't enough to see him for what he was.

I hadn't been able to see my father truly either. Once upon a time, he'd been the man who took me to Belle Green Park to play, who held me in his lap and did stupid magic tricks just to make me laugh.

But David Boswell was a thief. A liar and a conman who used his ability to taste emotion—by touching a person's skin—to prey on his own friends, siphoning their assets to finance his illegal activities, using their clean money to launder his own. Because he could always tell what they were feeling, he was uncannily disarming, easily able to gain their confidence and assuage their fears. He played TJ Wiles's father like a card, then tossed him aside when the stakes got too high, before disappearing altogether five years ago.

TJ had lived in Belle Green once, in a huge brick house with a manicured lawn as green as the golf course it nestled up to. But after TJ's father went to prison, TJ's mother committed suicide and TJ was left to live with his uncle here in Sunny View trailer park. A football scholarship had become his only hope for getting out—the same way the chemistry scholarship had become mine. He'd played hard, like his entire future depended on it, until the day he blew out his knee, and his entire future went with it.

My father hadn't just hurt TJ and his family. He'd ripped TJ apart, leaving a dark hole inside TJ's chest where his heart used to be. A space TJ imagined he could only fill by taking from me everything he'd lost. Two months ago, TJ testified that his hatred of my family drove him to kill four of my classmates in an attempt to frame me and exact some kind of twisted retribution against my father. TJ's victims—kids I'd been tutoring, kids I'd cared about—were gone and they were never coming back. Posie, Teddy, Marcia, and Kylie. They'd still be alive if it hadn't been for what my father did.

TJ hadn't succeeded in destroying my life like he'd planned. But he had taken my chance at a scholarship, my two best friends, and my ability to trust people without imagining the worst in them.

I'd spent years looking for messages from my father, scanning newspapers, mapping out the places I thought he might have been since he disappeared. I had so many questions—the kind my mother couldn't answer because she had no idea what my father and I were capable of—that conman David Boswell and his daughter, Nearly, were both capable of tasting other people's emotions just by touching their skin. I'd believed that if I found my father, I'd have all the answers and my world would make sense.

But the one person I had more in common with than anyone on the planet had caused so much damage that four people were dead.

Knowing who my father was, how could I keep searching for him? What if the only place left to look for him was somewhere in myself?

I pulled out the red thumbtacks from the map on the wall of my bedroom. One for every city where I suspected my father had been—Jersey City, New Orleans, Las Vegas, Los Angeles. I tried not to wonder how many other lives my father had ruined along the way.

The pins prickled the inside of my fist. I dropped them into the wastebasket, massaging the marks they left in my skin and watching them fade. A scientist named Locard came up with the idea that we leave trace evidence of ourselves in every encounter, and that we in turn take something from everyone we touch, even if we can't see it.

And those traces of my father—the pain he'd left behind in the people he'd stolen from, the genes I carried that made me just like him—terrified me.

I

Gravel crunched in front of my trailer and the muted bass of a stereo blew in through the open windows. I licked peanut butter from my fingers and pulled back the curtain. The fabric smelled like smoke, even though my mom had quit smoking two months ago.

Outside, heat waves radiated from the hood of the old black Mercedes that blocked my front porch. Reece Whelan sat in the driver's seat, wearing aviator sunglasses, his lips moving to lyrics I couldn't make out.

I threw open the front door as he eased out of the car.

"Where's your bike?" I asked, letting the screen door slam behind me.

He leaned back, his arms thrown wide to showcase the Benz. "What, don't you like it?"

I bit my lip, taking in the way his T-shirt stretched across the broad planes of his chest. "Oh, I love it. But doesn't it belong to *Detective* Petrenko?"

Reece took the front porch steps two at a time and pulled me into him, looking smug. I still hadn't quite gotten used to his tightly shorn hair, the soft prickly way it felt against my fingers when I ran my hands through it. His shirt smelled like Armor All and car leather. Different from the worn leather jacket I loved to bury my face in on the back of his bike. But under all that was the familiar citrus and sandalwood smell of his cologne and I drank him in.

He dangled the keys between us. "He probably won't miss it. Want to take it for a spin? It has air-conditioning," Reece teased.

He leaned in to kiss me but I held him at arm's length. "Wait. You *stole* Alex Petrenko's car?"

He arched a pierced brow. "I didn't steal it. I borrowed it. I stopped over at Gena's place to check in. Petrenko was there. They were . . . otherwise occupied." Reece let his eyes brush over me in a top-down way that still managed to make my knees watery, even when I wanted to strangle him.

I fought back a smile. "Okay. I get it. And?"

"And his keys were on the kitchen counter. I knocked on the bedroom door, and shouted 'Can I borrow your car?' He screamed something that sounded like *Yes, yes. Hell, yes.* Then Gena hollered something about getting the hell out of their house. So I did. And here I am." He beamed, still waggling the keys. "With air-conditioning."

The Benz dripped condensation from its underbelly onto the gravel. With every drop, I counted the number of ways we could get in trouble for this. Gena was an undercover narcotics officer tasked with supervising Reece, who was working as an informant in exchange for being let go after a drug bust last year. She was also engaged to Detective Alex Petrenko.

"Don't look so freaked out," Reece said. "Petrenko probably doesn't care. The police department issued him a freaking Charger with his promotion last month. This thing's just been parked on the street in front of Gena's place collecting dust. In a couple months, it'll be mine anyway. I only owe Alex a few more payments—"

"Wait, you're buying Alex's car?" I'd seen what he'd earned during the school year narcing for the Fairfax County Police Department. And I'd seen the checks he brought home all summer working in the kitchen at Nico's Pizza. He barely made enough money at either job to cover rent on his crappy apartment in Huntington. I didn't need AP Calculus to do the math. "How?"

He stepped toward me, his eyes fixed on mine, making me take a step back. "I told Nico's I'd work part-time through the winter." He took another step into me.

"What about school?" I asked, backing up against the door.

"It's only a few nights a week. I'll manage," he said when there was no space left between us. "But I might need a few extra tutoring sessions to keep up." He brushed peanut butter from my lip with his thumb, knowing full well that I could taste every sweet and wicked thing he was feeling through his skin. His intentions were decidedly more decadent than sharing sandwiches.

"What about your bike?"

"In a few weeks, it'll be too cold to ride anyway." His lips hovered close to mine. "Besides, the bike doesn't have a backseat," he whispered.

My mom cleared her throat loudly through the window screen.

"I'll get the sandwiches." I sighed, pushing him away.

"No sandwiches. We're going to Gena's for a barbeque."

Reece followed me inside. My mother stood in the kitchen in her bathrobe, cradling a mug of coffee in her hands.

"Hi, Mona." Reece handed her one of the PB&Js I'd made for us, and then he proceeded to scarf down the other. My mother raised a sleepy eyebrow at him. As much as she liked to lecture me about "taking things slow" and "being careful," she adored him in her own distant, cautious way. She dipped the crust in her coffee and smiled to herself.

"I'll get my books." I snatched a corner of the sandwich from his hand.

"Leigh, it's Labor Day! Also known as The Day Nobody Does Any Labor Because We're All Stuffing Our Faces With Pie and Deviled Eggs." Reece followed me down the hall, as did my mother's watchful eye, so I left the door open.

"You are aware that school starts tomorrow and we still have two chapters of algebra to cover before your placement tests this week?" Reece had been suspended twice last semester because of me, and I was determined to get him caught up so he wasn't stuck in remedial classes his senior year.

"No books," Reece said in a low voice when we were alone in my bedroom. "I don't plan on studying." He made a clumsy grab for my waist and groaned when I reached for my backpack.

He wasn't like anyone I had ever met. He walked into every room—into my life—with a reckless confidence. Like he had nothing to lose.

"Did you get your orientation packet?" I asked.

"Yes." He plucked the backpack from my hands and dumped it on the floor.

"Can I see it?"

He pulled me in close and nuzzled my ear. "I'll show you mine if you show me yours."

"Deal." I pushed him away and handed him the school letter off my nightstand.

He sighed and fished a folded envelope from the back pocket of his jeans. I sat on the edge of my bed and peeled it open. My heart sank at the return address on the envelope.

"You're going to Spring Run? That's all the way on the other end of the county."

Reece shrugged. "It's my safest option. Too many people know me here, between West River and North Hampton."

I tried to picture the city bus route from Sunny View trailer park to his school, but gave up after the third transfer.

Reece was thin-lipped as he read my letter from West River. He eased down beside me. "Are you going to be okay? You know, going back there?"

I pasted on a convincing smile. "I'll be fine."

He cupped my face and traced a thumb over my cheek. His touch was bittersweet, a mix of compassion and concern. "Are you sure it's not too soon? I could talk to Nicholson. Maybe he could find a way for you go to Spring Run with me." As soon as the words left his mouth, I tasted how foolish they sounded to him.

"As much as I love the idea of being in the same school together, I live too far out of the way for you to drive me. And besides, you'll be working. It's not like we'd be able to hang out."

"What if the nightmares start up? You just started sleeping again." The dreams had plagued me all summer—images of TJ staring at me down the length of a barrel in the moment before he fired the gun, the dead faces of my friends, TJ's voice telling me I hadn't been smart enough to save them. The nightmares had only subsided after his conviction. After the news channels and papers had finally stopped showing his face.

"Have you looked at my class schedule? I'm not going to have any time to think about what happened last year, much less sleep. I'll be fine." I had to be. College applications would be due in December, which meant I only had a few months left to sharpen my cumulative grades and my test scores.

Reece studied my class schedule, as if committing it to memory: AP Government, Introduction to Spanish, AP Physics II, Computer Science, AP Calculus, and AP English Lit. His gaze lingered on my new locker assignment. It was close to the main office—too close for Reece to risk being caught visiting me on campus. "Guess you'll have a pretty heavy load this semester."

"You too." He'd be juggling two jobs, between the pizzeria and narcing for the police. "I'm not worried," I said, trying not to sound worried. "We'll figure something out."

Reece snatched his school schedule from my hands and tossed both of them over his shoulder. "Screw this. School doesn't start until tomorrow. Right now, we've got more important things to do."

"More important than school?" I teased. He pulled me in close and fell back against the mattress with a glance toward the door.

"So much better than school." His rich, low voice tickled my ear. He peeled off my glasses and tossed them aside. Then he gently pulled the ponytail holder out of my hair which fell in disheveled brown waves over my shoulders.

"Aren't we supposed to be going to Gena's?"

"I can be quick," he said, kissing a trail down my neck.

But I didn't want what was left of our summer to be quick. I wanted it to linger. I wanted to savor it, like the lazy Saturday summer afternoons we'd spent curled up together on a picnic blanket under an old tree in Jones Point Park, Reece's textbooks abandoned in the grass.

"We don't have to go to Gena's," he said. "We could go to my place."

"If my mom found out, I'd be grounded for the rest of the year," I said, wriggling out from under him. I fished around the comforter for my glasses. It was our last day of summer with Gena too, and I didn't want to let her down. "Besides, you have to return Alex's car. Maybe he'll be more forgiving over a burger."

Reece flopped over on his back. "Fine, we'll go to Gena's."

I pulled him to his feet. I wrapped my arms around his neck and kissed him, reconsidering our options. He kicked the door shut with his heel. My mother cleared her throat again, and he smiled mischievously before wiping his lips and opening it.

"Later, Mona," he said.

"Not *too* late." She glanced up from the newspaper she'd been pretending to read, clearly noticing the absence of my backpack. Her sly expression said "Don't do anything stupid," in the same direct-and-yet-totally-indirect way the condoms had when she left them on my nightstand back in June.

My face felt hot when I kissed her good-bye. She tasted faintly amused. And maybe a little nostalgic.

Reece held the passenger door open. The interior of the

old Benz had been vacuumed, and the dashboard shone. A "new car" air freshener dangled from the mirror.

I got in and thought about my neighbor Lonny Johnson and his obsession with his Lexus. How it projected an image of what he wanted to be—a rich, successful businessman rather than the neighborhood teenage drug dealer struggling to get out of Sunny View trailer park. Detective Petrenko used to sell drugs alongside Lonny when he was working undercover as a narc. He'd driven the Benz back then. Now Reece would have it. My eyes crossed toward Lonny's trailer, but there was no sign of him or his car.

Reece drove to the end of my street and pulled in front of the Bui Mart.

"Why are we stopping?" I asked. A white Honda Civic was parked beside us. It belonged to my ex–best friend, Jeremy Fowler.

"I asked Gena what we should bring. She put us in charge of soda and chips."

"There's a 7-Eleven up the street."

"We're already here," Reece said, unbuckling his seat belt and getting out.

I sunk lower in my seat. "I'll wait in the car."

Reece eased back in. I stared out the window at Jeremy's Civic. Reece took my hand and gave it a squeeze, infusing me with a little shot of confidence.

"You can't avoid them forever," he said. I wished he were

wrong. The two people I'd cared about most, besides Reece, treated me like I didn't exist. Which sucked, because Anh Bui and I would probably end up lab partners, like we had every year. And since Jeremy and Anh were dating, seeing them together at school seemed inevitable.

I followed Reece into the store. The bells on the door announced our arrival and Anh looked up from the register. Her brother, Bao, the store manager, must have had the night off. Jeremy was perched behind the counter. He glanced at me over the rim of his glasses and, clearly finding me unworthy of his time, returned his attention to his magazine. Anh's face floundered and settled on a non-committal half smile, like she wasn't sure where her obligation to customer service began, given that our friendship had ended. I saved her the headache of figuring it out and headed for the walk-in cooler at the back of the store. It was probably warmer in there anyway.

I opened the heavy glass door and stepped inside, rubbing the chill from my arms. The walls were lined with shelves of beer and soda on one side, and big glass windows on the other that looked out into the store. I was grateful for the posters Bao had papered over the glass, so I wouldn't have to feel Jeremy and Anh staring at me. I grabbed a two-liter of Coke and some Diet for Gena, while Reece hit the ATM machine and picked out some chips.

Anh rang up our total. "Nineteen dollars and eighty-three

cents. Please," she added quietly, like she didn't want Jeremy to hear. Her eyes lifted to mine, then quickly away as she bagged my purchases. Reece dropped a twenty on the counter and Jeremy snapped the page of his magazine.

"Tough crowd," Reece observed when we were back in the car. The entire summer had gone by and they still hadn't forgiven me. Anh's family was still angry that I hadn't gone to the police when the murders began last spring, before she'd been drugged and abducted by TJ, and almost killed. And Jeremy was still angry about a lot of things, not the least of which that he'd spent the entire summer in outpatient rehab. It was hard to believe we were the same people who used to share twin packs of Ho Hos and sneak into each other's houses when our parents weren't home, just to spend time together. That we used to talk every day, about everything.

"I told you, nothing's changed." I dug around in the grocery bag for the salt and vinegar chips. My hand closed on something spongy. A Twinkie.

"You didn't have to buy this just to make me feel better," I said, peeling the wrapper open.

Reece watched me inhale the first bite. He raised a thoughtful brow and smiled as he pulled out of the lot. "I didn't."

My mouth was full of cake and cream. I stopped chewing. Anh must have slipped the Twinkie in the bag with our groceries. I hunted for the receipt. We hadn't been charged for it.

I ate it slowly, savoring it. It felt like a peace offering, and it tasted like hope.

We rode to Gena's with our fingers twined, the radio low in the background, Reece belting out familiar song lyrics while he used my hand as the fret board of an air guitar. His contentment filled me. At the next stoplight, I caught him looking at me. Caught my smile reflected in his sunglasses. This was different from holding on to his waist as the wheels on his bike hugged the turns. Sitting side by side, seeing him looking at me with that smile when his contentment turned to longing.

The Benz idled in front of Gena's row house. "They don't know we're here. We can still change our minds and go to my place," Reece said, leaning in for a kiss. He mumbled something about tasting like Twinkies and kissed me again more deeply.

We both jumped at a loud knock on the window. Alex stood beside the car with his arms folded. He didn't look happy.

Reece rolled his window down and Alex held his hand out for the keys. "Next time you steal my car, I'll have you cavity searched."

"I didn't steal it. It's thirty percent mine."

"Great. I'll be sure to invoice you for your thirty percent of the insurance, fuel, and maintenance." Alex grinned tightly, like it was all he could do to keep from smacking Reece's head. "It's due for a tune-up and an alignment, by the way."

Reece rolled his eyes and dropped the keys in his hand.

"And it only takes premium unleaded," Alex shouted as he walked into the house.

Reece flipped him off, fighting a smile.

We grabbed the chips and sodas and followed Alex.

"In here!" Gena called. The intoxicating smell of grilled onions and biscuits drew us to the kitchen. Gena was pouring apple filling into a piecrust. Her apron said "Kiss the Cook" and Reece obliged with a peck on her cheek. He scraped the bowl with his finger and licked it, and she swatted him with a spoon. His eyes rolled up in his head, euphoric.

"Back off, little man. She's already spoken for." Alex handed Reece a cold soda from the fridge and shoved him playfully out of the way. He tossed me a Rubik's cube from the counter. It was a special cube, smoother than the one I had, with the ability to make faster turns.

"What's your best time?" he asked me.

"A minute and twenty-seven seconds," I said. It sounded silly, compared to his ten-second wins, but he'd had a few more years to practice. Alex had given me my own cube in the days just after TJ's arrest, when the nightmares first started and I hadn't been able to sleep, as if he knew my brain needed an outlet from the madness—an algorithm of simple solutions to a complex problem. The cube was a puzzle that made sense, a game where no one got hurt. It was a way to measure myself getting better.

He raised an eyebrow. "Not bad."

Reece planted a proud kiss on my cheek. "Back off, Detective. She's spoken for."

Alex wrapped his arms around Gena's waist and watched her put the finishing touches on the pie. Alex was soft when he was with Gena, all denim and cotton and easy smiles. Nothing like the undercover narc who'd been posing as Lonny Johnson's lackey when I'd first met him last year at school.

Gena nudged him with her hip and put the pie in the oven. She handed Alex a set of tongs and sent him to the backyard to fire up the grill. I pulled a stool to the counter and watched Gena cook. There were so many facets to her. Some of them shone so brightly—her confidence, her looks, the brash character she portrayed to the world—it took me a while to see the layers underneath. Gena worked undercover in the local high schools. She and I hadn't liked each other much, back when I'd mistakenly thought she was closer to my age and dating Reece. But over the summer, we'd grown close. She was like an older sister to Reece, the only family he had left after his brother died and his mother disowned him.

Reece leaned back against the sink with a peaceful expression. If I touched him right now, he'd probably taste just like that pie. All sweetness and comfort. Like coming home.

"So, are you ready for your first day back to school?" There was a crinkle of concern in Gena's smile, and I knew what she was really asking me. Was I ready to go back to the place where the nightmares all began.

"As ready as I'll ever be," I said through a sigh. "How about you? Any chance you'll be assigned to West River?"

"The department is farming me out to a school in Arlington," she said, rolling her eyes. "Rush hour on I-395 every morning is going to be hell. I'll be lucky if I don't spend the entire fall semester stuck in in-school suspension for tardiness."

"Too bad. I was hoping we could study together. I'm taking Spanish for my language elective this year."

She looked up from her deviled eggs with a curious expression. "I thought you were taking Latin?"

I shrugged. "Learning Spanish just seemed more . . ."

"Practical?" she offered.

"No. More important." I pressed my lips tight. Reece and Alex both knew enough Spanish to understand Gena when she relaxed into a quiet dialog with herself. Or when she exploded in a fiery string of arguments she didn't expect anyone to answer. I guess I wanted to understand her too.

She smiled, like she knew what I was trying to say. Wiping her hands on a dishrag, she said, "I have something for you." She reached into her handbag and withdrew a large envelope. "Open it."

The letterhead inside bore the insignia for the Fairfax County Police Department. Cautiously, I thumbed through the contents: a generic-looking application for an internship position, plus two letters of recommendation—one signed by Officer Gena Delgado, and one by Detective Alexander Petrenko.

"You did it?" I asked, hardly believing the papers in my hand. "You got them to approve a forensics internship?" I had asked Gena if she thought there was a chance I could do my senior internship in the regional crime lab, but when she'd inquired, she discovered that the director of forensics had never approved an internship for a high school student before. I thought for sure I'd be stuck behind a desk all year, shelving books in a university medical library or washing petri dishes for a pharmaceutical company.

"It's not finalized yet. You need to have your mom sign the permission forms, and you'll need a copy of your transcripts from the school. Lieutenant Nicholson's agreed to be your official sponsor. Bring all the signed documents and the application with you tomorrow. He'll meet with you at the station after school."

I looked over at Reece. Then at Gena.

"I don't know what to say."

Gena tapped her lip and looked at the ceiling. "How about, *Estoy muy agradecida. Gena Delgado es la mujer más maravillosa, increíble, y bella en todo el mundo*—"

Reece threw a dish towel at her and laughed.

She rested a hand on my cheek. "Just say you'll work hard

and make us proud. You deserve this, Leigh." Her eyes were shiny with emotion. Pride. It was a bold and effervescent burst of tangerine that never failed to take me by surprise. "Oh, and one more thing!" She reached up to the top of the refrigerator and pulled down a couple of boxes wrapped in confetti-colored paper.

"What's this?" I pulled carefully at the paper's edges and opened the first box. Beneath the delicate tissue was a soft white collared blouse and crisp pair of pleated khaki slacks. The prices had been torn from the tags. In the second box was a shiny pair of matching flats, exactly my size.

"For your first day at the forensics lab. My mother always told me to dress the part," Gena said. "If you want to be a professional, you have to look like one."

I trailed a finger over the silky buttons of the shirt. I'd never given a moment's thought to what I would wear to an internship. Part of me wanted to throw my arms around her, if only to remind myself that she really believed I deserved all this. That she believed I could be the person inside these boxes.

"They're perfect."

"Good," she said, returning her attention to the bowls on the counter. "You can wear them to the wedding too. We're going to keep it simple. Just a few close friends and a Justice of the Peace, if we ever get around to setting a date."

Some of my pride fizzled. Alex and Gena had postponed

their original wedding plans because of the trial. The magazines and catalogs were all gone from her living room. The ones with the big poofy gowns and fancy china patterns.

"I thought you wanted a big wedding?"

She dropped a stack of mixing bowls in the sink. "Now that the case is over, I just want to be married. Thank God TJ took that plea bargain back in June. Otherwise, Alex would be so tangled up in court dates, we'd be old and gray before we could take enough time off for a honeymoon." Gena peeled off her apron and set it on the counter. "It's over. TJ's in prison and it's a new school year, and we can all move on with our lives."

"Amen!" Alex poked his head through the screen door. "Burgers are almost ready."

• • •

After dinner, we sat around the patio table, talking until the sun began to set, then we all helped clear the dishes. Alex put on Gena's apron and started in, while Gena organized the leftovers, singing softly to a song on the radio while she moved about the kitchen. I watched, feeling warm and full and drowsy.

Reece reached for my hand and led me to a patch of grass in the backyard. We lay there, staring at the sunset, my head on his chest and his fingers tangled in mine. He rolled onto his side, wincing from the lingering stiffness in his shoulder. Even though the bullet wound from TJ had healed, it still ached from time to time, and he bore it silently, like a penance.

"Close your eyes," he said, leaning into me.

"What?"

"Just do it." I felt a crisp, peppermint thrill as he pulled me to my knees. Reece was nervous, excited.

"What is it?" I giggled.

I felt his fingers at the nape of my neck, unfastening my pendant . . . his pendant. Its absence felt strange. I hadn't taken it off since he'd placed the chain holding his brother's class ring around my neck that night in the hospital back in June. I pushed away the unsettled feeling in my chest and resisted the urge to open my eyes, trusting in the sweetness of his emotions instead. Any doubts I had were overcome by the cool spill of a chain falling against my skin and the press of his lips to my cheek.

Reece's breath was shaky when he whispered, "Open them."

I blinked my eyes open. His brother's pewter ring was gone. In its place was a silver thistle charm, its leaves delicately curled around a flower made from a tiny purple stone. The thistle was a symbol Reece associated with his brother—a kid who wasn't afraid to do the right thing, even if it meant risking his own future. A reminder of the person Reece was trying so hard to be.

"If you don't want it, I'll understand. I mean . . . I don't want to take the ring from you . . . It's just . . . I want you to have something from me, but . . ." Reece held his brother's ring and its heavy chain, like he was waiting for permission to put it on. To put it back where it belonged. I drew it over his head.

The winding thistle tattoo on his arm slid around my waist. He pulled me in close and kissed me. His emotions seemed to mirror the changing colors of the sky, layers of deepening feelings with blurry edges I couldn't quite define. I slipped my hands under the hem of his shirt, up his stomach and over his chest, my fingers finding the smooth pucker of scar tissue just below his right shoulder. His heartbeat was steady and strong beneath my wrist, but everything inside him tasted uncertain.

"What's wrong?" I asked him.

I kissed the hard line of his jaw and it relaxed into a smile. "Right this second? Absolutely nothing."

And I knew exactly what he meant. That everything was completely right, but there was nothing we could do to keep this last day of summer from dissolving away.

2

MY LOCKER MADE A HOLLOW SOUND when I snapped it open, and my chest felt tight. The first day of my senior year should have felt great, like a new beginning. New classes, new books, new schedule. And yet, starting a new year without Jeremy and Anh—without Teddy's laughter and Posie's smile—felt like starting over alone. But I wasn't alone, I reminded myself. I had Reece. I had Gena. I had an internship.

I inspected the scratched interior of my locker. A new prepaid cell phone caught my eye on the shelf and a smile pulled at my lips. Reece used to leave prepaid cell phones for me last spring, because I couldn't afford (and didn't care enough) to buy one of my own. When we'd first met, I'd resented the idea of being connected to him. And now I couldn't stand being apart. The knot in my chest loosened as I thumbed through to the inbox.

One new text message.

Knock 'em dead today. I'll pick you up at your place after school. I miss you. Reece.

I glanced toward the front office, hoping he hadn't been caught. He must have broken into the school before daybreak to leave it for me. His new school was as far from his last assignment here at West River as Lieutenant Nicholson could put him. My smile flaked away as I touched the thistle pendant, and I tried not to think about the miles between us, or the long day of classes ahead of me.

I organized my notebooks on my locker shelf in order by period. Put my sack lunch on top. Snapped my small magnetic mirror in place inside the door. When I looked into it, a cluster of girls were whispering and pointing in my direction. I slammed the door shut and headed to my first period class.

Computer Science. Mr. Hurley. Computer Lab 269.

I navigated the halls with my head down, ignoring the conversations that seemed to hush as I walked by. My classroom was easy to find and I slipped into an open workstation at the back of the room. But with one glance at the door, I wished I hadn't picked the seat farthest from it. The whiteboard beside it said "Teacher's Assistant—Jeremy Fowler," and for a moment, I considered walking out. I'd never dropped a class before, but there was a first time for everything. Then the bell rang and Jeremy closed the door. He stood by the teacher's side at the front of the room.

Mr. Hurley prattled on about attendance and bathroom passes and tardy slips, and Jeremy walked up and down the aisles, handing out syllabi. I could feel Jeremy's gaze brush mine, neither of us looking directly at each other. Anh sat in the front row. I saw Sharissa Winters and Eric Miller from chem class last year. And Vince DiMorello, sitting with a few of his teammates at the other end of my row.

"For the purpose of this class, you will each set up an e-mail account today. You will use this account to submit your homework and to access your weekly assignments and your grades. You may also use these accounts to communicate with your assigned partners. To keep things simple and orderly, you will create your e-mail address using the following format: Your last name. Dot. Your first name. At our school domain." Mr. Hurley scrawled a sample on the board.

"The workstation where you are seated now will be your workstation for the remainder of the semester, and your lab partner will be the person seated beside you, beginning from the left of each row."

There was a rush of grumbles and whispers. Eric Miller sat to my right, and I cringed inside. He'd been Alex Petrenko's lab partner last year and neither one of them had done a bang-up job of keeping their collective grade above a C. Eric chewed a fingernail, looking equally dismayed, probably at being stuck with the school pariah for a lab partner. I gave him a small wave. He waved back. I guess it could have been worse. I could have been stuck with Anh.

Mr. Hurley stepped out of the room, leaving Jeremy in charge and instructing us to log on and get started. I studied the syllabus: Computational Thinking, Elements of Programming, Software Engineering. I didn't have a computer at home. I'd always used Jeremy's or Anh's, or reserved a workstation in the library. The other students had already signed on to their machines, pointing and clicking like it was second nature, as if they were completely at home.

"What's wrong, trailer trash?" Vince teased me as soon as Hurley was gone. "Never seen a computer before?" His friends laughed. Jeremy didn't intervene. Eric reached over and dropped a slip of paper on my table. A hastily handwritten bullet point cheat sheet for getting started.

"Thanks," I said quietly, so Vince wouldn't hear me.

Eric shrugged. "Do you have a computer you can use for our assignments?"

My face felt warm and I looked away. Eric lived in Belle Green. His father had been friends with my dad, but that was a long time ago, and if he didn't know I lived in Sunny View before Vince's outburst, then he did now. "I'm doing an internship this year. Maybe I can use one at the lab."

"Where'd you land an internship?" He actually sounded interested.

"The Joseph Bell Regional Forensic Lab." I felt myself swell with pride. I wasn't used to being the weak link in a lab partnership. Maybe that's why I wanted to impress him.

His eyebrows lifted. They were auburn, like the reddish brown hair that curled over his ears, and the spray of freckles across his cheeks and nose.

"How about you?" I asked. "Are you interning anywhere?"

"Nah. I didn't finish my community service requirements last year. Still catching up." Eric shook it off. "I'm just tutoring a couple days a week. It's not so bad."

We did that awkward thing when two people with nothing in common are forced to talk—looked at each other and then everywhere else, not knowing what to say.

He took a deep breath, scratched his head, and gestured to the cheat sheet. "Um . . . okay. Let me know if you get stuck on anything." I nodded, feeling small again as he turned back to his computer.

After a few minutes, I looked over at Eric, but his eyes were glued to his own screen. He was already reviewing the assignment for the week. Maybe having Eric for a lab partner wouldn't be so bad. After a little trial and error, I managed to set up my e-mail account. I used Eric's cheat sheet to find the group documents and began skimming the first assignment.

An alert popped up on my screen. Two new e-mails.

One from Mr. Hurley that said "Welcome and Introduction" in the subject line.

The second . . .

A chill raced down my arms. It was from wiles.thomas. *TJ.* It said "I'm watching you."

I looked around the class. Everyone was working. A series of quiet giggles escaped a girl from Vince's corner of the room. I thought about raising my hand, reporting it to Jeremy. Vince and the girl began cackling, curled in on themselves and gossiping in hushed tones. Jeremy didn't look up. Someone in the class had a messed-up idea of a joke.

"Everything okay?" Eric asked.

I took a deep breath and clicked DELETE. "Everything's going to be fine."

• • •

I threw open the door of my trailer after school, zipping room to room and calling my mother's name. She'd worked the late shift last night, and I hadn't had a chance to tell her about the internship. She wasn't home and her work shoes were

gone, so I ran back up Sunny View Drive and crossed Route 1
to find her. Her shifts had been screwy lately and I hoped
I would catch her between sets. I banged on the back door to
Gentleman Jim's, waving at the security camera in the alley
behind the strip mall. The bar was usually quiet around this
time of day, but I never used the front door. Walking in on
your mother when she's naked is awkward enough, but walking in on your mother and waving a permission slip while
she's dancing on a stage would take discomfort to a whole
new level. A moment later, Butch, the bar's bouncer, threw
the door open.

"Hey, sweetheart," Butch said, taking in my breathless state.
He scratched the back of his shaved head. "Everything okay?"

"Everything's great! Is Mom here?" I dug into my backpack for the internship forms, all business. I only had a few
minutes before Reece showed up at my trailer to take me to
the station.

A curious smile spread across Butch's face. "Come on.
She's in Jim's office."

She was dressed in a pair of jeans and a T-shirt. Her hair
was piled high on her head, and she was wearing her reading
glasses. I must have looked surprised.

"I came in early to help Jim with the books. The man is
mathematically challenged. We'll be lucky if he doesn't run us
into the ground." She smirked. "Don't look so excited about it.
My regular shift starts at eight." Her gaze drifted to the police

insignia letterhead clutched in my hands and her smile fell away. "What's this?" She reached for it as if it might bite her.

"I got an internship . . . at a forensic science lab." My mother was silent, her face expressionless as her eyes traveled over the form. "Gena recommended me, and Lieutenant Nicholson said it would be okay, and I really want to do this, but he said I had to get your permission first." The words came out in a rush, taking all the air in my lungs with them.

"You'll be working in a crime lab?" I could hear the worry in her voice.

"A *science* lab."

"What about school?"

"It won't interfere with school."

"But what about your grades?"

"That's exactly why I need this." In a few weeks, I'd be filling out college applications, competing against hundreds of students with high GPAs and perfect test scores vying for a handful of coveted academic scholarships. "I lost the chemistry scholarship in June. I can't afford to lose a chance at another one. This internship is an opportunity for me to stand out. To prove myself."

Butch handed my mother a pen. She didn't take it. "We'll be fine without the scholarship. You have all the money your father left you—the cash, plus the account he set up for you in Butch's name all those years ago."

It didn't matter that the money had filtered through some

out-of-state investment banker with fancy credentials, or that it was placed in my account through automated deposits and had probably never touched my father's hands. As far as I was concerned, that money was dirty. It had been stolen, manipulated by a psychic conman out of people who'd trusted him. "I don't want Dad's money."

"It's not your father's money. It's yours. It should be more than enough for next year's tuition, and if it's not, we can apply for financial aid. You should use this year to ease back into your studies. And maybe have a little fun."

My mother had never used words like *ease* when discussing my education. She didn't believe in financial aid. She believed in focus and sacrifice and merit scholarships. She'd always pushed me to do my best. "You don't think I can handle this?"

Her face fell. "It's just so soon after everything happened. Going back to school after everything you've been through will be stressful enough—"

"I'll be fine!"

Butch laid a hand on my mother's shoulder. She sighed, her eyes creased with worry lines.

I took her hands. "Please, Mom. I can do this." I felt her anxiety melt away around the edges, yielding to something minty and sweet. Despite all her fears, she believed in me. When I finally let go, she took Butch's pen.

We both held our breath as she signed her name.

• • •

When I got home, Reece was sitting on his motorcycle in front of my trailer, waiting. I hopped on the bike behind him before he could kill the engine, and we rode the entire way in silence. When I'd wrapped my arms around his waist and slipped my hands under his shirt, his emotions felt muddy with a taste that was hard to place.

"It's okay if you don't want to come in," I said as Reece darted glances around the rear parking lot of the police station, pulling his hoodie low over his eyes.

It would be too easy for someone—a student or an acquaintance or a dealer he'd narced on—to recognize him. Only a handful of people knew about Reece's ties to the police, and the fewer who knew, the safer he was.

He took me by the shoulders and looked at me from under his hood. "I want to come in. This is a big deal." He pulled me to him, and I took a deep breath, holding my internship papers tight to my chest, ready to get this part of the process over with. Police stations made both of us nervous.

"You know, you don't have to do this," he said into my hair. "You have your father's money. It's enough for school."

I pulled away. "You sound like my mom, Reece. This isn't just about money. I want to do this."

He brushed the hair back from my eyes. "I know, and that's what scares me."

"What do you mean?"

He was quiet for a moment. "I'm proud of you," he finally said. "I don't want you to think that I'm not. It's just . . ." He looked at the sky, like he was searching for the right words. "When I first accepted my deal with Nicholson, I thought working as a narc would make up for the night my brother died. But this job . . . these things I do, and the things I see . . . I relive that night my brother was shot every day."

"I don't understand what this has to do with my internship."

"Just . . . ask yourself why you chose this. If you really want to work in a crime lab, I'm behind you every step of the way. But don't do it for the same reasons I did. You're not your father," he said quietly. "You're a good person. You don't have anything to prove."

But he was wrong. In a lot of ways, I was my father. Every time I touched someone, I was reminded of how much of him I carried inside me. Reece knew that.

"I need to do this," I said. I needed to get the ground under me again so I could walk out of my father's lies and crimes and into someplace new.

Reece nodded. He pulled my head to his chest and kissed it, letting his lips linger against my hair. Across the parking lot, a man leaned against a bus stop shelter, staring at us through the gap between the vans while we held each other.

"We should go," I said.

Reece led me to an unmarked door at the back of the build-

ing and buzzed me in with his card key. A uniformed officer
behind a counter asked for my identification. My father's face
stared back at me from the bulletin board behind him. David
Boswell, wanted for a long list of racketeering crimes: illicit
gambling rings, extortion, bribery. Head down, I slid my student ID across the counter. The officer copied my information without looking up.

Reece guided me down a corridor of white walls and fluo-
rescent lights that felt entirely too familiar, past small square
rooms. Hard, claustrophobic spaces, like confessionals. Like
the room where I'd first met with Lieutenant Nicholson last
spring.

Do you know the person who wrote these ads, Miss Boswell?

A jarring, hostile voice rose from one of the rooms: "But I
filed a missing persons report!"

"At eighteen, she's legally an adult. You can file all the
reports you want, but I'm not under any obligation to open
a search unless you can give me a reason to believe she's in
immediate danger."

The yeller lowered his voice. It was scratchy and familiar.
Lonny Johnson.

"She hasn't answered her phone in three days," he said.
"She was supposed to call. She didn't. Her mother hasn't seen
her. She left with a . . . guy. No one knows where she is."

"Does her mother know who she left with?"

"No."

"Did she mention who she might be meeting? Do you have a name?"

"She doesn't ask their names." Lonny's reply was low and angry, ground between clenched teeth.

"Let me see if I got this straight. She left with a buyer and never came home with your cut of the drug money. So now you want us to go out and find her for you."

No answer.

"Lieutenant Nicholson made you a pretty sweet deal back in June. If he finds out you've been dealing—"

"I'm not dealing," Lonny snapped.

"No, you're having your girlfriend do it for you—"

"It doesn't matter what she was doing!" he shouted back. "She's missing. That's the point. She's just a kid. Someone should be out looking for her."

"She's an adult," the officer corrected in a firm tone. "An adult with a history of substance abuse. She's probably shacked up with some other dealer across town. This kind of thing happens all the time—"

"This is bullshit!" A chair screeched and toppled over. "If she lived on the golf course in Belle Green, I bet you would be out looking for her. But a girl from Sunny View is a waste of your time?"

I froze, pulling Reece to a stop. Sunny View was a small neighborhood. Forty trailers or so. Someone was missing, and chances are, it was someone I knew.

"Thanks for nothing." A dark figure stormed through the open door. In one hand Lonny clutched a photo. His other hand scrubbed hotly over his white-blond hair. He muttered to himself as his Doc Martens ate up the hall. Then he looked up and his steely eyes met mine.

Lonny's gaze warmed as it moved, top to bottom over me. It dropped a few degrees by the time it got to Reece. "Look what the cat dragged in," he growled, coming to a stop in front of us. Lonny tucked the photo of a blue-haired girl in his pocket, but not before I got a look. I knew her—her hair used to be bleached blond, but her kohl-black eyes hadn't changed. She lived a few doors down from Lonny. Went to his parties. Hung out on his porch. She'd been partying with Reece—had been flirting with him—the last and only time I'd really bothered to notice her. That was almost three months ago, before school let out for summer break.

If Reece remembered Adrienne Wilkerson, he didn't let on. He reached for my hand, his fingers brushing mine, and I instinctively moved away from the acrid taste of his hatred for Lonny.

"Boswell," Lonny said, tipping an imaginary hat to me. "Be careful out there," he said. And then he was gone.

The "sweet deal" the officer had just mentioned to Lonny was a trade—keep the secret of Reece's identity as a narc and stay out of trouble—in exchange for dropped drug charges.

"I hate that guy," Reece said.

"He's not so bad." He could have left us in that cemetery to die. He could have let TJ kill us, but he didn't.

"Yeah, well, he's not so good either. I don't trust him."

"He promised Nicholson—" *Nicholson*. I checked the time on my phone. "We should hurry. I'm going to be late for my meeting."

We rounded the corner and I took a moment to compose myself outside the lieutenant's office, straightening my internship papers and smoothing out my hair. It was tangled from the bike helmet, and there was a tiny stain on my T-shirt. I should have worn the clothes Gena bought me, but there hadn't been time to change.

"Miss Boswell. Are you going to come in, or are you waiting for a formal invitation?" Lieutenant Nicholson spoke in the same gruff voice that had made me bristle the first time we'd met.

I took a deep breath and walked into his office. Nicholson looked over the rims of his reading glasses, toward Reece.

"How was your first day across town, kid?"

"Fine," Reece answered.

"Officer Delgado says she filled you in on what we're looking for. Think you'll have something worth sharing by next week?"

Reece leaned back against the wall. "I'm working on it."

Nicholson turned to me.

"Officer Delgado says you want to work in the lab?"

"Yes, sir." I cleared my throat and stepped forward. My face flushed hot. "I was hoping for an internship in forensic science."

I handed him my paperwork and he thumbed through it. "Is this GPA for real?"

"Yes, sir."

"What's that SAT score mean?"

"It's almost a perfect score, sir."

I watched as he scrutinized my transcripts and my mother's signature of consent.

"We've never offered an internship to a high school student before, and quite frankly, I'm not sure why we're offering one now, except that Officer Delgado felt strongly enough about your qualifications to send the request up the chain." He tapped the papers with end of his pencil, thinking. "I have to ask you one thing before I put my name behind this. Background checks are standard procedure for anyone who'll have access to sensitive information. Have you had any contact with your father in the last five years?"

I swallowed, my throat suddenly dry. "No, sir. I haven't had any contact with my father since he left."

Nicholson looked at Reece. Then at me. Then he picked up a pen in his stocky fingers and signed his name. My breath rushed out.

"Your orientation is on Thursday. Be at the forensics lab at four o'clock. Take these forms with you. Doc Benoit will be expecting you." The lieutenant slid a lanyard containing a card key and an ID badge across the desk. Unlike Reece's card, this one had a logo on it . . . a microscope over a star. A lump tightened in my throat. The badge bore my name, and the lanyard said "Virginia Department of Forensic Science."

The lieutenant extended his hand. When I shook it, his touch was uncertain and slightly acidic.

"Make us proud, Boswell," is what he said.

But in my head, all I heard was, *Nearly, don't screw this up.*

3

AT 3:53 ON THURSDAY AFTERNOON, I stood in front of the forensics lab and ran my key through the card reader, the way I'd seen Reece do to get into the police station a few days ago. Nothing happened. I swiped the card again.

"You might want to turn it over," said a voice behind me. I turned to see a young guy, probably not much older than I was. He didn't look like a lab geek. His hair was too long. He pushed it from his eyes to look me over, starting at my white button-down and khaki pants. He raised an eyebrow. "You must be the new kid."

Kid? I scrutinized his faded jeans and his untucked Star Wars T-shirt, then I noticed the lanyard draped over it.

"Raj Singh. Lab technician," he said, noticing the direction of my stare.

"Leigh Boswell. Intern," I replied cautiously.

Raj Singh, lab technician, juggled a thermos and a lab coat in one hand, and swiped his ID with the other. A lock snapped and he opened the door, bracing it with an elbow. "I'd shake, but . . ." He shrugged, grinning as the door started to shut between us.

"Do you know where I can find Dr. Benoit?" I grabbed the door and slipped in behind him.

"Follow me." Raj walked in long, bouncy strides, pointing things out with a jut of his chin. "Bathroom's down that hall. Vending machines and break room are to the left. Supply closet's around the other side, but you'll need a key. Veronica can hook you up. She's upstairs on the Administration floor."

My new flats were conspicuously slick on tile, making me feel clumsy and off-balance. I scrambled to keep up. "Sounds like you've been here a long time?"

"Since I graduated last spring."

I inched forward, trying to catch another look at his face. As if he could feel me trying to guess whether he meant high school or college, he clarified, "BS in Forensic Science from George Mason. I'm taking classes in the mornings. Working toward my master's." Raj interrupted himself, tipping his chin toward a set of double doors. "Deliveries come in there.

The Fridge is down that hall too. But Doc should be in the Bone Locker this afternoon."

I fell back a step. "The Bone Locker?"

He laughed. "Come on. I'll show you."

Raj stopped at a door marked "OSSUARY—authorized personnel only."

"Here, let's try your card this time and make sure it works." I swiped my key, but nothing happened. Raj took it from me to study the magnetic strip at the back. "Hm. Sometimes they crap out for no reason. I'll take it upstairs while you meet with Doc and see if I can get you a new one." He used his own card and popped open the door. "He's in the stacks." Raj pointed into a cavernous room with rows of floor-to-ceiling shelves. When I turned around, he was already gone.

The door clicked shut and the room was eerily quiet, the sound echoing back at me from the dim corners where the dome lights didn't quite reach. I called down the empty rows, "Dr. Benoit?" The hard floors seemed to magnify the sterile, cold feel of the place.

"Third stack from the left," a voice came back to me. "Femurs. Just past the clavicles."

The stacks were full of cardboard boxes and plastic containers. All marked. Numbers, dates, body parts. I snuck a glance into a clear plastic bin and two empty eye sockets stared back at me. A skull. Not the bright white flawless kind that hung from a hook in the biology lab at school. This one was moss-colored, rough and pitted. Most of the teeth were missing or cracked.

"Don't worry." I jumped at Dr. Benoit's disembodied voice. "They don't bite."

I hurried toward the sound, careful not to look at the boxes too closely. At the end of the stack, a man in a lab coat perched on a ladder, digging through a cardboard box. Dr. Benoit withdrew a long rod and handed it down. "Here, hold this."

I took it, balancing the ladder for him with my other hand while he descended. He appraised me over the rim of his glasses. "You must be Nearly Boswell." Instead of reaching for my hand, he reached for the rod I'd been holding, then frowned. "Gloves, Miss Boswell. We wear gloves when handling human remains."

I grimaced at the thing in my hand. Then quickly handed the leg bone over and wiped my palms on my pants.

"Lieutenant Nicholson's told me quite a bit about you. Some of the most interesting cadavers we've ever seen in our lab came out of that case you were involved in. Mr. Wiles had a rather creative spirit." He was talking about TJ. The people he'd killed. Marcia and Teddy and Posie and Kylie. My eyes drifted to the stacks, to the names on the boxes, and Dr. Benoit pursed his lips, as if only just realizing that the cadavers he was referring to had been my friends.

"Not these." He cleared his throat, following the turn of

my head. "These are all unsolved cases. John and Jane Does. Bits and pieces of remains that have yet to be identified or connected to a specific crime. Like the odd pieces of a jigsaw puzzle. These are the ones we've yet to figure out."

I nodded numbly.

"Every skeletal piece in this room tells a story. From this bone alone, I can make a fairly reasonable estimation of the person's height, age, and sex. Maybe even how or when they were killed. Do you see this?" He held the bone out for me, and pointed at a set of markings with a gloved finger. "These marks are indicative of carnivore scavenging."

"You mean they're teeth marks?" I looked closely at the deep scratches. "Is that what killed him?"

"No, these marks were made postmortem. Probably by a raccoon." He held the bone closer, letting me look but not touch, gauging my reaction. I peeked into the surrounding bins, curious about the stories they contained. "I don't normally take on interns. I find it takes a certain strength of stomach to work in this kind of environment. But given your grades, and your experience with . . . well . . ." He held the femur at eye level, and shut one eye, examining the length of it, then he blew off the dust. "Let's just say I was willing to give you a shot." Doc Benoit looked over my shoulder. "Where's Raj?"

"He went to see Veronica about getting me a new card key." I stared absently at the bone in his hand, still unsettled by his professional distance from all this. His "strength of stomach."

"Good. You'll be reporting to him."

"To Raj?" My attention was now fully on the doctor's face. The tight graying curls at his temples. The stern rims of his glasses.

"Raj has a heavy course load this semester and he can use the help." Dr. Benoit set the femur on a tray and stripped off his gloves. "Let's get you squared away in the Administration office. I've got a delivery coming that I need to sign for anyway. We can meet up with Raj there."

I followed Doc Benoit out of the Bone Yard, still trying to wrap my head around the fact that I'd be reporting to a lab tech who wore Converse high-tops and carried a Darth Vader thermos to work. I picked at my shirt collar, pulling it and smoothing it, frantically thinking back to the first moment we met, wondering if I'd done or said anything stupid.

Doc Benoit deposited me in Veronica's office. Raj perched on the edge of her desk, chatting her up. I'm pretty sure he was trying to look down her shirt.

"This must be your new intern?" Veronica smiled, standing to introduce herself. She wore a blouse like mine, only hers was filled out. Raj looked annoyed at my interruption.

"That's what Doc says," Raj grumbled.

Veronica extended her hand and I tried not to cringe. I hated introductions, but there was no way to avoid shaking her hand without seeming rude. I pasted on a smile, but it wasn't so bad. Her touch was warm and tasted like cinnamon rolls. She was pretty and polished, her hair pulled back in a stylish twist. She reminded me a little of Gena and I liked her right away. But there was something else, something gooey and sweet I'd detected when her eyes drifted to Raj. I wondered if Raj even knew . . .

I pushed away the thought. It was none of my business. I handed her my paperwork. She gave the transcripts and letters of recommendation a cursory glance, raising an eyebrow at my test scores.

"I believe this is yours, then." She winked at me, and handed me a new access card. Then she thumbed through the rest of the papers I'd given her. "Looks like everything's in order, except we seem to be missing a few standard forms. I'm getting ready to leave for the day, but you can fill them out when we take your fingerprints next week." She was all business when she turned to Raj, no trace of the crush I'd tasted moments ago. "The internship description says she'll work a minimum of two afternoons, or eight hours per week."

Raj thought for a moment and said, "You'll work with me on Tuesday and Thursday after school. We'll start with eight hours and see how it goes. If I like you, maybe I'll let you help out on the weekends. You can usually find me in the Latent Prints lab upstairs." His gaze dropped to my blouse, which he clearly didn't find as interesting as Veronica's. "Word to the wise? When you come back next Tuesday, ditch the duds."

Veronica shot him an annoyed look. "You look nice, hon. What Raj means is you should probably wear something you don't mind getting dirty. Things don't stay new around here for long."

• • •

The sun was low in the sky when I got off the city bus at the end of Sunny View Drive. I stopped at the mailboxes and began thumbing through a stack of bills, until I was startled by the thwack of a hammer nearby. Lonny Johnson stood at the corner, holding a sheet of paper flat to the post of the streetlight as he tacked it in place. One hand partly obscured the word *missing,* but I could clearly make out the photo of a girl with blue hair. Adrienne Wilkerson. I guessed she hadn't come home yet.

Lonny finished hammering. He wiped sweat from his brow and bent to pick up a stack of flyers from the ground.

I could understand why he was worried, even if the police didn't seem concerned. Lonny's girlfriend had been killed by TJ back in June. Kylie's murder had been gruesome and violent. The haunting kind of brutality that burns itself into your brain and plays over and over in your head and makes you imagine terrible things. "I can help," I heard myself say before I realized the words were out.

Lonny turned at the sound of my voice. He smiled around the nails he held in place between his teeth. Or at least, I think it was a smile. With Lonny, I was never quite sure. He handed me the flyers and I walked with him to the next post.

"I didn't see you in school this week," I said, making small talk. In all the years we'd been neighbors in Sunny View, we'd never had a single class together.

"I got my GED over the summer. I am officially a high school graduate at the ripe old age of nineteen."

"Congratulations," I said, sincerely happy for him. Lonny was smart. The "doing" kind of smart that didn't have time for textbooks and lectures. Or small talk.

He began tacking up the next flyer. "You know her?"

I nodded.

"She went missing five days ago. The cops aren't lifting a finger."

I looked at the photo while he nailed it in place. Her eyes were glassy and ringed in dark circles. Maybe the police were right, and she was just on a bender. "Maybe she's just—"

"I need a favor," he said, cutting me off.

I swallowed. "A favor?"

"I want you to keep an eye out for her. Let me know if you see anything that might give me some idea where to find her."

"Okay," I said. That seemed easy enough. "I'll keep my eyes open in Sunny View. I'll ask around at school. Maybe someone will know where she—"

"Going back to the crime lab anytime soon?" Lonny's eyes

shot straight to my lanyard, then bored into mine. I'd forgotten to take off my ID.

A knot tightened in my gut. "Tuesday. After school."

"Good. Poke around a little bit. You've got my number. If you hear anything that might have to do with Adrienne I want you to call me."

I had that slippery feeling. The kind that fired off warnings in every nerve cell, right before I did something wrong. "But I can't. What if I get caught?"

A cool smile crept over him. "This, from the girl who stood on the hood of my car and threatened me with a baseball bat? Come on, Boswell. I know you better than that. You don't scare that easy."

Back in June, I'd asked Lonny for help, and he'd come. He'd saved my life that night. Reece's and Anh's too. And if that wasn't enough, he'd come forward to testify as a key witness against TJ. This was not a choice he was giving me. He was collecting on a favor. Not begging for one. He put his hands in his pockets and leaned against the pole.

I nodded and handed him back his flyers.

"I knew I could count on you." He chucked me softly under the jaw with tattooed knuckles covered in thick silver rings. He tasted like relief and determination, with sharp metallic undertones. I watched him walk away. He would not let this go. He would find Adrienne at any cost, even if I had to be the one to pay it.

I headed for my trailer, kicking up loose stones in the street. There had to be another way I could pay off my debt to Lonny. Maybe Adrienne would turn up before next week.

"Flavor of the month? You sure know how to pick 'em." Jeremy stood in the shadow of my trailer. His voice was so thick with disdain, it took me a minute to place it in the dark. He'd been watching my conversation with Lonny.

"He's a friend, Jeremy. But you're right, I thought I knew how to pick those too. What are you doing here?" My stomach knotted to see his dad's BMW parked alongside my trailer.

He pushed up his glasses and gestured to the dingy gray aluminum siding where the words *trailer trash* had been sprayed in big red letters. "Your mother called my father about the lovely artwork someone painted on your trailer."

My face grew hot.

"Do you think it was Vince?" he asked, assuming the holier-than-thou tone he'd used to speak to me in computer class all week.

"Maybe. Or maybe one of his friends. It wouldn't be the first time," I mumbled, heading for my front porch.

I felt Jeremy's eyes, heavy on my back. I stopped and turned to face him. "If you have something to say, then just say it."

Jeremy shook a slip of paper at me. I didn't reach out to take it, so he pushed it closer to my face. Close enough for me to see the dark blue ink that formed crisp bold letters.

$$\sum F = 0 \Leftrightarrow \frac{dv}{dt} = 0$$

I instinctively stepped away from it, my heel connecting with the porch step. The message looked identical to the handwritten notes TJ had left for me last semester. The ones that always foreshadowed his next kill. "Newton's law of inertia. Where did you get that?"

"Someone left it on my desk."

"In what class?"

"Not at school." Jeremy looked anxiously at my trailer and lowered his voice. "I found it on the desk in my bedroom."

"Don't look at me. It's not like *I* put it there!"

"You're the only one besides Anh who knows how to get in my house!"

"For crying out loud, Jeremy! You keep your spare house key under a plastic rock in your front flowerbed. Everyone in Belle Green probably knows how to get in your house. Vince lives across the street. He's been watching you lock yourself out since you were twelve."

I snatched the note from his hand. "This would be just like Vince too. He toilet papered my trailer in July, left a flaming bag of dog shit on my front porch in August, and drunk-dialed me last weekend pretending to be the police. I wouldn't put it past Vince to have a little fun at your expense too. For that matter, I'm surprised he hasn't already."

Saying it out loud, it all made more sense. After TJ had

confessed, the media had run all the details of the story. From the scientific riddles TJ placed for me in the *Missed Connections* of the newspaper to the handwritten clues he left in indelible blue ink. Reporters dug up as much dirt as they could find on my father—the crimes he'd committed, how he'd left TJ's dad to take the fall alone, and how I'd been searching for him in the personal ads. They had broadcast it all on TV, because motives (as Gena explained to me) make for a great story. And I suppose the same was true in high schools too.

Jeremy pushed his glasses up his nose. "I got the flaming bag too, Leigh. I already knew that was Vince. I watched him scoop the poops out of his own yard! This is different."

But it wasn't different. Sure, the letters were written with the same blue ink. And the handwriting was a pretty close match. But it wouldn't be hard for Vince to mock up a phony message just to freak Jeremy out. No harder than it had been for him to create a fake e-mail account in TJ's name.

"Why are you here, Jeremy? What do you want me to do? Commiserate with you? Do you want me to feel sorry for you?" I pointed at the spray paint on my trailer. "These games, these stupid pranks! This isn't anything new! The only reason my mother probably called this time is because . . ." I almost choked on the words. "Because this piece of shit trailer belongs to your father!"

I raced up my porch steps just as the door flew open and

Jeremy's dad came out, pushing past me with a wad of rent money in his hand. "I expect the place painted this weekend. And don't bother sending receipts for reimbursement. Your rental agreement clearly states—"

"I know what my contract says, Jason." My mother sounded tired. Like she'd had enough of his bullshit. She leaned against the doorframe wearing jeans and an old T-shirt. Her glasses slipped down her nose, making it seem like she was looking down on him. I wondered if this is what Jeremy and I would look like in ten years. Like two people who knew too much about each other to ever be friends again.

Jeremy hunched in on himself as Mr. Fowler descended the steps. He grabbed Jeremy hard by the arm and shoved him toward the BMW. "I told you to wait in the goddamn car."

My mother put her arm around my shoulder.

"That man hasn't changed in all the years I've known him. I don't know how Jenna lives with him. If I was her, I'd have taken that poor boy and left that son of a bitch years ago."

I turned to look at her, surprised by the bitterness, the depth of her loathing. My mother, who didn't believe in leaving when things got tough, who'd stuck it out in this crappy neighborhood in our crappy house with her crappy job after my father left, believed—all the way to her core— that Jenna and Jeremy would be better off without a husband and father. Without Jason Fowler's job or his money or his house. We watched as the BMW pulled away, Mr. Fowler shouting while Jeremy melted into the interior. Between Jeremy and me, I wasn't sure which one of us had more reasons to feel ashamed.

4

THE COMPUTER LAB was bustling on Friday morning, everybody out of their seats and clustered in groups, talking about their weekend plans. I sat down behind my computer and logged in, doing my best to tune out the chatter about homecoming court nominations and football games and whose parents were out of town, leaving their houses ripe for a kegger.

The second bell rang.

"Take your seats, everyone," Mr. Hurley said. There were a few groans and protests from around the room as the class settled in. "Your assignment for the day has been posted. We are short an assistant today, so please be patient with your questions and I will do my best to get to everyone." Jeremy wasn't standing at the front of the class. Eric's chair was empty too. I sighed, and opened my e-mail.

A ball of paper hit the side of my head. I turned in Vince's direction. He was red-faced, laughing into his hand, pretending to read his screen. The girl next to him kicked him under his seat, but she was laughing too. Mr. Hurley was bent over someone's keyboard at the front of the room, his back to us. I sunk in my chair and ignored the fading giggles.

Two new messages. One from Mr. Hurley, outlining today's assignment.

And one from TJ Wiles. My eyes skipped cautiously back to Vince, but he was leaning into the aisle, whispering to his friends.

I opened the e-mail.

"Things are already in motion," it said. I scrolled down, but that was all it said.

Eric plunked down into his chair and dropped his backpack beside him. "Sorry I'm late," he said. "Did I miss anything?"

"Nothing worth worrying about," I muttered, deleting the message.

I clicked open the assignment from Mr. Hurley and skimmed it. "We're supposed to write a program that converts decimals to fractions using Euclid's algorithm," I explained. "It's due next Wednesday."

"Hey," Vince called out, raising his hand to get Mr. Hurley's attention. "This looks like math. This class is supposed to be an elective. I didn't sign up to take any extra math."

Mr. Hurley straightened and turned to the back of the room. "You're free to drop the class, Mr. DiMorello. I hear there's still an opening in first period Interpretive Dance in the gym."

A roar of laughter filled the room. Blood rushed to Vince's

cheeks and he slouched with his arms crossed, glaring daggers at his screen.

"I can handle the math part," I offered Eric.

"I'm not worried about the math," he said defensively.

I lowered my voice. "Well, I'd rather not do the programming part, if it's all the same to you."

I started at Vince's voice close behind me. He held a folded twenty dollar bill over my shoulder and whispered in my ear, "Hey, Boswell, how about a couple bucks for some help with the assignment?"

Anger boiled up in me. "Something tells me you don't need any help finding your way around a computer."

Mr. Hurley turned in our direction and Vince slipped the money in his pocket. "Whatever, trailer trash." Vince turned to Eric, like he'd just noticed him sitting there. "How about you, carrot top? We're neighbors, right? You live in Belle Green?"

Eric didn't answer.

"You any good at math?" The corner of the twenty was sticking out of the pocket of Vince's jeans, and Eric's eyes drifted to it.

"I do a little tutoring," he muttered. "Twenty an hour."

"What do you get for doing someone else's assignment?"

"Suspension," Eric said coolly.

Vince made a face. He grabbed a hall pass from a hook on the wall and slipped out the door.

"I'm impressed," I said. "You really know how to handle him."

Eric shrugged. "I've lived around assholes like Vince my whole life. He's only out for himself. Do business with a guy like that, and you're bound to get into trouble."

He started typing lines of code, his keystrokes heavier than usual, like maybe Vince had gotten under his skin as deeply as he'd gotten under mine. I tore a sheet of paper from my notebook and scribbled out a sequence of equations. I handed them to Eric as the bell began to ring.

• • •

I called Reece from my locker as soon as seventh period was dismissed. He picked up on the first ring.

"Is it Saturday yet?" he asked longingly. "You have no idea how badly I miss you."

"Come pick me up," I said, practically bouncing on my toes. "My mom's working tonight. We can go to my place and make ramen noodles and pretend to study."

He growled, frustrated. "I wish I could. I'm working the late shift at Nico's tonight."

"I can come with you. I can grab a booth and do some homework or something."

"Friday nights are busy. I won't have time to hang out. We'll spend the whole day together tomorrow. I'll pick you up at ten."

I sighed. "Bring me a cannoli?"

I could hear his smile through the phone. "With extra chocolate sauce and two spoons. I promise."

• • •

I woke on Saturday morning to the sound of a car door slamming. I jumped out of bed and peeled back my curtain, hoping the sound of the car door had been the Benz. Maybe Alex had let him borrow it. But no one was there.

I checked my phone. It was almost eleven a.m. Where was Reece?

One new text message.

Didn't want to call and wake you. Can't make it today.

Left you something on your front porch.

My shoulders slumped like someone had just let all the helium out of me. I trudged to the front door and threw it open, half expecting a soggy chocolate cannoli with one lousy spoon. Instead, I found a bouquet of wild daisies—the kind that grew in the weeds behind my trailer. Next to it was a paint can, wet gray paint still dripping down its side, the same gray color of my trailer. Anchored under the edge of the can was a note, scribbled on the back of a gas receipt.

> I miss you. Picked up an extra shift at Nico's.
> Working a double. I'll call you tomorrow.
>
> RW

I descended the porch steps with the daisies. The whole side of the trailer was repainted, and the graffiti was gone.

I looked up the street, but his bike was nowhere in sight.

Sunny View Drive was empty, except for the man standing in front of one of the streetlight poles, staring at one of Lonny's flyers. Only I had the weird feeling he was really looking at me. I crossed my arms over my pajama top, feeling a little creeped out.

A white van slowed at the stop sign at the corner. When it eased forward again, the man at the streetlight was gone. I was still staring at the place where he'd been standing when the van pulled up beside my trailer. Butch got out, swinging a paint can in his hand.

"Oh," he said with a look of surprise, and maybe a little disappointment. "I guess your mom didn't need any help after all." He set the can down and rubbed his shiny, shaved head, admiring Reece's handiwork. "Did you do this?"

"Not hardly. It was Reece," I said, tucking the daisies behind my back.

"Is Reece this boyfriend your mother's told me so much about?"

"What do you mean?" Butch had my full attention. "What is Mom telling you?"

"Everything." He grinned, watching the color rush to my cheeks. "Hey, Leigh." Butch took my chin in his hand. He was the closest thing I'd had to a father figure since my dad left. He tasted like love and worry and pride. "It sounds like Reece is a good kid. But if he's an informant . . . if he's ratting his buddies out to the cops . . . that's a dangerous line to walk. I've known good men who've been killed for a lot less. And I don't want you tangled up with the wrong people. It would destroy your mother if anything ever happened to you. Just . . . be careful, okay?"

Butch had never met Reece. He'd never seen us together. He couldn't know that I tasted all the same things when Reece touched me too. "Reece is careful. He would never do anything to hurt me." I held on tight to the sagging daisies in my hand. "He promised. You'll see."

5

ON MONDAY MORNING, I got to the computer lab early to finish an assignment I hadn't done over the weekend. I peeked my head in the door and heaved a sigh of relief. I had the room to myself, at least for a while. Or at least, I'd thought I did.

Jeremy ambled in after me and set his backpack down with a hard thunk. He sat on the teacher's desk and frowned at me, adjusting the rolled cuffs of his long sleeves. He pulled them just low enough to cover the darkest part of the fading bruise his father had probably left on his arm Thursday night.

I turned to my screen and began typing, biting my tongue. He didn't want my help or my concern anymore.

I logged into my e-mail account. One new message.

From TJ Wiles. "I can't be stopped so easily."

Damn Vince and his stupid friends. I gritted my teeth and fired off a reply. "Who is this?"

My message bounced back. "This user does not exist." Exactly what I thought.

Jeremy heaved an exasperated sigh. "Do you seriously think Vince DiMorello has physics formulas just floating around in his big meathead?"

"Excuse me?" I started at the sound of Jeremy's voice and looked up from my computer.

"This note I found in my bedroom," he said, waving it at me again. "I know you don't care, but I do. I want to know who broke into my house and put it there."

I clicked DELETE with a little too much force, making Jeremy flinch. "I already told you my theory."

Jeremy chewed on his thumbnail. "It couldn't have been Vince." I wasn't sure if Jeremy was talking to me or to himself. I kept typing, so Jeremy raised his voice. "Spray paint and toilet paper is his MO. Not physics formulas. He's an idiot. A total moron."

"Anyone can Google a formula."

"He's too lazy for that."

"Got something to say to me, Fowler?"

Vince stood inside the door of the computer lab.

Jeremy tucked the note close to his body, but I was certain Vince had already seen it. His eyes narrowed on it. He grabbed

Jeremy by the neck and pinned him to the whiteboard. "If this is your idea of some kind of joke, it isn't funny, Fowler!"

I leaped from my chair. "Let him go!" I pulled at Vince's shoulders. It was like trying to move a boulder.

Vince gave Jeremy a last shove, then dropped him to the floor. He reached into his shirt pocket and tossed a folded slip of paper at Jeremy's feet. The paper leached heavy blue ink.

Vince waved a thick finger back and forth between me and Jeremy. "I know it was one of you! What the hell is this supposed to mean anyway?"

Jeremy rubbed his throat and pulled himself to his feet. I reached down to pick up the note. It was eerily similar to the one in Jeremy's hand.

$F = ma$

"Where did you get this?" I asked Vince.

He looked first at me, and then at Jeremy, like he wasn't sure if he should say. "Someone left it in the front seat of my car. It was there this morning when I left for school."

If it wasn't Vince, then who'd broken in to Jeremy's house?

"Show him," I said to Jeremy.

Jeremy hesitated. "Someone left this in my bedroom Wednesday night."

Vince took it. His face crinkled, confused.

Jeremy shot me an I-told-you-so look.

"They're Newton's Laws of Motion," I explained. "Jeremy's

note is the mathematical representation of the first law. Basically, it says that an object at rest will remain at rest unless acted on by an unbalanced force. Your note represents the second law, which gives the exact relationship between acceleration, force, and mass."

Vince and Jeremy shared the same expression my tutoring students used to wear when I'd completely lost them.

"You know, the idea that it takes more force to move an object if it has a greater mass? Like the two of you. You guys are the same height, but your mass is way different. I would need to apply a lot more force to push Vince than to push you."

Jeremy's face reddened and he shoved his glasses up the bridge of his nose. "Fine, I get it. But that doesn't answer the question of what it means."

"The first two laws have to do with inertia and . . . momentum . . ." My voice trailed off. I had a nagging feeling, like an itch in my brain.

I can't be stopped so easily. Had the e-mails been empty threats? Or had they been something more?

Vince jerked his chin at me. "So what did your note say?"

The question shook me from my thoughts. "What?"

"You said these are the first two laws. So that means there are more, right?"

Vince was right. And the nagging itch burrowed deeper under my skin. "I didn't get any note. Unless you count those stupid e-mails you keep sending me."

Vince made a face. "What are you talking about? I didn't send you any e-mails."

"Sure. Whatever. Because you wouldn't have any reason to send me e-mails during computer lab pretending to be TJ just to mess with me!"

"Oh, you want to play that game? Fine. How do we know it wasn't you who wrote the notes? I've seen you digging around under that fake rock and letting yourself into Fowler's house before. Maybe *you're* the one who's messing with us."

"This from the guy who spray painted my trailer last week?"

"That doesn't count. I was inebriated." He shoved Jeremy's note at him. "That still doesn't answer the question of which one of you broke into my car."

I took a deep breath and tried not to think about strangling him with a computer cable. As much as I hated him, and as much as didn't want to feel like I owed Jeremy anything, I was just as curious as they were to figure out who was behind the notes.

"Did you lock your car last night, Vince?"

"I always lock it."

"Was your window smashed?"

He recoiled. "No."

"Could someone have jimmied the lock?"

"No. It would have triggered the alarm. What are you getting at?"

"Occam's razor. The simplest answer is often correct. Who has your spare key?"

Vince hitched his thumbs in his pockets, shifting from foot to foot. "What spare key?"

I stood with my arms crossed, waiting.

Vince stared back, with nothing to say.

Jeremy checked his watch. "Well, we have a few minutes before class. Want to hit the vending machines?" he asked me.

We started toward the door. For a split second, everything felt right and familiar between us. Like all this time, we'd just needed a common enemy to bring us back together, even if it was probably just a ploy on Jeremy's part to get Vince to talk.

"Fine!" Vince yelled before we reached the hall. "I keep a spare. Big deal. No one knows where it is."

"You've never used it?" I asked.

"No, it wasn't for me. It was for . . ." Vince's mouth clamped shut, trapping the rest of his thought between tight lips.

"It was for who, Vince?"

He didn't answer.

"Do you want to figure this out or not?"

"It doesn't matter." He shook his head. "It couldn't have been him anyway."

I didn't like the look on Vince's face. I couldn't quite tell if he was shaking off a thought, or if that thought had made his whole body shudder. I touched his forearm. Felt the hair rising from the goose bumps on his skin. Vince DiMorello was scared, and it left a horrible familiar taste in my mouth.

"The spare belonged to TJ, didn't it?" I was certain of it.

He winced and jerked away. "He was the only one who used it. He kept stuff in my glove box. Stuff he couldn't keep in his locker or his uncle's trailer. Pain meds for his knee, Oxycontin and shit he'd bought on the street. But that doesn't have anything to do with this. TJ's in prison. And Powell Ridge is like four hours away. I've heard the place is like fucking Alcatraz. I doubt he's allowed to talk to anybody."

"Who else knew about the key?" I asked.

"No one." Vince blinked hard and looked away.

"Emily Reinnert," Jeremy said. Vince's face flushed. "She was dating both of them. She would have known about the key." Jeremy was right. It made perfect sense. Emily was TJ's accomplice and girlfriend. She'd been so closely involved with him, she'd been a key witness in his trial in exchange for a reduced sentence. She had also been cheating on him with Vince. It had been one of the final straws that had broken TJ, when Jeremy had shown him photos of Vince and Emily kissing.

"No," Vince said firmly. "It couldn't have been Emily. She's on house arrest. She can't go anywhere without her parents or the police knowing about it."

The first bell rang. Students began filtering in. Vince was still eyeing me suspiciously.

"When you figure out who else knew about the spare key, you'll know who was behind this. Meanwhile, there's no reason to freak out. The notes are bogus. They don't make any sense. Someone's probably just screwing around." I sat down at my computer, wishing I believed that.

"I'm still not convinced you didn't have something to do with this, Boswell," Vince said, making heads turn. Jeremy and Vince stood beside each other, staring at me with dubious expressions. Last year, everyone ignored me. Now it seemed like everyone was watching, like they all knew my father had created the monster that TJ had become and it was only a matter of time before I did something wrong too.

"You're not the only one," I muttered.

6

ON TUESDAY AFTER SCHOOL, I found Raj where he'd said he would be, sitting in front of a cluttered workstation in the Latent Prints lab. A "Han Shot First" bumper sticker was taped to the side of the desk. He stretched and yawned.

"Feel like bringing me a cup of coffee?" he asked, scratching the Star Wars logo on his T-shirt.

Pecking order was one thing. Being a self-serving asshat was another. "Not really."

"I had a feeling you'd say that." He rubbed his eyes and gave me a once-over. I'd followed his lead, opting for sneakers, jeans, and a T-shirt Reece had given me for my birthday that said "Stand Back, I'm Going to Do Science." Raj read my shirt and laughed. "You have much to learn, young padawan. Come on, I'll show you where we keep the sterilizing equipment. That is, if your commitment to feminism doesn't preclude you from washing beakers and pipettes."

"Very funny." I followed Raj. He handed me a pair of latex gloves and a plastic basin and showed me through the building, lab by lab. We collected dirty glassware and lab tools, hand-washing and loading them into sterilizing machines. "Why can't I just help you with whatever you were doing in the Latent Prints lab?" I asked. "I know how to work a computer."

"Believe me," he sighed, "I would like nothing more than to dump that load on some poor unsuspecting high school gopher, but I can't. You'd need special clearance and your own password to get into the AFIS system, and gophers don't qualify."

"AFIS?"

"The Automated Fingerprint Identification System. It's a regional database of fingerprint records, most of them collected from crime scenes or arrest records. It's available through a network to various departments of law enforcement, usually for the purpose of identifying a person suspected of a crime, or linking them to other crimes in the area that haven't been solved yet. Which is why you'd need a password. Doc can't let padawans go poking around in there."

"So that's what you're doing? Identifying fingerprints?"

Raj looked sheepish. "I wish. Only licensed fingerprint examiners get to do that. I just scan and enter the data."

"So we get the mindless cleanup jobs," I said, setting another full bin of glassware on my cart. "But who gets to do the glamorous stuff?"

"Crime scene investigators get to pull the actual prints from the scene." Raj cocked an eyebrow and grinned. "Want to see something cool?"

I couldn't help but smile at the mischievous look on his face. As soon as I did, Raj motioned me to follow. We left the cart and headed back upstairs. He shut the door to the Latent Prints lab behind us and began pulling supplies from a cabinet. Then he drew on a pair of latex gloves.

"What are we doing?" I asked.

"We're going to process your fingerprints. The examiner's on vacation, which is why you haven't had your fingerprints taken yet. She'll be back tomorrow, but I can do it now since you're here." He was entirely too eager as he fumbled with the supplies.

I looked around for an inkpad but all I saw was a brush and a container of black powder.

"Do you know what you're doing?"

Raj rolled his eyes. "Please, I've watched her do this a million times."

"Why aren't we using ink?"

"Because inkpads are for cops and sissies, not scientists."

"But I thought you said we weren't doing science."

"Only when no one's looking. Here, put your hand on the plastic sheet. Don't press too hard. It'll push the ridges too close together. Yeah, that's good." He gently lifted the corners of the plastic from the table and carried it to an opening in a large piece of equipment. "Ever heard of cyanoacrylate?"

"No," I said, watching him clip the sheet inside.

"Sure you have. It's Super Glue. Now check this out." Raj locked the chamber door, pressed a few buttons, and we watched the fingerprints process through the glass window. Tiny white crystals began to form ridges and whorls, and from an oblique angle, I could just begin to make out my own fingerprints. "This is a fuming chamber. All you need is a heat source, a little water, and Super Glue. The heated cyanoacrylate changes to a gas, and if there's enough humidity in the chamber, the Super Glue fumes bond with the proteins in your sweat. You can put all kinds of things in here . . . beer cans, glass, firearms . . . anything non-porous should work. When the Super Glue crystals harden, we'll be able to handle your fingerprints without smudging them. Then we can use black powder to give them enough contrast to be scanned into the AFIS database, and your prints will officially be on record."

A sick feeling snaked through me as Raj carefully removed the plastic sheet from the fuming chamber.

"What if I don't want to be on record?"

"Everyone who works in the lab has to have a set of elimination prints on file in AFIS. In case evidence was ever contaminated, we'd need to be able to rule you out as a possible suspect."

"Does that happen often?"

Raj set my fingerprints in a drying chamber. "Do you have any idea how many people go tromping through a crime scene before CSI teams get there? Trust me, you want your prints on file. It makes the examiner's job a lot easier. Besides, when you graduate and go off to some fancy college next year, some poor schlep like me will have the honor of purging you from the system. It'll be like you were never even here."

I held out my opposite hand. Let him press and roll each finger. Watched my fingerprints develop and harden in a box of smoke.

Next, Raj scanned my prints into the computer. Seeing my name on the AFIS screen felt strange, even though Raj had checked the box indicating they were elimination prints. Once my fingerprints were entered, my reasons for being in the system wouldn't matter. I'd be just another set of random markers in a database of criminals, waiting to be identified and sorted.

Raj looked pleased with himself. "Pretty cool, huh?" His face fell, suddenly serious. "And if anyone asks, we used ink. Okay?"

"Sure." I'd had enough of fingerprinting lessons for one day. "I'm going to go finish the sterilizing."

"Do me a favor and stop by the Fridge. Doc had a body coming in today, and he'll probably have some stuff that needs to be cleaned."

Raj turned back to his computer and I headed downstairs to pick up my abandoned cart. I followed signs for the Ossuary, remembering that the Fridge was somewhere off the same hall.

I pushed through the set of double doors Raj had pointed out during my tour. A delivery driver waited on the other side. His truck was backed up tightly against an open garage bay; its rear doors swung wide, revealing a long black body bag on a gurney. I stood against the wall with my hands in my pockets while Doc Benoit signed for the delivery.

When he was finished, I said, "Dr. Benoit? Raj asked me to come down and see if you need me to—"

"Here, hold this," Doc said, plucking a small brown bag with a yellow biohazard sticker off the top of the gurney. I stepped forward to take it, holding it at arm's length.

"Miss Boswell," Doc Benoit said, shaking my attention

from the bag. "Do you mind?" He gestured to my feet. "You're standing on my scale." Beneath me was a large rectangular cut-out in the floor. Beside it, wires climbed up the wall to a monitor that flashed 112.3 lbs. I stumbled out of the way and the monitor flashed back to 000.0. The driver wheeled the body bag onto the scale and Doc Benoit recorded the weight.

"Follow me to the Fridge," he said.

He wheeled the gurney to a large metal door and swiped his card. A cool rush of air escaped when Doc Benoit pushed it open. It smelled like the air in the biology lab at school during dissection week, but stronger. Formaldehyde and phenol, chemical smells that grabbed at the back of my throat. I blinked, my eyes watering as I stepped into the cold.

The "Fridge" was a storage room containing a row of gurneys. Along the wall were metal shelves, lined with plastic trays labeled with the names of body parts. Teeth, jaws, skull fragments, phalanges. I didn't look inside.

"Well, first things first," Doc said, pulling on a fresh set of latex gloves, blue booties, and a surgical cap, then handing me a set. I stared at them, sick at the thought of putting them on.

Doc stood there, waiting.

Make us proud, Boswell.

I put on the booties and cap first, then the gloves, the smell of latex inviting a rush of memories. TJ's gloved hand over

my mouth, his gun at my temple. I breathed through a wave
of nausea.

"Ready?" Doc asked.

Don't screw this up.

I steadied myself against a rolling tray containing various
sizes of labels and specimen containers. Doc unzipped the
body bag from the middle, pulling it wide to reveal a woman.
Her arms were an unnatural color, covered in a film of dirt.
Her scant clothes were caked with it. Her hands were covered in paper bags and before I had time to wonder what they
were for, Doc removed one.

Her short nails were polished, a garish shade of electric
blue, and bitten around the purpling cuticles. Clipping off
a small piece of fingernail, he placed it in another paper bag
and handed it to me. Doc Benoit carefully inspected both
hands, using small tools and swabs to collect trace evidence,
he explained. When he was finished, I had a collection of
small paper bags, which I labeled according to his instructions. Under the space for her name, I wrote DOE, JANE.

"Let's see if we can figure out who Miss Doe really is," Doc
said, rolling the tip of one of her fingers in ink and pressing
it to a small white card, then handing it to me. "If her prints
aren't in the system, then we can check against the missing
persons reports for distinguishing marks." Doc pulled a small
voice recorder from his shirt pocket and pressed a button.

"Victim is a Caucasian female. Approximate age, late teens

to early twenties. Cause of death, strangulation. Ligature marks on the victim's wrists." I had the urge to swallow, to keep swallowing to hold down my revulsion. I looked at the tray, and tried to stay focused on the bags that contained her cut fingernails and the residue Doc had dug out from underneath them. The room began to swim.

I heard Doc opening the body bag further.

"Multiple piercings in both ears. Eye color . . . brown. Hair color, light brown at the root," he said to the recorder. To me, he said, "Put this in a bag and label it 'hair sample.'"

I turned back to him and reached for the tweezers, struggling to keep pressure on the prongs, focusing hard on the small pointed tip so I wouldn't see the dead face inside the bag.

The hair in the tweezers was blue.

A sour burn climbed up my throat.

The tweezers clattered to the floor.

Adrienne, was my last thought as I dropped to the floor beside them.

• • •

"You're back," Raj said, pulling smelling salts from my nose.

I wasn't sure where Raj had come from. I was on a gurney in the hall outside the Fridge. "What happened? Where's Doc Benoit?" My mouth tasted sour. Raj helped me sit up slowly. My head pounded and the walls were moving a little.

"You passed out cold. Hit your head on the supply cart

on the way down. It took both of us to get you off the floor. Anyway, Doc asked me to look after you. Between you and me, he doesn't deal very well with vomit."

I wrapped a hand over my stomach, breathing shallowly. My T-shirt and jeans were wet where I touched them, and smelled like puke.

"Don't be embarrassed," Raj said when I tried to cover them. He bit his lip to keep from smiling. "It's happened to all of us. Everyone gets sick their first time seeing a body. It just doesn't normally happen on the first day."

A body.

Adrienne.

The body in the bag had been Adrienne's.

I grabbed Raj by the shoulder, ready to tell him. But how would it look to Doc Benoit if I told them I knew yet another victim? Four black bags had already been delivered to him, with the bodies of people who'd gone to my school. People I'd known. Even though Adrienne's murder had nothing to do with the others, Doc would probably tell me I was too close to the victim to stay involved. They'd probably recuse me from the lab. Maybe from the internship.

I let go of his shoulder.

Raj helped me off the gurney. He walked me to the water fountain and I drank slowly, hoping it would stay down. "I get it now," I said between small, cautious sips. "No nice shirts in the lab."

He smirked.

"I'll be fine next time. I promise," I said.

Raj scratched his head. "I'm not sure there's going to be a next time for a while."

"What do you mean?" My heart fluttered. What if they already knew?

"You're just an intern, so technically you shouldn't have been in the Fridge during a procedure. And you definitely shouldn't have been taking evidence from a homicide victim. I don't know what Doc was thinking taking you in there with him. Sometimes Doc's so preoccupied with dead people, he sort of loses touch with those of us who still have a pulse. Veronica's going to kill me. You haven't even signed your non-disclosure agreement yet."

"Non-disclosure agreement?"

Raj sighed and rubbed his eyes. "The very important legal form we all have to sign that says we promise not to tell anyone about the specifics of the cases we've worked on inside the lab. I was supposed to have you sign them when you had your fingerprints taken. I guess I sort of forgot. This was a huge breach of protocol."

"Am I in trouble?"

"Of course not," Raj said with a dismissive wave. "It was my fault. But let's just keep you out of the Fridge for a while. At least until we get all your paperwork wrapped up." Raj looked at my eye and cringed. "You should go home, put some ice on that shiner and get some rest."

I reached up to the small pulsing ache above my right eye. The knot was tender and sore to the touch.

How was I going to keep my word to Lonny if I wasn't allowed to tell him that Adrienne's body was here? And if I wasn't allowed back in the Fridge, how would I find out what had happened to her?

"Do you have a ride home?" Raj asked, shaking me from my thoughts.

"I'll take the bus. I'll be fine." I didn't want to face Gena or Reece after blowing my first real day.

Raj took off his lab coat and slipped it around my shoulders to cover the puke stains on my shirt. It was long enough to cover my jeans too. "How about I take you home? On the way out, we'll run Jane Doe's prints through the computer and drop the evidence bags in the lab. You know, intern stuff." He winked, like it was all no big deal. Just trace evidence. Not bits and pieces of a person I knew.

7

I ASKED RAJ to drop me off in the parking lot of the Bui Mart. I didn't want him to see the "missing persons" flyers Lonny had plastered throughout Sunny View. The print quality wasn't great, but if Raj had seen the body when he'd come to pick me up off the floor, then the blue hair was a dead giveaway. He'd know I'd recognized the victim and had kept it to myself.

I waited at the intersection for the light to change and walked with my head down when I crossed the street so no one would stare at my swollen eye. My shoulder brushed a man who passed too closely from the opposite direction. When I looked up, his head was down too, but I'd had the nagging feeling like he'd been staring at me. The same feeling I'd had all day at school. The same feeling I would have the next time I stepped foot in the lab. Like people were watching, waiting for me to do something wrong. Like I was being judged.

My head throbbed, and I glanced in the direction of Lonny's trailer, half expecting to see him sitting on his front porch, watching me too. I would only have to keep this from Lonny for one more day. When we had run the fingerprints through the Automated Fingerprint Identification System an hour ago, Raj said the examiner would probably have a conclusive result in a few days. Homicides were prioritized, so the print would be matched quickly if Adrienne had a police record, and I was pretty sure she did, judging by the conversation I'd overheard at the police station last week. Once police knew the body was Adrienne's, it would all be out in the open and I'd be off the hook with both Lonny and Doc Benoit.

But for now, no one in Sunny View knew Adrienne was dead. Not Lonny. Not her friends. Not her mother . . . a fact that tugged at my chest, making me stop and turn toward Lonny's trailer. A light was on in his kitchen window. His car was parked outside. I hadn't signed any non-disclosure agreements yet. But leaking the details of a homicide to a drug dealer with a criminal record would be a mistake. A mistake that could cost me my internship.

My feet kept moving, but my eyes kept wandering back toward his trailer. Lonny was a friend, sort of. He'd come through for me. And we had an agreement. But if I told him, he'd roll right down to the station and demand information, and then how would I explain my breach to Doc Benoit, and Raj, and the investigators working on Adrienne's case? I lowered my head and kept walking. I didn't look up until I was at my own door.

• • •

I put the key to the lock, but the door swung open under my hand.

Our trailer was always locked. Even when we were home. The importance of this had been drilled into me every day since I was old enough to stay home alone.

I looked over my shoulder, wishing I'd let Raj drive me all the way home. The street was empty and quiet. I stepped just inside the opening. The living room was dark, the evening light too dim to penetrate the closed drapes.

They'd been open when I'd left that morning. I was certain of it.

I slipped off my shoes and used one to prop the door open. That's when I smelled it. Cigarette smoke, clinging to the heat of the room. So fresh I could still smell the strike of the match.

I reached into the corner. My hand closed over the blunt end of the baseball bat my mother kept in the entryway, and I waited for my eyes to adjust. I blinked, making out the rumpled yellow slipcover on the sofa, the juice glass full of butts and ashes on the table beside it.

Someone had been here.

A man's button-down shirt was draped over the back of a kitchen chair.

Someone was *still* here.

I turned toward my mother's bedroom. The light was off, the door was closed. But I swore I saw something move in the gap underneath. I reached into my pocket and pulled out my cell phone. Scrolled to Reece's name and started typing a message.

A floorboard creaked.

My fingers froze on the keys and I set the phone on the table, my message unfinished. I gripped the bat with both hands and raised it over my shoulder. Someone—a man— was in my mother's room. I crept toward it, flattening myself against the wall. I listened for the sound of my mother's voice, her breath. But it was silent. Like whoever was on the other side was listening to me too.

My phone jumped to life, vibrating against the table. Someone was calling. Probably Reece. I was supposed to call him when I got home. I didn't move. I held my breath as I watched the phone skitter toward the edge.

It dropped onto the floor, and then everything happened at once. My mother's bedroom door flew open, an arm snaked out, grabbed me by my shirt front, lifted me off my feet, and shoved me hard against the wall. The bat clattered to the floor. The hall light snapped on, and I blinked against it, heart pounding under the huge hand at my chest.

"Nearly Faith Boswell! You scared me half to death!"

Butch. It was just Butch.

He let out a relieved breath and eased me to the floor. "Jesus, Leigh! I could've killed you. What are you doing, sneaking around in the dark? And what the hell happened to your face?"

My knees wobbled and I let the wall hold me up as relief washed over me. My mother held the light switch in one hand and clutched the front of her robe tight to her chest with the other. The man in her bedroom was just Butch. An awkward giggle escaped my throat. My mother rushed to my side and inspected my eye, prodding it with her fingers.

"Who did this to you?"

"Ow!" I swatted her wrist. "No one did anything to me. I slipped and fell in the lab." I felt some of her worry rush out of her. Out of both of us.

My mother was safe. Butch was here. She pulled her hand from my face, but not before I tasted it. Something secretive, hard to place, hiding under my tongue. She darted red-faced looks between me and Butch. He bent down and picked up the bat, avoiding my eyes.

Butch was here. With her. Inside the trailer.

Inside my mother's room.

Butch and my mother.

Butch stared at the floor, scratching the back of his big bald head, awkwardly trying to cover the red smudge on his shirt, just below his neck.

My mother fidgeted with her robe. "Butch was just picking me up for work."

"Aren't you late?" I asked, my tone thick with accusations.

"We were just leaving," they said at the same time, which should have made it seem like they were telling the truth, but didn't.

"Where's his van?"

"I walked," Butch said, still not quite looking me in the eye. "It's just across the street." He threw a thumb in the direction of Gentleman Jim's.

Neither of them spoke.

It occurred to me that maybe he had been picking her up

for work all summer, and I'd been spending so much time with Reece, I just hadn't been around to notice. That maybe Butch had been parking his car in Jim's lot to keep our nosey neighbors from talking about it. Maybe he'd been inside our trailer before—inside my mother's room.

"I'll wait in the living room," I said, snatching the bat from Butch's hand and storming down the hall. My mother hadn't had the nerve to tell me. In the hospital, we had promised each other, no more secrets. That we would trust each other. But looking around my trailer, seeing Butch's shirt hanging over the chair and the fresh cigarette butts in the glass on the table, I wasn't so sure.

The floor creaked. I knew Butch was standing behind me, but I couldn't look at him. I returned the bat to its place behind the door and grabbed up the glass of ash and butts. "She's smoking again," I said without turning around. The lipstick on the butts matched the stain on the neck of Butch's shirt, confessing all the secrets my mother hadn't told me. I shook them into the trashcan under the sink.

"She had a rough day," he said softly, as though this should be enough. He pulled my shoe out from where I'd wedged it inside the security door and leaned against the frame, taking up the whole of it as he stared down the street. He always looked tough, but tonight he seemed troubled, and I'd never seen Butch troubled before. He tossed my shoe at me. "Be sure to keep the door locked when your mother's at work tonight."

"It was unlocked when I got here," I said with a little too much sass.

"That's because I was here."

I rolled my eyes. "Oooh, Butch Reynolds, the big bad bouncer."

"I'm serious, Leigh. I want you to be more careful." Butch's face was stony. There was a worry behind it I'd never seen before.

"What's wrong? What happened?"

He looked at me for a long moment, as though he wasn't sure if he should answer. He glanced toward my mother's closed bedroom door.

"Your mother got a letter from the state yesterday." Butch scratched the back of his head, hesitating.

"And . . . ?"

"Reggie Wiles is out on parole."

TJ's father.

"Since when?" I asked.

"Two weeks ago."

"What do you mean, two weeks ago?" Reggie Wiles wasn't serving time for violent crimes, but that didn't mean he wasn't capable of them. "Why didn't the state notify us two weeks ago?"

"The letter was mailed a month ago, but the mail carrier put it in the wrong mailbox. Apparently, it's been sitting in a stack of unopened mail on Mrs. Moates's coffee table. She noticed it when she finally got around to paying her phone bill and brought it by yesterday morning after you left for school."

Butch rested a hand on my shoulder. "Don't worry. Reggie's living in a halfway house in Arlington. He's closely monitored and he's got a curfew."

So did plenty of kids at my school, but a curfew didn't keep them from sneaking out either. "For how long?"

Butch hesitated before answering. "Three or four weeks. Then they'll release him to live with an approved family member."

An approved family member. Probably the same one they'd assigned TJ to live with when he was orphaned. With his drunk uncle Billy, four trailers down from our own. "No! They would never let him live that close to us."

"We don't get a say," Butch said, shushing me and looking down the hall like he didn't want my mother to hear. "He's served his time. Technically, he's a free man. We have no reason to assume he's a danger to you or your mother. And you know I would never let anything happen to either of you."

Butch's hand brushed my cheek. His worry had a sour center, but it was cocooned in something I recognized. Something thick and honey-sweet. The way Reece had tasted all summer when my hands wrapped around his waist on the back of his bike. Or his wrapped around mine while we were supposed to be studying algebra.

How had I never seen it before? When Butch talked about my mother, all his hard angles melted into something soft and warm.

My mother came into the living room, bringing our conversation to a quick close. Neither of us wanting to worry her any more than she already was.

"Ready to go?" she asked, grabbing her keys and purse, then pausing over the cigarette-ashen glass in the sink. Her eyes met mine. She pulled a crinkled pack of lights from her pocket and tossed them into the trash.

"Mom, you don't have to—"

"No, no more cigarettes. I promise." She kissed my head and didn't let go. Butch stepped outside, and she spoke softly into my hair. "I'm sorry I didn't tell you about us."

"Why didn't you?"

"I guess I was worried about how you would feel about Butch and me . . . being together. I love him. I think I've loved him for a long time. But you were so obsessed with the notion of finding your father, and I didn't know what it might do to you, if I were to bring another man into your life. Then after everything happened in June, and you were in the hospital, Butch was the one who was there for us. And your father . . ." She didn't have to say it. I had almost died, and my own father hadn't even called. "By then, you knew the truth about David. And I thought, maybe it was time I started facing up to some truths too. Like my feelings for Butch. He makes me happy. I won't apologize for that, Nearly, but I'm sorry if you're not ready for me to move on."

Her shame tasted like ash on my tongue and I didn't want to make her feel that way. "I'm not upset about that. You know I love Butch. And I want you to be happy. But you shouldn't keep secrets from me. Not when those secrets affect both of us."

"I'm sorry." She smiled. "No more hiding cigarettes and boyfriends. I have to go. Don't forget to lock up behind us." She kissed my forehead and left with Butch.

I watched them twine their fingers together and walk slowly over the rutted gravel. My mother didn't clutch her purse to her side, or pinch her coat tightly around her neck. She never once looked over her shoulder, even in the dark. She was happy. She was safe. The two things she'd never been with my father.

I locked the door and scraped my cell phone off the floor. The battery and cover had come loose when it fell, and I snapped it back together just as Reece's motorcycle skidded to a stop outside my trailer. Shit, I hadn't called him back.

"Leigh!" Reece pounded on my front door. "Leigh! Are you—?"

I threw the deadbolt and opened the door. Reece's fist hung, knocking in midair, his expression frozen somewhere between relief and what-the-hell-happened-to-your-face.

Reece took my chin in his hand and turned my cheek to

the light. I swallowed back salt and hot metal. Felt the rise of his blood pressure in my own veins. "Who did this to you?"

I stepped aside to let him in, and then locked the door after him. "I did it to myself. I saw something in the medical examiner's lab. I guess it freaked me out. I fell and hit my head."

Reece watched me check the locks again, then studied the bruise. "Does it hurt?" he asked, wincing.

"It's better than it was." Reece touched my brow with the tip of his finger, awakening the pain, and I flinched. He headed to the kitchen and put some ice cubes in a plastic bag. Then he eased down beside me on the sofa, carefully pressing it to my face. I shut my eyes against the cold, then smiled at the soft warmth of his lips against mine.

"What did you see?" he asked me when I'd opened them again. His face was close to mine, and his eyes were a dark, deep blue. They were hard to look away from and easy to get lost in.

"A body," I said.

He set the ice on the coffee table and wrapped his arm around me, drawing his fingers through my hair.

"She was young, and she'd been murdered. I passed out—maybe it was the smell, or the color of her . . ." I swallowed hard, stopping myself before I said too much. "Or the color of her skin. I don't know. I hit my head on the autopsy cart when I fell."

"Leigh, are you still sure . . . ?"

"Reece. I'll be fine. Raj took care of me—brought me home. He said it happens to everyone on their first day." Actually, Raj said it happens to everyone when they see their first body. Adrienne's was hardly my first, but I didn't want to give Reece another reason to worry.

"Raj?" Reece pulled away and raised an eyebrow. "Should I be worried that you're hanging out with some sexy CSI guy?"

"No, just a geeky lab tech. But if I had a thing for Star Wars T-shirts, I'd be a goner."

He laughed and nestled in beside me, resting his arm around my shoulders.

I glanced down the hall toward my bedroom. "Reece, do you know anything about halfway houses?"

He pursed his lips. "Why?"

"Reggie Wiles was released from prison a few weeks ago."

"Huh."

"'Huh'? That's it?" I asked, looking up into his face.

"Well, I'm sure he has a lot of people keeping tabs on him." He rested his lips on my forehead. A tang like cider vinegar crept over my tongue. His concern was muddled with something a little too sweet, like he was intentionally trying to hide it from me. "Don't let it worry you, Leigh. You're just starting to feel better after everything that happened. You're happy again. Don't let Reggie Wiles distract you from school or your internship." He stroked a delicate finger over my bruise. "Or me," he whispered, lips against my ear. "There's nothing to worry about, Leigh. Not while I'm here." He lay down across the cushions, and I sank into him.

Reece ran his fingers under my shirt, up my rib cage, tasting sweet and hot. His nose brushed mine, then his mouth, his tongue tracing my lips before sliding between them.

Reece's phone vibrated silently in his pocket. He groaned, then reached to pull it from his jeans. He squinted at the screen. "It's just Gena," he said, declining the call and setting the phone on the coffee table beside the bag of ice. He eased back down to the sofa, pulling me with him. His lips and tongue tickled my neck.

The phone began rattling on the table. Reece's fingernails dug into my jeans. "Your shirt smells terrible. I think we should take it off," he said, pushing the fabric up my sides until his hands found my bra.

I giggled. "It's probably Gena again. Aren't you going to answer it?"

Reece fidgeted with the clasp. "Ignore it. Maybe she'll go away."

"I'll talk to her." I lifted my head from Reece's chest and scrambled for the phone. He moaned and threw a pillow over his face. I expected to see Gena's name. Instead, the screen read "Private Caller." Odd, she'd just called from her own cell. I'd seen the number when he'd put the phone on the table. Unless she was calling from a different line, hoping to fool Reece into picking up this time.

I untangled myself from the sofa and climbed over him to take the call in the other room. Maybe I could find a way to convince her to check on Reggie without throwing up any red flags.

"Reece can't come to the phone," I said, trying not to sound breathless. "What's up?"

The silence on the line was heavy and too long.

"Are you there?" I asked.

"Who is this?" a girl asked. The tentative voice in the receiver wasn't Gena's.

I peered around the wall at Reece. His face was still buried in the pillow, his chest rising and falling in a shallow, steady rhythm.

"Who is this?" I asked the girl.

Reece stopped breathing. The girl didn't answer.

Reece sat up and was across the room in three long strides. He snatched the phone and disconnected, dropping it face down on the table, like it had burned him.

"Who was that?" I hated that my voice sounded like the girl on the line. Fragile and uncertain.

"Nobody," he said, scrubbing his face and inching away. Like he didn't want to touch me. Like he didn't want me to feel something. But he was too late. I'd felt his skin when he'd taken the phone: a rush of hot panic that left a searing guilt.

My mouth was still dry with the charred taste of it.

"Nobody?" I repeated. I'd been *nobody* once. Someone who'd made him feel guilty. Someone he kept secrets for. "Is she your . . . Is she a . . ."

His pause was too long. Like he was weighing words. He reached for me, but I moved away. He'd had too much time to focus his thoughts, to steady his emotions. He was good at hiding who he was inside. *"You're* my girlfriend. You're the only girl I want to be with."

"Then who is she?"

"She's just part of the job."

"I was part of your job."

"I didn't want you to worry over nothing. She's nothing. In a couple days, she'll do something stupid and get herself arrested and it'll be over. It's just a job, Leigh. It doesn't mean anything."

"If it doesn't mean anything, why hide it?" Maybe for the same reasons my mother had been hiding her relationship with Butch, and Reggie's release from prison. Because they *did* mean something.

"I have to go," he said. I didn't know if the sting was the bristle of his lips on my bruise, or the fact that he was probably leaving to console some girl who wasn't supposed to know he had a girlfriend.

He paused before opening the door. I could feel him standing there, waiting for me to look at him. I didn't move. Didn't say anything. He closed the door hard behind him.

Exhausted, I turned the deadbolt and headed to my bed-room.

I fell to my bed and stared at the wall. A photograph I'd never seen before of my father and me was pinned to the map. My eyes skimmed over my desk and my bed. Everything was there—my books, my pajamas, the shoes Gena had bought for me, and the old Rubik's cube Alex had taught me to solve—everything was the same. Only the photo was new.

I was maybe five in the photo, just a kid with frizzy pigtails and grass stains on the frayed knees of my jeans, sitting in my father's lap in the Fowlers' dining room, around a table littered with poker chips and playing cards. We had identical smiles.

I pulled the pin from the wall and smoothed the hole it left in the image, perfectly centered on my father's forehead. The placement of it felt angry. Intentional and hurtful. My mother wouldn't have left me a photo like this. Even if she had saved any photographs of my father, pinning it this way—ruining this image of my father and me—wasn't some-thing my mother would do. Unease crept through me. I held the picture close to my face. The photo didn't smell old. It smelled pungent, like fresh ink.

I turned it over and my blood ran cold.

$$F_A = -F_B$$

The formula was written in bold blue letters.

Newton's third law of motion.

For every action, there is an equal and opposite reaction.

8

THE NEXT MORNING, I walked to school early and waited at Jeremy's locker. He and Anh rounded the corner, holding hands and talking softly to each other. Jeremy's smile slipped from his face when he saw me. Anh looked back and forth between us. She kissed Jeremy's cheek and told him she'd catch up with him later. Behind his back, she gave me an awkward wave before disappearing around the corner.

I stepped aside so Jeremy could get to his locker. Instead, he dropped his backpack between his feet, like he didn't trust me enough to dial his combination while I was standing there, which was saying a lot, coming from the guy whose idea it once was to put a house key in his front yard to make it easier for me to sneak into his room.

I pulled the photo from my pocket and held it out to him, but his gaze lingered on my bruise.

"What happened?"

"Nothing. Just an accident." It was the same thing Jeremy always used to say whenever someone noticed a mark he couldn't cover.

Jeremy took the photograph. "That's my house. Where'd you get it?" He turned the picture over, and his face paled.

"It's Newton's third law."

Jeremy shoved it back at me with an annoyed look. "I know what it is! Where'd you find it?"

"Tacked to my bedroom wall." Just saying it out loud made my skin crawl. Someone had been in my home. In my bedroom. Had probably gone through my things.

"Still think it's just a joke?" Jeremy asked.

I used to read the personals every week, laughing over the triteness of the ads. Until I saw one that felt wrong, different from the others. The phone calls and spray paint, the dog shit on my porch. Those were all stupid childish pranks, the kind of thing Vince and his friends would do. But this photo? This series of carefully placed physics formulas?

I caught his eyes and held them.

"I don't know," I said.

The first bell rang. Jeremy picked his backpack off the floor. I picked up mine. He adjusted his glasses and kicked the floor with the toe of his shoe.

"So what do we do?"

"Change our locks?"

Jeremy sighed. "Okay. But if you change your locks, don't forget to make a new set of keys for my dad. He gets pissed off when tenants change the locks and don't tell him." And from what I'd seen in front of my trailer last week, that kind of anger would probably manage to fall back on Jeremy.

"Are you going to be okay?" he asked, gesturing loosely to my eye.

"Yeah," I said. "You?" I looked up at his face. Three months ago, I would have reached for his hand when I asked him how he was feeling, just to make sure he was telling the truth. Now all I could do was hope he was being honest with me.

"Yeah." A million unspoken words seemed to pass between us, all of them uncertain. "Are you coming to class?"

I bit my lip. "I'll be there in a minute."

He headed to the lab with his head down. When he rounded the corner, I pulled my phone from my pocket and hit Gena's number on speed dial.

"Aren't you supposed to be in first period?" she answered.

"Second bell hasn't rung yet. I know this sounds silly, but I need a favor. Butch told me that Reggie Wiles was released from prison. Can you pull some strings and see if he's been anywhere he shouldn't have been in the last few days?"

"What do you mean? Like where?"

"Like Sunny View."

Gena was quiet. "Why do you ask?"

The bell rang and I plugged my ear. "No reason."

I could practically hear her rolling her eyes. "You're worrying for nothing. The halfway house program is structured and closely monitored. There's no reason to be concerned. This is exactly why I didn't want you to know."

"But I just found out yester—" The subtext slid into place with a shocking clarity. "Wait, how long have you known?"

Gena was quiet.

"You knew Reggie was out of prison the whole time and you didn't tell me?"

"When you didn't get the letter, we thought maybe it was for the best."

"We? Did Reece know too?"

Her silence was a punch to the gut. It knocked me breathless. He knew, long before last night. And he'd kept it from me.

"You should have told me."

"Look, if it'll make you feel better, I'll have Alex talk to Reggie's parole officer."

I gritted my teeth. She thought I was paranoid. "Fine."

"I'm telling you, you're freaking out over nothing. I'll call you after school."

I disconnected and headed toward my first period class, feeling like an idiot. They all thought I was fragile. Like I needed to be protected from my own imagination. But I wasn't imagining this, was I? If it wasn't Reggie, then who else could it be?

My phone buzzed. One new text message.

I need to see you. I want to explain. Pick you up after school? RW

Great, Gena must have texted him. I hesitated, fingers over

the keys. I would have to change the locks after school, while my mother was at work. And if Reece knew I was anxious enough to change the locks on my trailer, he'd freak out and tell Gena. And she already thought I was freaking out over nothing. Better to wait until I had concrete proof that Reggie wasn't where he was supposed to be.

I replied:

Study group after school. My place at 6?

His answer came hours later, like an afterthought, sometime during fifth period.

Sorry. Have to work. Catch up with you on Saturday.

I wanted to throw the phone across the hall. By Saturday, I'd be a steam kettle ready to explode. Or else I'd be missing him so badly, I'd forget why I was angry with him in the first place. I knew Reece was only trying to protect me. The same way my mother and Gena were. But if everyone was keeping things from me, how was I supposed to protect myself?

My phone buzzed again. This time, it was Gena.

We checked with Reggie's parole officer. You're worried over nothing.

I clung to the hope that it was true.

• • •

Later that night, three new trailer keys rattled in my pocket as I headed for Gentleman Jim's—one for me, one for my mom, and one for Jeremy's dad. I spent the whole day trying to think up some reasonable excuse for changing the locks, some plausible explanation that wouldn't worry Butch or my mother. I stood on the sidewalk in front of the flashing neon lights outside the club, putting the finishing touches on some elaborate story about neighborhood kids sticking chewing gum in the keyhole, just as Butch pushed open the paint-blackened door. Music spilled out with him. In his hands, he held two boys by their shirts, like bags of trash he was hauling to the curb.

One of them was Reece.

He went limp when our eyes met, all the fight slipping out of him. The guy he was with jerked around in Butch's grip, clumsy and drunk, cussing loudly and making a scene.

"Keep it up, and I'll call the police," Butch growled.

"No cops, man." The kid swayed on his feet, doing his best to look sober. "We're cool."

I stood frozen on the sidewalk. "What are you doing here?"

Reece's cheeks flushed and he darted a guilty look across the parking lot. It had only been a quick glance, but I followed his gaze. A girl sat on the hood of a car, smoking a cigarette and watching us all with an amused smile.

His friend looked me up and down, unimpressed. "Who's this?"

Reece ignored him. His eyes flashed, bloodshot and full of words he couldn't say, wouldn't say. Not here.

Butch's grip on Reece seemed to soften. He and Reece had never met, and as many times as I had imagined this moment, I'd never pictured it happening like this.

"I'll let you off with a warning. You boys sneak in my club again, either of you," he said, jerking Reece's collar hard, and the other boy's even harder, "and it'll be the last time you sneak anywhere. Got it?"

They nodded, and Butch let them go with a rough shove toward the parking lot. "Go sober up. You shouldn't let your mothers smell you like this."

Reece winced. He walked away, looking over his shoulder at me. His friend stumbled, muttering to himself while trying to light a cigarette. Reece pushed him hard in the back toward the girl's car. "I told you it was a stupid idea."

The girl tossed her hair back from her eyes and flicked her cigarette to the ground as Reece and his friend came near. She jumped off the hood. "Took you boys long enough," she said with a flirtatious smile, lowering her lashes at Reece. She looped her arm in his, but he shook her off.

"Let's get out of here," he said. Reece got in the passenger seat and slammed the door. He didn't look at me again.

Butch folded his arms over his chest. "That's Reece?"

I nodded.

"Do you trust him?"

My face burned and my eyes watered. I watched the girl's car shrink in the distance.

He'd said he had to work.

I held out a key. "I changed the locks on the trailer."

Butch stared at it, as if weighing its significance. His hand brushed mine when he took the key, and my tongue swelled thick with sympathy. The sting of it left tears in my eyes. He tucked the key in his pocket. "I understand. I'll make sure your mom gets it."

• • •

Later, locked inside my trailer, the shame gave way to a numbing fatigue. I skipped dinner and curled up in my bed. My phone buzzed. One text message. From Reece.

I'm sorry. I didn't have a choice.

I pitched the phone across the room. Lonny once told me that the thistle doesn't get to choose whose side it's on. That who it hurts is just a product of its circumstances. But that was bullshit. There was always a choice.

My hands shook as I unhooked the clasp and took off the pendant. I didn't know what to do with it, only that I didn't want to wear it anymore. I lifted my mattress, reaching for the Ziploc bag where I kept my father's things. I pulled it into my lap as I crumpled to the floor. The bag contained my collection of personal ads clipped from the *Missed Connections* over the years while I'd been searching for messages from my dad. It was where I kept each one that reminded me of him, the Google search results that Jeremy had once printed for me on all of my dad's fake names, the old photo of my dad's poker club that Jeremy had found in his father's office last spring, and my father's

wedding ring. I opened the bag, ready to toss Reece's thistle inside with all the other messed-up pieces of my life I
didn't know what to do with.

But the Google searches were gone.

There was a newspaper clipping in their place—one I
hadn't put there.

Someone hadn't just broken into my trailer to leave the
photo on my wall. My room had been searched. Whoever
had left the photo had taken the Google results. He was looking for my father and he wanted me to know.

I unfolded the newspaper clipping. The headline read:
"Local Business Man Charged on Multiple Racketeering
Charges: Police Seeking Anonymous Caller Credited With
Providing Information Leading to Arrest."

Reggie Wiles's face appeared in a mug shot, dated June 28,
2009. Then again, in a photo taken outside the courthouse,
his shoulders hunched to avoid the cameras of the reporters. This was the man who used to play poker every Friday
night at Jeremy's house with my dad. But he looked different
from the man I remembered. Different from the faces in the
photo in my lap, of all the other Friday night players—Jason
Fowler, Anthony DiMorello, Karl Miller, and Craig Reinnert—wearing Belle Green Poker Club shirts, smiling, arm in
arm. Reggie's face in the poker club photo had long ago been
torn away, and I had always imagined it looked happy like the
others. But in these photos, Reggie Wiles wasn't smiling. His

eyes were hooded and his jaw was set hard and square. Angry.

I held the photo close to my face. Had I see this man before?

In the posture of the man in the bus shelter outside the police station?

Or maybe in the hunched shoulders of the man who'd bumped me in the street after Raj had driven me home?

The different images began to click together, to form a face.

Had it been the face of the stranger I'd seen staring at Adrienne's picture under the streetlight? Or had he been staring at me?

For every action, there is an equal and opposite reaction.

Gena was wrong about Reggie. She had to be.

"Want to talk about it?" My head snapped up and my breath caught in my chest. My mother stood in the hall, dangling the new key from her fingers.

"I didn't hear you come in." I folded the article without looking at it, trying not to draw my mother's attention. "I thought you were supposed to be at work?"

"This is more important." She sat on the edge of my bed, looking at the bag I held on my lap, my father's ring and Reece's pendant and the poker club photo in plain view. The last time she'd seen the photo, she'd been angry. She'd told me to get rid of it, that she never wanted to see it again. She reached for the article, and I let her take it. Her brow furrowed as she read the headline. "Butch told me what happened with Reece."

I looked away.

"I'm really sorry," she said. "I think I know how you feel."

"You do?"

She nodded, folding the article and placing it in my hands. No anger. No reprimands. "It's hard when someone you love does something that makes you feel ashamed. I know in my heart that your father always had the best intentions—that he wanted a better life for us—but the choices he made hurt people. And rather than move on, I carried that burden. I let his mistakes define me. I lost a lot of friends."

"Like who?"

She thought for a moment, staring at the faces in the photo through the bag. "Like Jenna Fowler. Like Mary Reinnert, and Karl Miller. They were good people. Loyal friends."

"But I thought *they* stopped being friends with *you*. Because of Dad."

My mother shrugged thoughtfully. "Maybe. Or maybe I was too ashamed to try. Maybe I didn't think I deserved them." She wiped a tear from her eye. "I regret that. I miss them sometimes."

"It's hard to believe our families used to hang out together." I shook my head. "Vince, Emily, Eric . . . even Jeremy. I can't imagine us even wanting to be in the same room together. I mean, I remember those Friday nights watching our dads play poker, but we're all so different now. What were their fathers like?" I withdrew the photo of the poker club from the bag, more curious than she would ever realize, as I placed it in her hands.

She smiled an old smile as she traced the edges with a finger. "Anthony DiMorello. He was handsome and reckless. Drank like a fish. Always finding trouble. He wasn't the brightest, but his heart was usually in the right place.

"Then there was Karl. Karl Miller was a sweet man." She shook her head and her smile fell away. "It never made sense to me, that a guy like Karl could leave his wife and run off with some other woman. He was too good a man to do something like that. I used to think that your father's friends were so connected, so dependent on one another, that together they made a whole person. Karl was the heart of that person."

"What was Anthony?"

"He was the muscle," she laughed. "I guess you could say Craig Reinnert was the conscience. The future city councilman; well-spoken, well-dressed, always trying to keep an upstanding face. Uptight, Anthony used to call him." My mother bit her lip, lost somewhere in a memory. "Then there was your father. He was the soul—the living, breathing, dreaming core. He was the glue that brought them all together, sweeping them all up in his big plans and his big ideas." She trailed off, as if she was watching him go.

"What about Jason Fowler. What was he like?"

She heaved a sigh while she thought about him. "Jeremy's dad was the brains of the club. And he never let you forget it. Heaven help you if you disagreed with him. He and Reggie used to go fisticuffs all the time." She laughed at the memory. "Then Karl would peel them off each other, and Anthony would take them all out for drinks until the fight was water under the bridge."

My mother handed the photo back to me, her thumb covering Reggie Wiles's missing face.

"Was Reggie Wiles a friend?" I asked.

My mother's smile was deeply sad. "He was once. Your dad's *best* friend."

"What was his role in the group?"

She looked away. "Oh, I don't know," she said with a dismissive wave. "I guess he was the id. All need and want and raw ambition. Reggie Wiles was always hungry. And when he wanted something, nothing could stand in his way."

"Were you afraid of him?"

Her smile crumbled, and I watched her struggle to build it back up again. She pulled me in close to her side. Her worry was a gnawing acid. It climbed up my throat and I felt her push it back down. "No more than you should be."

9

I AWOKE ON SATURDAY MORNING with my cell phone in my hand. More than two days since I'd seen Reece at Gentleman Jim's, and even though I wasn't exactly sure what I needed to hear or what I expected him to say, a not so small part of me ached for him to figure it out.

A car door slammed and I leaped to the window, still clutching the phone. Reece wasn't there. But my neighbor emerged from her trailer, still wearing her nightgown, leaning up on her toes to get a better look at some invisible point down the street.

I dropped the curtain and ran to the front porch, where I was greeted by the muted drone of a police radio. A crowd had gathered at the bottom of Sunny View Drive, all of them staring toward Lonny Johnson's trailer.

A strand of yellow-and-black police tape cordoned off a perimeter around Lonny's Lexus, his driveway, then wrapped around the narrow property surrounding his trailer. Two police cars parked alongside the gravel street.

I ran back to my room and got dressed. Grabbing my cell phone and house keys, I left, quietly bolting the door so I wouldn't wake my mother.

I wove my way toward Lonny's trailer, through the crowd of curious neighbors. Arrests in Sunny View weren't all that uncommon. And patrol cars did regular drive-bys almost every day. So why did it seem like the entire neighborhood was standing in the street watching? What had they all come to see?

Billy Wiles opened his door and squinted down the street. He scrubbed a filthy hand over his sleepy red eyes and the whiskers on his face, and scowled as I walked by, like the noise that had woken him had been my fault. Then he pulled on a tattered button-down and ambled off his porch toward the Bui Mart, like the show wasn't worth his time.

Mrs. Moates stood in a circle of the neighborhood gossips, one of her mangy-looking cats weaving in and out of her ankles. She held another tightly to her bathrobe while she stroked its head and talked too loudly. I listened, picking up bits of conversation. Piecing them together. The police had come that morning with a warrant. Had searched Lonny's car. And then his trailer. Adrienne Wilkerson was dead.

So that was it. Everyone knew about Adrienne now. But that didn't explain what the police were doing here. Or the yellow tape.

Deputies in uniform took up positions around the tight perimeter. Behind them, a detective I didn't recognize held open the trailer door. Lonny appeared, with his hands cuffed.

Our eyes caught and held. His stare was insistent, demanding something from me as he slowly descended his porch steps.

I surveyed the scene, the faces of the cops. The strange man standing off to the side that didn't look like a cop or a neighbor. I stood on tiptoes as someone stepped into my way, desperate for a better look. But the man was gone.

The detective escorted Lonny under the police tape toward a line of parked police cars. Lonny watched me from the corner of his eye. If I let them arrest him, I might not get another chance to talk with him. To find out what happened.

I ran alongside them. "Please," I said. "I'm a friend. Can I talk to him, just for a minute?"

The detective ignored me, directing Lonny into the back of a waiting cruiser. Lonny's eyes never left mine as they took him away.

• • •

Three hours later, I sat in an empty interview room in the police station, my forehead resting on the cool metal table and my phone hot in my hands. I lifted my head to check the screen again. No missed calls. No new messages. Reece hadn't called since I'd seen him at the club. Hadn't sent a single text message to apologize, or even try to explain. I'd called Gena for a ride to the station, and nagged her until she finally conceded to talk to Alex and arrange for me to see Lonny.

My head snapped up when the doorknob turned and Alex came in. He looked tired. Inconvenienced. It was long past the end of his shift, and he probably wanted nothing more than to go home. He dropped into the chair across from me.

"What's happening to Lonny?" I asked.

Alex clenched his jaw, and I wondered if Gena would ever hear the end of it for making him help me. "Lonny's in a temporary holding cell until his attorney can get here. I pulled some strings and bought you five minutes. That's all you've got. Get in, say what you need to say, and get out. Got it?"

"What's he being held for?"

"He's in for questioning. He hasn't been charged yet."

"Charged for what? Why is his trailer all taped off?"

Alex looked me over. If I were anyone else, the conversation would have been over.

"A girl named Adrienne Wilkerson was murdered. Her body was found by hikers in Mount Vernon District Park." Alex paused. "She lived in Sunny View. You know her?"

I shook my head. "Not well. What does this have to do with Lonny?"

"Maybe the question you should be asking is, what does this have to do with you?"

Truth was, I had asked myself the same question. Over and over again. "I'm just trying to help."

Alex muttered a frustrated curse. "You don't owe him any favors. He's been in and out of this place so many times, Nicholson might as well install a revolving door with Lonny Johnson's name on it."

"So you're saying he'll be out of here soon? That they'll let him go?" If that was the case, I could just go home.

"No. What I'm saying is he can't be helped, Leigh. I know you've got a thing for bad boys and all, but—"

"What's that supposed to mean?"

"It means he can't be fixed. Lonny's rap sheet is a mile long and with his record, it doesn't look good." Alex took a weary breath. "Look, I shouldn't be telling you this, but the investigators got a lead from someone who claimed they saw Lonny and Adrienne together the night she disappeared. Lonny doesn't have an alibi and the evidence suggests he was involved."

"What kind of evidence?"

Alex shook his head. "Come on, Leigh. You know I can't tell you that."

"Do you think he did it?" I blurted without thinking. Alex knew Lonny Johnson better than anyone. He'd spent nine months undercover as Lonny's right-hand man. They'd gotten close. Lonny had trusted him.

Alex paused, thoughtful. If I touched him, I suspected he would taste like disappointment and regret. Like maybe I wasn't the only one who wished I knew how to save a guy like Lonny Johnson. "I don't think he'll walk this time," he said quietly. "So you don't need to worry about repaying any favors. But if you want to take your five minutes and say good-bye, they're probably going to transfer him to county detention later tonight."

Alex led me to the desk in the holding area. He asked permission before checking my clothes for contraband, then directed me inside. The holding area was exactly what I'd imagined —a narrow corridor lined with cells. A uniformed officer stood beside an open cell door. Head down, I almost bumped into the prisoner emerging from it. I uttered an apology, but when I looked up into his face, my throat filled with something hot and sour.

Reece stood in the corridor in a rumpled shirt, dumbfounded and staring at me, waiting as the officer opened the adjacent cell and released a girl with bloodshot eyes. She slipped her arms around Reece's shoulders, letting her sleep-matted hair fall over them.

"What's the holdup, babe?" Her voice was raspy. She looked up at him with a full-lipped smile, then at me. Her eyes lit with recognition. "Wait, isn't that the girl from the club?" I watched, my chest clenching like a fist as her fingers snaked into his. Eyes burning, I stared at their hands. This was her. The girl on the cell phone. The one at Gentleman Jim's. I stood, blocking the corridor, waiting for him to shake her off, but he didn't.

He darted a quick look at Alex. Past me. Through me.

Alex cleared his throat quietly, pulling me gently aside to let them pass. Reece grabbed the girl's hand and pulled her to the door.

"I'm so ready to get out of here. Want to go to my place?" the raspy-voiced girl asked Reece. Alex nudged me on, and the door to the holding area shut before I could hear Reece's answer.

A knot swelled in my throat. It was all that was holding back the tears.

"It's not what it looks like, Leigh," Alex said.

"You're defending him?" I choked out.

"No. I think he's an asshole. You deserve better."

"Better than what?"

"Better than someone who spends more time in lockup than in class."

"I thought you all were supposed to be on the same side."

Alex cast a wary glance at the cells. All but one was empty— Lonny's—but Alex lowered his voice anyway. "He's an informant, Leigh. Not a cop. And people only become informants for two reasons. Because they need the money. Or because they need to get out of trouble."

"So you're saying Reece is a criminal."

"No, I'm saying he doesn't narc out of the goodness of his heart. He does it because he has to."

I didn't know what to say. Suddenly, I felt so stupid. It's exactly what Reece had been trying to tell me. That he'd taken this job for the wrong reasons. That he hated it. All this time, I'd been telling myself that Reece was good at his job because he was noble and heroic. But he was just good at pretending to be bad because he wasn't really pretending at all. Maybe that's what he meant when he said he didn't have a choice. That he couldn't choose to do the right thing because inside he was still the same person he'd been before. He'd liked taking Alex's car. I'd tasted the cool rush of adrenaline when he did. Did being with this girl make him feel that way too?

As if reading my thoughts, Alex took me by the shoulders and looked me in the eyes. "If it makes you feel any better, I've spent more nights than I can count on the wrong side of those bars, with the wrong people, when all I really wanted was to curl up with Gena at home on my couch."

I nodded, but it was small consolation, remembering the way Reece felt in my arms on my own couch a few nights ago. The way it all seemed to change the minute that girl called.

"Alex, did you ever . . . you know . . . have feelings for any of the people you got close to when you were narcing?"

"We're all human, Leigh. We can't get close to people without feeling something." He glanced toward Lonny's cell. "His attorney's going to be here soon. Do you still want to see him?"

I nodded, wiping my eyes as Alex led me to the last cell.

Lonny sat alone on the cot in the small enclosure, his head tipped back against the wall. His eyes were closed, but one of them opened lazily when Alex rapped on his cell door. "You've got a visitor. Five minutes. Your attorney's on his way."

All afternoon I wanted to talk to Lonny, but now, looking back at him through the bars, I didn't know what to say.

"Did you mean what you said?" His voice sounded so weary and rutted, I could almost taste the resignation in it. "You told that detective you were my friend. Did you mean it?" This was a test. The way every interaction with Lonny was a test.

I lifted my chin as he stood up and strode toward me.

"They're going to convict me, Boswell. For the same reason my attorney is going to let them. Because it's human nature. Because we make decisions that support our preconceptions of what's right. The cops think I'm bad. So they assume I'm guilty. They'll cherry-pick the evidence that proves that they're right. They'll stuff the DA full of everything he wants to hear. That I cut Adrienne up into little tiny pieces and dumped her body in the woods. But it's bullshit—"

"Wait," I said, thrown suddenly off balance. "What did you say?"

"I said it's all bullshit. I didn't kill her."

I'd seen Adrienne's body in the Fridge. She hadn't been cut. She'd been strangled. So why would Lonny think she'd been chopped up unless the cops had led him to believe it. Unless they intentionally misrepresented how she died to trick him into some kind of knee-jerk attempt to correct them. It's like they were hoping he'd react, or say something incriminating, something that might prove he knew exactly how she died.

I withdrew my hands from my pockets and stepped close to the bars, placing them over his. They were cool and dry. There was no conflict. Nothing difficult to place. Underneath his anger and grief, a confidence lingered, crisp and cold on my breath.

He hadn't corrected them. Because he couldn't. Because he didn't know how Adrienne died. Because he wasn't the one who'd killed her.

I began to pull my hands away, but he held me in place. Held my stare.

"I know you didn't kill Adrienne," I said. "The evidence they found is probably just circumstantial. Maybe that's why they haven't charged you yet."

"What are you going do about it . . . friend?" He stared at our joined hands. Then glanced over my shoulder at the duty officer who was watching us closely. And at Alex, who was pretending not to. My face burned. I wanted to snatch my hands from his.

There was nothing I could do for him. Nothing I would do if it meant jeopardizing my internship. "They can't hold you forever. Eventually, they'll have to let you go."

Lonny laughed. His syrupy-hot cynicism stung my throat. It left an ache in my chest.

What was it Alex had said?

. . . *the evidence suggests he was involved.*

"What did they find?" I asked.

"I don't know. They won't tell me. Whatever it is, they're going to make it stick." Lonny believed this, and it was difficult to think logically while his resignation, the hopeless acceptance of his circumstances, tried to settle in my heart.

"Think." I pulled my hands from his to clear my head. "Did the police find anything of Adrienne's in your house when they searched it? Could she have had anything of yours when she was killed?"

Lonny rubbed his eyes, looking frustrated. "My lighter and phone went missing the afternoon Adrienne disappeared."

"Is it possible Adrienne had them?"

"I don't know." He shook his head. "She'd been at my place that day. I guess it's possible. I left them on my front porch, we went inside. She was there for twenty minutes or so, and then she left. When I came back outside, they were gone."

If Adrienne had taken his phone and his lighter, and that's what the police had found, they would have been transported to the lab for examination. Raj said murder cases were prioritized above most others, so it would be processed quickly. The prosecutor would have to produce evidence beyond a reasonable doubt that Lonny had committed the crime in order to indict him for murder. If the evidence against Lonny was purely circumstantial, they couldn't keep him locked up. His lawyer would make sure of it. But if it wasn't . . .

What if the evidence against Lonny was more than circumstantial? What if I had misjudged him the same way I had misjudged Reece? What if *I* was the one who was only seeing what I wanted to see?

I took a step back from the bars. "I'll find out as much as I can on Tuesday after school when I go back to the lab." If he really was innocent, he'd be released by then anyway.

"I'm not going anywhere," Lonny said, as if he could read my thoughts.

"Five minutes are up," Alex said.

I said good-bye, and had almost turned away when Lonny spoke.

"'Petrenko's right, you know. Reece is an asshole. But he's no idiot. He has to know how lucky he is to have you."

My eyes burned and the room became watery. I turned for the door. "I know what I saw."

He grabbed my arm through the bars. Waited until I looked him in the eyes. "I know what you're thinking. You're wondering if you put your trust in the wrong person. If you're a bad judge of character. I'm just asking . . . just . . . please . . ." Under all his bitterness and fear, I tasted one last sweet drop of hope. Like maybe I could save him. "Don't believe everything you see."

10

I snapped open my locker on Monday morning, bleary-eyed and only half-awake.

It snapped shut in my face, loud and jarring. A hand pressed against it. Reece's hand. I followed the thistle tattoo up the length of his arm and turned to find him standing over me, his brother's ring hanging from the silver chain around his neck. He looked down at me with weary blue eyes, looking sullen and as sleepless as I felt. "You're supposed to be in school."

"I am in school."

"You're not supposed to be in this one!" I snapped. Girls at the end of the hall stopped to stare. They whispered behind their hands.

"Does it matter? I'll probably be in a different one next week."

"You shouldn't be here."

"I need to talk to you."

"I don't need to listen."

Jeremy stood staring at the end of my locker row and I felt my face grow hot.

"Please," Reece said quietly. "About last week. What you saw at the club . . . I told Kurt I didn't want to go. I tried to get him to go someplace else. I'm sorry . . . I didn't mean to put you in that position. I don't want Butch or your mother to think—"

"To think what?" I dropped my voice low, hoping no one else could hear it. "That you're a drunk and a creep who sneaks into strip clubs? That you like lying to your girlfriend and tricking girls into falling in love with you?"

He made a face like he'd been punched. "So that's it? So that's what you think of me?"

"I'm trying not to think of you at all." When I did, it hurt too much. And made me question who I was for wanting him so badly. "You should have told me about her."

Reece put his hands on his hips and rocked his jaw back and forth. "There was nothing to tell."

"Is she the same one who called your cell phone?"

"I told you. She's nobody."

I turned and walked away.

Reece stepped in front of me. "Is that why you changed your locks? Because of me?"

I froze. "How do you know I changed my locks?"

"What did you expect me to do? You're not answering my calls. I came by your trailer and Butch was there. He wouldn't let me in to see you."

"So you tried to break in to my house?"

"No!" he said, taken aback. "I just wanted to leave you a note. I wanted a chance to explain."

"I promise," I said, disgusted by the very thought of finding another note in my bedroom. "It wouldn't have gone over well."

"Is this loser bothering you, Boswell?" Vince stood beside me in a freshly pressed button-down and a varsity jacket, smiling crookedly at Reece.

"Back off," Reece said. "This is none of your business."

"You're trespassing on school grounds. You don't belong here, Whelan. When Principal Romero finds out —"

"Principal Romero can kiss my ass," Reece fired back.

"Looks like Boswell doesn't want you here either." Vince put a hand on my shoulder, and Reece let loose with a hard, fast punch to his face.

They flew at each other, grappling and slamming against the lockers.

"Reece!" I shouted as people gathered around to watch. "Stop it! Just go!" All I wanted was for him to leave before anyone got in trouble.

Security arrived, pulling them apart and holding them at opposite ends of the hall. Reece's ear was bleeding, and Vince's lip. Reece wouldn't look at me. He jerked out of the security guard's grasp and stormed out the front door.

Principal Romero showed up, just in time to see Reece straddle his bike through the windows.

"Should we go after him?" the guard asked.

"No," he said, turning toward me. "I know who he belongs to. And I know exactly who to call to report it."

He walked toward his office, with security and Vince in tow. No doubt, Lieutenant Nicholson would be Principal Romero's next call.

I watched Reece's bike disappear, wishing he'd never come.

Then I opened my locker and restarted my day, trying to imagine he'd never been in it.

II

ON TUESDAY AFTERNOON, the door to the Latent Prints lab was closed. I stood on tiptoes to look in the window, but it was covered with a sheet of black paper. I cracked the door. The room was dark inside, and I flipped on the light.

"Hey!" Raj shouted. He sat cross-legged in the middle of the floor, squinting and covering his eyes. "Turn that off, will you?"

"Sorry." I turned off the overheads. Raj switched on a flashlight. The only light in the room was the beam it cast across the floor. He set it gently on the tile. I blinked, letting my eyes adjust.

"What are you looking for?"

Raj smiled wide. "It's not what I'm looking for. It's what I've found. Check it out." He pointed in the direction of the beam. "Look closely at the floor. What do you see?"

The smooth tiles in the path of the light glimmered with

dust. A lot of dust. Footprints of differing shapes and sizes.

"Where'd all this come from?" I whispered, awestruck by the number of tread patterns that crisscrossed under the beam. The floors in the lab were always spotless. The custodians mopped every night. "Did you sprinkle something on it?"

"Nope."

"Then how'd the floor get so dirty?"

"It always looks like this. You just can't see it."

"Why are we seeing it now?"

"It's the oblique angle of the light. When we shine a light on something straight on, there's not enough contrast to see the impressions. But when we lower the angle, casting the light from the side, the shadow effect increases the contrast, and voila! Footwear, hairs, fibers—latent evidence becomes visible."

Raj crawled along the beam, looking hard at the impressions in the dust.

"Aha! I've got you, you bastard!" He pointed at a line of shoe marks, moving the flashlight to reveal their path from the door to a cabinet on the far wall. He leaped up, grabbing a small device from his lab coat pocket, some electrical wires, and a long sheet of black Mylar film from the counter behind him.

Raj placed the film gently over a set of footprints and clipped a wire to its edge. The device in his hand was a stun gun. My mother carried one just like it in her purse. I backed away.

"Um . . . Raj? What are you doing?" Playing with Super Glue and fingerprint powder was one thing. Playing with electricity was entirely another. "Whatever it is, I'm not sure it's a good idea."

"Someone's been stealing luminol from my cabinet."

"What's luminol?"

"It's a spray used to reveal latent blood evidence."

"Why would someone want to steal that?"

"Because it's fun to play with. Luminol has chemilumines-cent properties. When it reacts with an oxidizing agent, it makes a seriously cool blue glow. I mean, I get it. We've all done it. But this bonehead's screwed up my inventory three months in a row. He wants to play detective? Great, let's show him how it's done."

He thumbed on the stun gun and I thought about taking another step back, when he touched it to the wire clipped to the film. I crept forward to watch over his shoulder. The sheet vibrated with a static charge, lifting a perfect dust impression from the floor. Raj flipped on the light and studied the prints. "Size ten Crocs? Pathetic. But they shouldn't be too hard to find." Raj tossed the film into the trash. As soon as it touched the plastic liner, the dust dispersed and the footprint disappeared.

Raj scratched the stubble on his jaw. "Hey, you okay? You look like you were up all night."

My eyes felt puffy and raw under my glasses. I hadn't been sleeping much. I couldn't stop seeing the image of Reece with that girl. I spent my energy trying to resist the urge to return the handful of missed calls and text messages from him.

I shrugged it off. "Just a little insomnia. Nothing a few really boring gopher tasks can't fix."

Raj sat down in front of the computer. "Boring I can definitely help you with." I watched Raj log himself into AFIS, typing a string of numbers into the password field, then working through a list of names. One by one, he deleted their prints from the system.

"What are you working on?"

"About once a month, I get a report with a list of records that need to be purged from the database. Usually dropped charges, or people who were found not guilty during an appeal. Sometimes minors whose charges were expunged by a judge. In those cases, we remove their prints from the system. After I'm done, I'll get back to scanning the old prints. Gotta feed The Monster." Raj patted the top of the monitor.

"The Monster?"

"It's what we call AFIS. She's an amazing beast. We have to keep feeding her if we want her to work for us. The more records we feed her, the bigger she grows, the more possible matches she can find for us. Kind of like you and donuts."

"What's that supposed to mean?"

Raj smirked as he voided the last record in the pile. "I don't need an electrostatic dust lifter to know you're the one who's been snarfing down all the chocolate frosted donut holes in the break room."

"No one else was eating them," I said defensively.

"No one else had a chance," Raj laughed.

My cheeks warmed.

Raj sighed as he plucked a new stack of print cards from a box. I watched as he scanned them into the computer, waiting for him to tell me to go wash dishes or something equally mundane. But he seemed to like the company.

"Raj?" I asked. "Did CSI find any fingerprints in the Adrienne Wilkerson case?"

"A print was lifted from a cigarette lighter found at the dump site. It's the only one that didn't match the prints of the victim or the guy they arrested."

Which meant the lighter could be the key to ruling out Lonny as a suspect.

"Are you going to run it through The Monster? Can I watch?"

Raj shook his head. "I'm only allowed to scan old print cards. A licensed fingerprint examiner is the only one qualified to handle prints collected from a crime scene. She'll be the one to enter them into AFIS and determine the search criteria."

"Then what happens?"

"AFIS'll spit out a list of possible matches. The examiner will use a comparison microscope to identify the right one.

Then she'll have another licensed examiner verify her findings." That sounded like it would take a while. Maybe days. Three had already passed since I'd gone to see Lonny. How many more would he spend behind bars until he could be eliminated as a suspect?

"I thought The Monster would just spit out a match. You know, like boom, here's your guy."

Raj laughed. "Contrary to the gross exaggerations propagated by Hollywood screenwriters, fingerprint identification is still a manual process. And if the right suspect hasn't been fingerprinted and put in the system before, we may not find a match at all. Hence the importance of the cheap manual labor you and I are so generously donating to the State of Virginia." He cocked his head and looked at me sideways. Then he glanced at the door. It was still shut, the window still blacked out. He pushed the computer mouse toward me. "You want to drive?"

"Who, me? I thought you said—"

"You've been watching, right? I mean, it's not rocket science or anything. Here." He gave me his seat and stood over my shoulder while I scanned the first few records. "See. Piece of cake. If you get through that stack of records before the end of our shift, donuts are on me." Raj playfully patted my head. The saccharine sweetness of opportunity left a curious tingle on my tongue. Like maybe this wasn't the only mundane task he was looking forward to delegating off his plate.

"Very funny," I muttered, sinking back into the chair. At least this was more interesting than washing beakers.

Raj snuck across the hall to pick up some toxicology reports to be delivered to Doc Benoit's office, leaving me with firm instructions to tackle at least half the card stack before he returned. I stared at the mouth of The Monster, wondering who I might be feeding to it.

I picked at the edge of the card on top. Then set it back down.

Instead, I typed a name into the search field.

Reece's name. His record appeared, every one of his fingerprints. Anything he touched for the rest of his life would bear the latent print of who he used to be. And even though I was still pissed at him, I wanted to kick in the screen. Because this was the reason he had been in lockup holding hands with another girl. A girl he shouldn't be with. This was the piece of himself he was trying to expunge.

I cleared the screen of Reece's record before I did something permanent. Something wrong. The cursor blinked at me from the search field.

I typed another name.

Boswell, David.

No fingerprint records returned. Which only meant my father had never been arrested for his crimes. And while part of me was relieved to see an empty screen beside his name, a deeper part of me recognized that it shouldn't have been empty at all.

Curious, I typed in Lonny's name. Johnson, Leonard.

Lonny's prints were already there, connected to a series of crimes dating back to 2007. According to The Monster, Lonny was twelve when he'd committed his first B&E on record. Then came the drugs, the larcenies, the assaults. It all spoke to Alex's point. That Lonny had been consumed, he was too deep in the belly of The Monster. All it would take was a partial print to dredge up every crime he'd ever committed. To a jury, he'd look guilty. They'd never think to see him in a different light.

Don't believe everything you see.

I stared at The Monster. There was no changing the past. Lonny was already inside the system. But maybe that would work in his favor. Raj had said it himself. They'd found one print that *wasn't* Lonny's. The real killer was still out there, but maybe his print was in here.

• • •

When I got home that night, the trailer was locked and dark. The baseball bat stood propped in the corner behind the door. And yet, no matter how many lights I turned on, I couldn't shake the feeling that I wasn't alone. My mind wandered to the stranger at Lonny's trailer when he was arrested on Saturday morning. To the man under the light post who'd been reading Lonny's flyer. Everywhere I went, I had the shadowy feeling that someone was following me.

I pulled my phone from my pocket. Five missed calls and two voice mails from Reece. My finger hovered over his number. Everything inside me ached to call him, but would the sound of his voice just make me feel worse? I stuffed it back in my pocket and checked the locks again, leaving the chain unfastened so my mother could get in when her shift ended at four.

I made myself a sandwich and brought it into my bedroom. I took the baseball bat with me and sat cross-legged on my mattress with the bat across my lap, picking at the bread crusts. Gena had to be wrong. Reggie's parole officer must have made a mistake. It had to be Reggie Wiles who broke in to my trailer. The notes had all started showing up after his release. And he was the only person I knew of with a reason to want to find my father. Gena might not believe me, but I just needed more proof.

For every action, there is an equal and opposite reaction.

I looked around my room. If Raj could figure out who'd been stealing from his cabinets in the lab, there had to be a way to identify the person who'd broken in to my trailer. I set aside my sandwich. The only smooth surface the intruder would have walked on was the square of linoleum by the front door. I grabbed a flashlight from the junk drawer in the kitchen and switched off the lights. Squatting beside the foyer, I held the flashlight low to the floor. It was dusty all right. And there were footprints. Lots of them. The three-by-three sheet of flooring contained days of prints since I'd last bothered to mop. Mine, my mother's, Butch's, Reece's, and even Mr. Fowler's. All of them jumbled together, a scramble of random shimmers, no one print clear enough to make anything useful of.

I turned on the lights, thinking about what Raj said, about how oblique lighting can reveal hidden things. I returned to my room, trying to see it from a different angle. What about fingerprints? Only where would I look to find them if I still wasn't sure exactly how the intruder had gotten in?

As far as I knew, the intruder had only touched one thing in my room that no one else had. No one but me.

I stood beside my bed and lifted the edge of the mattress, plucking out the plastic bag. If Reggie Wiles had been here, inside my trailer—if he'd put that article inside my bag— then there was only one way to prove it.

12

THE NEXT MORNING, I found Anh alone in the library studying before school. I set my books down and eased into the chair beside her. I should have been grateful we could just be in the same room studying together. I didn't really need her to help me with the fingerprints.

But I missed the sound of her voice on the phone. The way she teased me about the Einstein shrine in my bedroom. I missed arguing with her over who would wash the petri dishes in lab, and I missed the geeky stuff we did together, like making Mentos volcanoes out of two-liter bottles in the parking lot of the Bui Mart after school.

"Can we talk?"

Anh closed her book, her hand still in it, holding her place like she might change her mind.

"Never mind," I said, my voice close to breaking. I scooped up my books. "It was a bad idea. I'm sorry—"

Anh let her textbook fall shut, reaching fast for my hand. Her grip tasted like every summer day we hadn't spent together. "I miss you," she whispered.

I made a noise somewhere between a giggle and a cry. "Want to see something cool?"

• • •

Anh met me at the Bui Mart after school. She waved at her brother, Bao, without making eye contact, and we both zipped through the store aisles, grabbing the supplies we needed off the shelves with a frenetic energy.

"I'm all out of peppermint Mentos," Bui said dryly, turning back to his *People* magazine. "And if you get Cherry Coke on my car again, I'll make you scrub the urinal for a month."

Anh ignored him and reached for a can of spray foam. I shook my head and picked up a roll of duct tape instead. We rounded the end of the aisle, almost knocking over TJ's uncle.

Billy Wiles was red-nosed and sullen. There were dried yellow sweat rings on the collar of his undershirt. People said he had tried to find a job after the trial. That he'd used the last of the money from TJ's trust fund to buy the beat-up Chrysler sedan parked outside his trailer. But for a long time, the media reporters wouldn't leave him alone, and he eventually gave up. He rarely came out of his trailer anymore except to buy his beer and some food, and I tried not to stare at him as he made his way to the walk-in cooler in the back.

Anh didn't seem fazed by him, and Bao just waved like Billy was any other regular customer. Which I guess he was. If you didn't count the fact that his brother was a felon and his nephew murdered four people in cold blood. Maybe I shouldn't be so critical. I guess, in a way, TJ had betrayed Billy too.

He took his six-pack, a can of hash, and a loaf of bread to the counter, and paid for it with a wad of singles and some loose change. Anh and I finished our shopping, and when the counter was empty, we dumped a tube of Super Glue, the duct tape, a bag of plastic clothespins, and a roll of wire down. Then Anh threw a bag of Ho Hos on the pile with sideways smile in my direction.

Bao's brows drew together. He closed his magazine and studied our purchases while Anh made a neat list on a three-by-five card of everything we were taking from store inventory.

"The only thing we're missing is the coffee can," she said.

"We sell coffee," Bao said.

"Not in metal cans," I pointed out.

Bao's dreams of earning an MIT degree died when he gave up college to help his parents run the store, but his inner geek was alive and well. "What are you up to?" he asked, sounding slightly amused.

"None of your business," Anh answered without glancing up from her list.

Bao turned to me. I couldn't tell if his frown seemed more curious or judgmental, which was the way he'd looked at me since June. "Tell me what she's up to and I'll buy you a Yoo-hoo." When I hesitated, he threw a vanilla Zinger on the counter. But it was the simple fact that he was talking to me, that made me want to tell him everything.

"Cyanoacrylate fuming chamber," I said.

Bao's eyebrows shot toward the ceiling and he turned back to Anh. "That's so freaking cool. Can I watch?"

"No!" Anh said, shoving our supplies in a paper bag and ushering me toward the door.

"Why not?"

"Does ammonium nitrate synthesis ring any bells?"

"Oh, come on! That was an accident!"

"You caught Mom's curtains on fire, and I got grounded for a month!"

"You have to admit, the pyrotechnics were pretty cool."

Anh rolled her eyes and pushed me out the door. "He's hazardous to my health. Let's go."

We crossed the intersection at Route 1 and Anh glanced back at the Bui Mart windows when we hit the corner of Sunny View Drive.

"Will he be mad?" I asked. As much as Anh pretended not to care about her brother's opinions, I knew she did.

"He'll get over it."

"Have you?" the question slipped out. Her footsteps slowed, and I was afraid of her answer.

"I'm not sure," she said. "I don't think the things that happened to us are the kinds of things we're supposed to get over. I think they're the kinds of things we're just supposed to get through. All I know is that I want things to be like they were."

"Me too." The thin breath I'd been holding eased out of me.

"Give Bao time. He's coming around."

"What about Jeremy?" I asked. It felt strange, to have to ask Anh how Jeremy was feeling.

"Don't take his silence too personally. He's had a lot on his mind."

"You mean with the notes?"

Anh paused. "What notes?"

Shoot. "Jeremy didn't tell you?"

A crease pulled at Anh's brow. "Tell me what?"

I filled Anh in on the three mysterious messages, and the fact that TJ's father was out on parole. She was quiet when

I told her about the note in Jeremy's room. "I'm sorry. I thought you knew."

"It's okay," she said, but I could tell that it wasn't. "Jeremy and I haven't had much time to talk lately. His dad hasn't been letting us spend time together outside of school." She stared at the gravel, as if she was ashamed. "Who do you think wrote the notes?" she asked.

I didn't want to worry her. "Probably one of Vince's friends," I lied. "But it can't hurt to rule out TJ's dad. If I can find a set of prints, I can run them through the database at work and make sure Reggie Wiles isn't a possible match."

"What if he is?" Anh stopped walking.

I turned. "Then I'll talk to Gena and Alex. They'll know what to do." It was the right answer. Going to the police is what a good person did when they were in trouble. It was exactly the opposite of what I'd done before. Which was the whole reason Anh's family had been so angry with me. And if I had concrete evidence that Reggie Wiles had been in my trailer, then Gena would have to believe me.

We made a quick stop at Mrs. Moates's trailer and negotiated a dollar and some loose change for one of the old thirty-nine-ounce metal Walmart coffee cans I'd seen storing random crap on her yard sale table last week. Back at my trailer, I dragged a chair from the kitchen and propped the front door open for ventilation. Anh dumped everything out onto the kitchen table. I washed and dried the empty can, and set it on top of an old rusted hot plate we never used. It was a perfect fit.

Next, Anh and I strung wire across the top of the open can, and I clipped my sandwich-sized Ziploc bag to the wire with a clothespin, careful not to crease it.

Anh looked confused. "I thought we were looking for fingerprints on a photograph."

"Super Glue only works on nonporous surfaces. But whoever left the photograph touched this bag."

I added ten drops of Super Glue to the inside of the can, then huffed a long hot breath inside it before sealing the plastic lid with duct tape. I turned on the heating element and waited. Fumes began to roll beneath the clear lid. Anh and I bumped heads trying to peek through it, and it felt good to be sitting at my kitchen table laughing with her again. When condensation began to form, we turned off the heat, used potholders to carry the can out on the porch, and leaned our faces away as we pried open the lid.

I pinched the corners of the bag and held it against the dark backdrop of my neighbor's trailer. The white crystals formed several distinct print patterns. Now all I had to do was let it dry, transfer them to a card, and scan them through AFIS without getting caught. I could do it after school tomorrow.

Anh leaned over my shoulder to look. She sucked in an awed breath. The fumes clung to her hair and she smelled like the chemistry lab at school. "That is the coolest experiment we've ever done," she said. "Can I keep the coffee can? I'm going to see how much Bao will pay me for it."

I handed her the fuming chamber with a smile. "Only if we split the profits."

"Deal." Anh packaged up the supplies and sealed the can. "So, where's Reece? I haven't seen him around."

Hearing his name hurt all over again. Reece loved that I was smart, and how excited I got over stupid, geeky things. He used to set a timer and watch me solve the Rubik's cube, to see which algorithms yielded the fastest time. He'd laughed like crazy when we got in a marshmallow fight, and I beat him with a catapult I'd made out of a mousetrap and a plastic spoon. And I'd never forget the look of amazement on his face, that stifling hot day back in August during a power outage at Gena's house, when I made ice cream out of her milk, cream, and sugar, by lowering the freezing point of the ingredients with salt. We'd all sat in her kitchen, spooning it out of the plastic bag, and when Reece had kissed me, his lips were cold and sweet.

That Reece would have loved watching this experiment. I hesitated before answering. "He's at a different school this year. Principal Romero wouldn't let him come back."

"Does he know about all this?"

"No. Not all of it. Are you going to tell Jeremy about Reggie's parole? I sort of left that out when I talked to him." If

Anh told him I'd been holding information back, he'd be pissed at me, and we'd be back to square one when I finally felt like maybe we were on the road to fixing things.

Anh balled up a wad of used duct tape. She looked torn. "I probably shouldn't keep it from him."

"Why do you think Jeremy didn't tell you about the notes?"

"Probably because he didn't want me to freak out and jump to ridiculous conclusions."

I raised an eyebrow.

"I know. I know," she sighed. "I see your point. Jeremy has enough to worry about. Okay, we'll keep this between us for now. But promise me you'll let me know about the fingerprints."

"I'll know by Friday."

Anh carried her new toy to the door. I moved the chair out of her way and held it open for her. "We don't have to wait until Friday to talk, right?" she asked. "I mean, you could call. Or something."

I smiled. "Or something."

Anh walked backward away from my trailer, her own smile bright in the fading light as she waved good-bye.

13

THE NEXT AFTERNOON, I ducked out of seventh period early and took the bus to the lab. I found Raj in the break room, chatting up an evidence courier, the firearms examiner, and the pretty blond DNA examiner's assistant from the second floor.

He excused himself when I walked into the room, looking smug as he glanced at his watch. "Ditching class, Leigh? You're not due in for a couple hours."

"Early dismissal. No homework. Thought I'd come in and help out." I had at least three hours of studying to do and a paper to write. "Want me to work on that stack of latent print records?"

Raj looked anxiously over his shoulder and lowered his voice. "You can't do that. You don't have access. You'd need a password."

Clearly, Raj was not planning on letting me use his. I bit my lip. Telling him I remembered the string of numbers he'd used to log in last time would probably not go over well.

"Can't you just log me in?"

He eyed me skeptically.

"What? You promised me donuts. I'm motivated."

He broke into a smile. "As much as I would love to never

scan another fingerprint card again, I can't. Besides, I don't have time to run you upstairs. Doc has a body delivery in about twenty minutes and he'll probably need a hand. How about helping me with some evidence returns while I wait?"

"Evidence returns?" I winced.

"Don't look so glum. It won't take long. Just administrative chain-of-custody stuff. After that, there's a cart full of glassware in the DNA lab that needs sterilizing, and some autopsy tools that need to be returned to the Fridge."

I dragged my feet as I followed Raj to the mailroom, and only half listened as he explained that evidence was sorted in bins by case number, not by name, showed me how to log the evidence out of the lab, and told me how to figure out where it needed to be transported.

Then he dropped a bin on the table in front of me, jolting me back to task, and gestured that it was my turn to demonstrate that I'd actually been listening.

I reached inside and began pulling out the contents. Then paused. The bag containing the switchblade was cold and heavy, and I quickly set it down. This was Lonny's knife. I'd seen it before, when he'd held it to Emily Reinnert's throat the night TJ was charged with murder.

"You know that Jane Doe they brought in on your first day? The one with the blue hair?"

I started at Raj's voice. The room slid back into focus.

"She was killed on August twenty-ninth. Doc thinks it

happened sometime between nine and ten p.m. This is the evidence from her case." He emptied the rest of the contents from the bin. "Doc matched the ligature marks on the victim's neck to a piece of rope found in the suspect's trash can. The lab found strands of blue hair on it. We're waiting on some lab results, but we're pretty sure it's the murder weapon."

"That doesn't make any sense. Why would the rope still be in his trash can two weeks after she was murdered?"

"He probably watched the news and panicked when he saw her body had been found, then tried to get rid of the rope before he got caught. Criminals will do pretty stupid things to avoid getting busted with evidence . . . swallow drugs, toss guns out of car windows, throw murder weapons in their own trash cans." Raj looked down at the pile of evidence and shook his head, like he'd seen it all so many times before, there was no point in examining it any closer. "Clearly, this guy isn't too bright. The asshole's cell phone was the icing on the cake. He'd taken pictures of the victim minutes after he killed her. Cops found the phone in his car when they searched it. That's how Doc was able to estimate the time of death so closely. The time stamps on the photos were right around ten o'clock, and her skin still had some color, which suggests *pallor mortis* hadn't set in yet."

No. This all sounded too easy.

I know a set-up when I see it, Lonny had said to me once.

And this didn't add up. The sloppiness of the crime. The obvious loose ends. Lonny was smart. Careful.

My hands are clean, he'd said, proud of his ability to conceal his crimes from the police. If he'd actually killed Adrienne Wilkerson, he wouldn't have left any trace.

I picked up the paper evidence bag containing the lighter and studied the label. It described a brass Zippo, engraved with the letters *LJ.* I set it down hard on the counter.

"But you said the prints on this lighter didn't match the guy in lockup."

"*One* of the prints didn't match, but that's not all that unusual. It could have been left by one of the investigators."

"But then it would have been eliminated by AFIS."

Raj shrugged.

"What ever happened to innocent until proven guilty?"

"You weren't here when they dropped off the evidence. You didn't talk to the cops who brought the guy in. The guy's got a rap sheet longer than Lieutenant Nicholson's man bits."

"That doesn't mean he's guilty of *this* crime."

"No, the evidence does." He shoved the bin toward me. I turned my back to him to rifle through it.

"So one print doesn't match," he went on. "The lighter still belongs to him. The rope was found on his property. And the phone was registered to an account in his name. The car they found the phone in? Also registered in his name. And it was parked in his driveway. How much more proof do you need?"

"What about DNA tests? Have they looked for the killer's DNA on the corpse, or on the rope? What about tire marks or footwear impressions at the dumpsite? Or prints from the car? Or—"

"Too expensive," Raj interrupted. "And the detective didn't need it. Besides, DNA tests can take months to process. They have enough to convict him without it."

He slapped a label on a shipping box and stretched packaging tape over the seams.

"But what if he didn't do it? You can't assume he murdered her just because his lighter was found near the body. I thought you were a scientist."

"I'm also a realist. He had photos of the body on his phone! Face it. He's a conviction waiting to happen."

Lonny was right about one thing. He'd already been found guilty by everyone who mattered.

"If we're done in here, I'm going to wash glassware." I shoved my hands in my pockets and left Raj alone in the mailroom with the sealed box of evidence.

Minus one piece.

The black evidence bag containing Lonny's smart phone pressed against my hip as I climbed the back stairs to the Latent Prints lab. I walked fast, skipping every other step, sweat beading down my back.

I didn't steal it. I was only borrowing it. They'd already processed the evidence for the police. Checked it for prints and copied the photos. All I needed to do was search for something the investigators and examiners missed. Then return it before anyone realized the chain of custody had been broken.

I snuck quietly into the Latent Prints lab. The black paper still lined the window from Raj's flashlight experiment on Tuesday, but I left the lights off so no one would notice them under the door. I leaned with my back against it, staring at the evidence bag in my hand. There were photos on the phone of Adrienne's dead body—her blue skin and purple lips and the angry bruises around her neck. My finger hovered over the seal, but I couldn't make myself open it.

I just needed some time. I would come back and check the photos when I was certain I was alone. If the phone never left the lab, was the chain of custody really broken? Or was the phone merely misplaced? But where to hide it?

I looked from cabinet to cabinet. All were well used. The only place Raj wasn't ever likely to see was . . .

The bottom of the box of fingerprint cards. He'd been working through it for months, and at the rate he was going, I had weeks, maybe longer, until he got to the bottom of that stack. I tucked the cell phone deep inside the box, careful to make sure it was covered.

Heart still racing, I dropped into the rolling chair in front of the AFIS machine. I logged in, mimicking the password keystrokes Raj used before. I was in!

I dug around in my lanyard pouch for the pieces of the

plastic bag I'd fumed for fingerprints with Anh, then dusted them with black powder. I typed my own name into the search field and laid the transferred prints into the comparison microscope at The Monster's side. One by one, I eliminated my own prints. An index finger. A partial thumb. Until I was left with a set of prints that weren't mine.

I typed "Reginald Wiles" into the search field. Waited for a crisp, clear full set of prints to appear on the screen. I enlarged the image, enhanced the focus. I counted ridges under my breath, looked for matches in the shape and direction of the whorls, finding nothing. The prints weren't a match. Whoever had put the article in my bag hadn't been TJ's father.

This couldn't be right, could it? I'd seen a strange man in Sunny View on two separate occasions. But looking back, I'd never really gotten close enough to be certain they were the same man at all. I wasn't even sure what Reggie Wiles would look like after five years in prison. My gut had been telling me it was Reggie, but there was no arguing with the facts. The fingerprints on the bag weren't his.

So if it wasn't Reggie Wiles who'd left the note in my room, then who was it?

I checked the clock. Raj would probably be done helping Doc in the Fridge soon. I stashed my fingerprint samples inside my lanyard pouch and stuffed the half-empty container of black powder in my backpack, so he wouldn't find it and become suspicious. Then I logged out of AFIS, clearing the screen just as I heard a card key slide over the scanner. I threw on the lights, and was already across the room, clutching an empty glassware bin with white knuckles by the time Raj poked his head in the door.

"Oh good, you're still here," he said, short of breath. There was sweat on his forehead, like he'd run up the two flights of stairs and his smile curled toward the side of devilish. "There's something downstairs you're going to want to see."

• • •

I followed Raj to the Fridge.

"They brought him in a few hours ago," he said. "They're calling him the Golf Course Corpse. Someone dug him up last night and left the bones on the Belle Green golf course in plain sight. Doc's requesting a forensic anthropologist from the Smithsonian to confirm the age of the bones and cause of death." He paused, one hand on the door. "Are you sure you're going to be okay in here?"

I was sweaty and flushed, still shaking from the close call in the lab upstairs. He probably thought I had a weak stomach. I pushed him out of the way to open the door myself. "I'll be fine."

On a gurney in the middle of the room were mud-brown bones. I walked closer and saw that they were laid out in a disconnected pattern, assuming the loose shape of a human skeleton.

"Isn't he amazing?" Raj whispered, circling it.

I cautiously breathed through my nose. But the corpse didn't smell sweet and putrid, the way I'd imagined. Instead, it smelled earthy, like a pile of overturned dirt and wet leaves. The bones seemed benign, peaceful, except for a section of broken and jagged pieces that had once been his skull.

"What happened to his head?" I asked, bending to peek at the remains.

"Probably a homicide. Looks like someone brained the guy and buried the body to keep from getting caught. But who knows who dug him up? Doc thinks the victim is an adult male, between twenty-five and forty years of age, in the ground at least three years. Detectives think probably five. We can't confirm that yet."

I winced. "Would a blow to the head really do this much damage to the skull?"

"Not one," Raj said. "This was multiple hits. Someone was seriously pissed at this guy. Probably some rich country-club schmuck who cheated on his wife. They found him under a false front on the golf course."

"What's a false front?"

"It's a slope on the green. But it angles the wrong way. If your ball lands on it, it rolls away from the hole, instead of toward it. They're designed into the greens to make them more challenging."

"Belle Green, you said?"

"Yup. The groundskeeper found the exposed grave and called the police early this morning. Whoever dug up the remains wanted them to be found. But that's not even the weirdest part. Check this out." Raj pulled on a pair of lab gloves and leaned over the bones. "Can you see this?" He pointed to a spot on the anterior side of one of the femurs.

I squatted until I was eye level with the lightly colored scratches in it. "What are those? Scavenger marks?" I asked, remembering my conversation with Doc Benoit in the Bone Locker.

"Get closer," Raj nudged with an excited grin.

The scratches were numbers.

90179257433275. A fourteen-digit number had been lightly etched in the victim's bone. "What does it mean?"

Raj snapped off his gloves. "That's what detectives are trying to figure out. It's too long to be a social security number or a phone number. Their best guess is that it's some form of tracking or serial number. But a number this long might take some time to crack."

"It looks fresh." The bones were covered in dirt, but there was no dirt inside the grooves where the cuts were made. It seemed reasonable to assume those numbers were carved after the body was exhumed. "Why would someone do that?"

"Clearly, whoever dug up the body wanted to leave some kind of message."

"Then why not just come out and say what they wanted to say? Why write it in code?"

Raj thought about that for a minute. He dumped his gloves in the biohazard bin with a nostalgic smile. "When I was a kid, my older brother and I used to leave each other secret messages. We had this whole encrypted system for communicating. The beautiful part was that we could leave the messages anywhere—right out in the open, so they were easy to find. And no matter where we left them, my parents could never figure out what they said. My guess is, someone wanted to make sure the message was found, but the message wasn't intended for just anyone to read. It was intended for someone specific. Which makes this whole case even more incredible."

I studied the rest of the remains, a canvas of fragmented clues. What kind of person would exhume a body that had been buried for years, and carve a message in his bones?

"Who is he?" I asked softly, not realizing I'd said it aloud until Raj answered.

"No idea. He wasn't buried with any identification. But detectives have a pretty strong lead. The body was hidden in a highly visible public place. Which means the hole was probably filled at night, when the golf course was closed. Most likely, he was buried while the false front was being constructed, or else someone would have noticed the cuts and imperfections in the turf. The false front was built about five years ago. If the detectives can confirm the dates between the time the front was back-filled and the turf grass was laid, they can cross-reference it with a list of missing persons from the same time period." Raj scratched his head. "The condition of the poor guy's teeth isn't going to make it easy to ID him, but a forensic anthropologist can do a facial reconstruction of the skull fragments, and a forensic artist can use that to sketch the victim's face. If they can find a possible match, Doc will be able to confirm an ID by sending DNA samples to the mitochondrial lab in Richmond."

"When will we know?" I asked, trying to steady the tremor in my voice.

"Depends," he said thoughtfully. "Days. Maybe weeks."

I straightened slowly. A man, dead five years, buried in the golf course near my neighborhood. I hadn't heard from my father since he disappeared . . . five years ago.

• • •

That night, I listened to Reece's voicemail messages, saving them and replaying them over again.

I told myself I didn't want Reece in my life anymore. That I didn't need him. The same way I'd told myself I didn't need my father. But lying here, alone in the dark, I wasn't as sure. I had told Nicholson I hadn't had any contact with my father in five years. I had made myself believe it. It was wrong to keep looking for him, to want him in my life. But now, all I wanted was to know he was alive.

I climbed out of bed and turned on the light. Then I fished

around in my desk for a handful of pushpins. One by one, I put them back in the empty holes in my wall.

"Are you out there?" I whispered to them. "Is it you?"

14

THE NEXT DAY WAS FRIDAY, and I headed straight for the computer lab before school. There had to be a way to find my father.

I started to Google one of his aliases. Then backspaced through the letters until his name was deleted. It was a stupid idea anyway. Searching for him this way made no sense. I just wanted reassurance that he was alive. Somewhere. Anywhere but in pieces on a gurney in a cold room.

I bent down to pick up my backpack.

"Need a hand with . . . ?"

Jeremy looked over my shoulder and studied the blinking cursor on the search screen, even though there wasn't anything left in the search field to see. His glasses slipped down the bridge of his nose and his eyes caught mine over the rim. Warmth spread over my cheeks, like I'd been caught doing something wrong.

"Still looking for him?" he asked. I couldn't tell if he was mocking me. I stood up, almost knocking into him when he didn't back out of my way. "Because I can help. If you want me to," he added quickly. "There are all kinds of new facial recognition software and cell phone tracking and social media sites we've never tried. We could look for him, you know . . . like old times. If you want to find him."

"I don't care where he is," I said.

"Oh." Jeremy's face fell.

I let out a long breath. "I need to figure out where he's *not*."

Jeremy pushed his glasses up his nose. An uncertain smile touched his lips, then retreated again. "I don't understand."

"It's okay." I rolled my eyes at my own foolishness. No matter how technically savvy Jeremy was, he couldn't use a computer to prove my dad hadn't been lying in a hole in Belle Green for the last five years.

Not unless he could use that kind of technology to prove my father was actually . . . somewhere else . . .

I suddenly thought of Lonny. The photos of Adrienne's body on Lonny's phone. They were time stamped.

Lonny didn't have to prove he wasn't at the park when Adrienne was murdered. He just needed to prove he'd been somewhere else. Far enough away that he could never have made it to the park where Adrienne's body was found by the time the photos were taken. Police said he didn't have an alibi, meaning there was no one to corroborate his location, but that didn't mean he hadn't left any tracks. There were always tracks. Some were just harder to see.

Maybe there was a way I could help Lonny without risking my internship. Maybe I could prove he was innocent without having to break any rules. All I had to do was retrace Lonny's steps the night Adrienne was killed.

"Jeremy, you're a genius." I said, my mind buzzing so loudly, I was hardly aware of the first bell ringing, or the students filtering into the room.

Jeremy looked confused. "I didn't do anything yet."

But with any luck, maybe I could.

• • •

After school, I got off the bus at the corner of Sunny View Drive and Route 1 just as TJ's uncle made it to the end of the crosswalk with a six-pack tucked in the crook of his arm. He glanced up as I descended the bus steps, and I wondered if we were both thinking the same thing . . . that it would be awkward to have to walk side by side all the way home, neither of us saying a word to each other. I was glad I didn't have to.

Instead, I crossed the street and headed for Bui's, feeling more and more confident in my theory. Billy Wiles had walked across the street to buy his beer at the Bui Mart every afternoon for as long as I could remember. Bui's was easy. Bui's was close. It was the nearest opportunity to satisfy an addiction, if you lived in Sunny View.

Lonny said his phone and lighter went missing the last time he'd seen Adrienne, which was several hours before she'd been killed. But Lonny had been smoking like a house on fire since he was twelve. At least a pack a day. If his lighter went missing before he left the house, he would have stopped somewhere for matches, or a cheap lighter on the way. Bui Mart would have been his first stop. Bao had been skittish after a series of break-ins last year, and if he'd been concerned enough to mount a gun under the counter, there was a good chance he'd installed cameras too. If I could prove Lonny had been at Bui's, maybe it would be enough to prove he wasn't at the crime scene.

AC/DC wailed through the overhead speakers inside, too loud for Bao to hear the bells jingling on the door. He stood behind the counter, rocking out with an air guitar and thrashing his head, his voice peeling out a whiny falsetto to "Back in Black." As I neared the counter, the charred scent of burning popcorn filled my nose. Across the store, the microwave beside the slushie machines belched out black clouds. I sprinted past the counter to shut it off, catching Bao's attention. The music cut off suddenly, and then Bao was at my side, waving a magazine in the air to disperse the smoke.

We both coughed and covered our mouths.

"Jeez, Bao," I said, plucking the singed bag out of the microwave. There were still ninety seconds left on the timer. "How long did you set it for? There's a popcorn button on the front of the machine."

"It wasn't me!" Bao took the bag and carried it into the men's room. He dropped it in the sink. "Billy must have forgotten it."

"Maybe he was too drunk to remember," I said sharply.

Bao emerged with a thoughtful expression. He inspected the inside of the microwave and sighed. "You get to know a lot of drunks working in a place like this. Billy's not the sloppy kind. He's just been through some rough times."

"You're awfully forgiving, considering what happened to your sister."

"Why shouldn't I be? Billy wasn't the one who kidnapped her. He wasn't the one who killed those kids. If I blamed him—if I took my anger out on an innocent person just because they were related to someone who'd done bad things—I wouldn't be any better than TJ. Would I?" He gave me a pointed look, before turning it inward. His lip quirked with a sheepish grin. "Sometimes I give great advice, huh?"

Bao propped open the store doors to air out the stink. Then he leaned back against the counter beside me. "Can we stop talking about Billy now? It's ruining it for me."

"Ruining what?"

"This fantasy I'm having, where we get naked and have crazy make-up sex behind the hot dog machine."

I tried not to picture it. But had Bao just apologized? It sounded like the same almost-apologies I'd shared with Jeremy and Anh. The kind where neither of us says we're sorry. We just sort of dance around the words and try to move on, like nothing's changed. "Is Anh here?" I asked.

"No." Bao's eyebrows shot up. He pointed to the hot dog machine. "Does that mean—?"

"No! But I do need a favor."

"What exactly do you need?" Bao wagged his eyes.

"Not in this lifetime. Name your price."

"Anh tells me you scored some kind of forensics internship. How about something cool from your lab, like . . ." He scratched his chin and thought for a moment. "I don't know . . . like one of those fancy UV lights they use to find evidence at crime scenes, or a human skull or something?"

"I can't just take a human skull out of the lab! And those fancy lights cost a lot of money."

"What about that cool luminescing spray they use to find blood spatter?"

I waited for the punch line. For the quirky smile that would give away the fact that he was kidding. "What on earth would you do with a bottle of luminol?"

He looked at me with an expression of utter disbelief. "Have you never watched *Dexter*?"

"There has to be something else."

"It's either that, or smokin'-hot sex behind the hot dog machine."

I sighed. It wouldn't be easy, but maybe there was a way to give him what he wanted without breaking any rules. Luminol was just a chemical with luminescent properties, and creating a chemical was no different than following a recipe. I made a mental list of ingredients and supplies . . . latex gloves, paint thinner . . . "I guess I could make it. I'd need a few days to—"

"No," he said. "None of this generic homemade kiddie-chem crap. I want the real deal."

"The lab doesn't just give this stuff away, you know."

"I don't care how you get it. But if you're going to ask me for a favor, it's either that, or lick pickle relish off my—"

"Fine!" I held up a hand. "I'll get it."

Bao did a victory dance behind the counter.

"I want to see your security footage from the night of August twenty-ninth."

He stopped dancing. "Who says I have security cameras?"

The guilty look on his face told me everything I needed to know. That he did have them. And that no one else knew. "Convenience stores have hidden cameras. So do creepy perverts. You're two for two."

He folded his arms and leaned a hip against the register. "So what if I did have this hidden camera? And I did let you see the recordings? You'd give up the goods?"

"I'd give up the luminol. And that's it."

Bao swung himself over the counter, dropping to the floor beside me with a wicked smile. "You don't know what you're missing, Boswell." He pulled a ring of keys from his pocket and unlocked the office at the back of the store. "Just don't tell Anh about this, okay?" He left the door cracked and sat down behind the computer. I wheeled another chair close beside him.

"What are we looking for?" he asked.

"I want to see who was in the store between nine and ten on the night of August twenty-ninth."

Bao clicked open a window, revealing a grainy black-and-white image of the store, from a vantage point behind the counter. Anh must have been on duty that night, because we had a clear shot of the back of her head. The footage sped up, the clock racing in the lower right of the screen. People walked in and out of the store at high speed.

Bao paused the shot. "I knew it!" he said, pointing at the screen. "I knew Little Miss Perfect had a weakness. You saw that didn't you? Anh took a Kit Kat. And she didn't put it on her tab!"

A noise from the store drew Bao's attention. He stood up, still shaking his head as he pushed the mouse toward me. "Here, knock yourself out. I have to be on the floor when customers are in the store. Just push the PLAY button to start the video again. I'll be back in a minute."

I slid his chair out of the way and scooted closer to the screen. Pressed PLAY and watched the faces come and go, trying to recognize Lonny in one of them. At 9:37, a white blond head stood at the counter. I paused the footage. Ran it back. Then slowed it down. It was Lonny. He paid cash for a cheap plastic lighter and a pack of cigarettes. This might be exactly what I needed to plant reasonable doubt in the prosecutor's mind. The Bui Mart was only a couple miles from Mount Vernon Regional Park, but if Lonny was at Bui's at 9:37, was it even possible that he could have abducted Adrienne and driven her to the park, then killed her in time to match the time stamps on the photos taken with Lonny's phone at ten o'clock? If nothing else, this should at least lend credence to Lonny's alibi, that his lighter had been missing.

Bao hadn't returned, so I left the office and found him scouring the inside of the microwave, his nose wrinkling over the smell. "Still reeks like smoke in here. I'm never going to get the smell out of this place."

"Can I get a copy of the video footage?" All I needed to do was get that information to Lonny's lawyer, and let him handle the rest. I'd have officially paid off any debt I owed Lonny Johnson for saving my life. I could return his cell phone to the mailroom before anyone knew it was missing.

"Depends. What else can you get me from the lab?"

"Don't push your luck, or I'll tell your mom about the camera you put in the women's bathroom."

Bao paled and stopped scrubbing to look at me. "How'd you know about that?"

"Lucky guess. Can you get me a copy or not?"

He slung the rag over his shoulder and stared at me with

his hands on his hips. Finally, he said, "Bring me the luminol and I'll make you a copy."

"Deal," I said. The acrid smell of burned popcorn followed me out the door.

15

I DUCKED INTO THE FORENSICS LAB that evening just before dusk. The supply cupboard where Raj had tracked the Croc prints contained rows of boxes containing plastic spray bottles. The crystals rattled inside as I held one under the red emergency exit light to check the label. I took a deep breath and stuffed the luminol deep in my backpack.

It was the right thing to do, I told myself. I would order a replacement bottle when I did inventory next week. And if I'd learned anything this week, it's that even if Raj noticed, he wouldn't suspect me. Because he already suspected someone else.

Heart still racing, I reached into the box of fingerprint cards and felt the evidence bag containing Lonny's cell phone. Still there. I hadn't yet gathered the nerve to open it, to see the photos of Adrienne's body that Raj had insisted were there. But if Bao came through—if the video from Bui's exonerated Lonny—maybe I would never have to. I covered the phone and slipped out of the lab, pulling the door shut behind me.

"Hey, I thought I saw you walk past the break room. Didn't expect to see you on a Friday night. Don't you have a hot date or something?"

I hid my backpack behind me. "I . . . um . . ."

"You don't have to explain," Raj whispered conspiratorially. "I wasn't one of the cool kids either. I probably would have preferred to spend my Friday nights in a lab when I was in high school too. But if it's any consolation, your timing's great." He held up a lab report. "We've got a list of missing persons that could be possible matches for the Golf Course Corpse. Doc wants me to cross-reference them against the DNA database for any existing records. Want to help?"

My breath rushed out. I was only half listening, my panic-addled mind unable to register anything but relief that this had nothing to do with the luminol in my backpack, or Lonny's missing phone. That I hadn't been found out.

Raj waved the printout in front of me.

A list of possible matches . . . that's what he'd said.

I snatched it from his hand and skimmed the search criteria. Adult males, ages twenty-five to forty reported missing or wanted by authorities during a set of dates.

Five years ago.

Five men.

Five names. Rodriguez, Miller, Nguyen, Brown, and . . .

Boswell.

I grabbed the nearest chair and dropped into it. Everything else slipped away.

I shook my head, unable to look away from the name. David Boswell.

This didn't prove anything, I told myself. It only meant he fit a very broad description. It only meant he was missing. And I already knew that. There were four other names. Four other people's fathers it could have been. It didn't have to be mine. It couldn't be.

Raj peeled the page from my hand, his smile gone. He looked at the names on the list and paled.

"Oh, man. Is that . . . ?" He swallowed, tripping over his words. "I had no idea. Boswell. Shit. I'm an idiot. I'm so sorry. I should have looked at it first. I was just so excited to . . ."

Raj straightened, his tone assuming a more professional distance. "Did you know David?" he asked. The question felt loaded, like he just needed the right trigger to set something in motion. The same way it had felt when Nicholson had asked me if I'd had any contact with my dad.

The sad part was, I didn't really know the answer. "He's my father."

Raj folded the paper, tucking it out of sight. "Then I have to tell Doc. He'll want to . . . you know . . . recuse you from any involvement in the case. At least until . . . until we can rule out David Boswell as a match."

I touched the ends of my hair. It was long, with impulsive

curls like my mother's. Yet somewhere inside it was a piece of my dad. I plucked a strand.

"It's not enough," Raj said, taking my hand as if reading my thoughts. He was salty and sweet and I almost gagged on his sympathy. "Mitochondrial DNA is passed through the mother. You would have to be maternally related to the victim for a hair sample to work."

I held the strand between my fingers, unable to let it fall. "Let me know if you find him."

• • •

The bus ride home that night was taking longer than usual. Traffic backed up for miles heading south on Route 1. Ahead, blue lights flashed and sirens blared. As we neared my stop, the bus crawled to a standstill. I slid up the aisle and tapped the driver's shoulder.

"Can you let me out here? I can walk the rest of the way."

"No, sugar," she said. "I can't let no one out in the middle of the street. I'll lose my job. Sit down and get comfortable. Looks like we'll be sitting awhile." The driver pointed out the front window, over the line of cars ahead of us.

Smoke clouded the night sky, engulfing the strip mall across the street from my house. I straightened, gripping the handrail as the bus inched forward, searching the fire for its source. Neon lights flickered from the windows of Gentleman Jim's, the club I'd always secretly wished would burn to the ground. I breathed a sigh of relief it was still standing and safe.

Farther down, ambulances and fire trucks fanned out from the Bui Mart. I scrambled down the bus steps, peeling the door wide enough to slip through, ignoring the shouts of the driver. I darted into the highway, between stopped cars.

The air was thick and choking, warmer the closer I got to Bui's. People crowded the parking lot, and I pushed through them, searching for Anh and Bao. An ambulance eased slowly out of the lot with its sirens on and my heart climbed into my throat.

I searched the crowd for their parents. For anyone who could tell me what had happened. Butch's head stood taller than the others, close to the smoking remains of the store, and I pushed my way toward him, calling his name. His arms rested around my mother's shoulders. She turned at the sound of my voice. Black streaks trailed down her face and I couldn't tell if it was makeup or soot. Until Butch turned too. He was covered in it, his skin glistening with sweat and filth.

"What happened?" I asked, breathless, my mouth dry from the smoke. "I can't find Anh or Bao."

"Anh's fine. She wasn't here when the fire started," my mother said, taking my hand in hers. It was hot and slick. She tasted like cool salt water, sadness, and relief.

"What about Bao?"

"No one's really sure," Butch said. "I couldn't talk to Mr. Bui. He wanted to ride with Bao." He waved away a paramedic. People rushed around in every direction, radios and lights and noise.

"Ride with Bao where?"

Butch wiped a streak of black sweat from his brow. "By the time I got in there, the store was already engulfed. I don't know long how Bao stayed inside, trying to put it out."

The fire was extinguished for the most part, the crowd beginning to thin. We crossed the parking lot to get some distance from the smoke. I crumpled onto the curb beside them and rested my head on my knees, still clutching my mother's hand. Butch made her feel safe, secure, with his strong arms around her. I held on to her tightly, stealing those reassurances and making them my own.

I tasted it, a heartbeat before I felt the shift in my mother's posture. An acidic burn that tightened my throat.

"What is it?" I lifted my head, sharp and alert, following the direction of her stare.

Across the parking lot, Billy Wiles stood in a crowd with his hands in his pockets, staring at the remains of the fire. As if he could feel us watching, he turned in our direction.

"Nothing." My mother's shoulders relaxed. The burn subsided as Billy walked off into the shadows. "In the dark, he looks so much like his brother. For a moment, I could have sworn . . . oh, never mind." She pulled me closer. "It must have been the smoke in my eyes."

• • •

The next morning, I sat in the shade of the bus shelter on the corner of Route 1, watching the fire marshal and arson investigators disappear inside the cooling skeleton of the Bui Mart. After a few hours, the yellow caution tape began to sag, the white trucks were loaded back up with equipment, and the parking lot slowly emptied. Mr. and Mrs. Bui were not there. When I'd called Anh that morning, she said they hadn't left Bao's side. His condition was critical.

I couldn't fight the suspicion snaking through me. That this had something to do with me. I'd just been in Bao's store, looking through security footage that would exonerate Lonny, and allow the police to focus on finding Adrienne's real killer. Now the videos were probably destroyed, and I had the sinking feeling that none of this was a coincidence.

16

THE NEXT WEEK was a blur. I tried to focus on classes and homework, but it was hard to keep my mind off the arson investigation and the tests being run on the golf course bones. It was hard to keep my mind off of Reece. At least I hadn't gotten any more cryptic notes since I'd changed the locks on my trailer, and neither had Jeremy or Vince. I spent every afternoon with Raj after school, trying to stay busy, listening to conversations in the break room, and watching reports and evidence boxes go in and out of the mailroom. Raj had laughed when I asked him what was taking so long, and why things couldn't happen more quickly, the way they did on TV. By the end of the week, I was no closer to knowing if the bones were my father's, or who had started the fire at Bui's.

The following Tuesday, I was back on the bus for the long ride to the lab. I curled into my seat and thumbed on my phone. It was full of messages, mostly texts from Reece. I'd answered the urgent ones that came in the late-night hours after the fire, letting him know I was okay and that I hadn't been involved. But then came the others, saying he wanted to see me, that we needed to talk. The longer I put off responding to them, the more awkward it felt to try. He began every text with an apology. But to forgive him seemed too easy, and to confess to missing him made me feel weak. I didn't know what else there was to say.

Instead, I texted today's homework to Anh. She had been excused from school to stay with her brother at the hospital, and I'd offered to check in with her teachers each day and communicate her assignments back to her, hoping the small gesture would alleviate some of the nagging guilt I still felt about the fire, and keep me posted on Bao's slowly improving condition.

My phone buzzed. Gena's number flashed across the screen, and I sighed before picking it up.

"I don't know what's going on between the two of you,"

she started in, "but whatever it is, don't you think you're being a little hard on him?"

"Hard on who?"

"You know who," she said, sounding snippy. "Come on, Leigh. The boy's a mess. I've never seen him like this."

Whatever. I shouldn't care. I told myself I didn't want to know. "What do you mean?"

"He's like a lovesick puppy with a hair-trigger temper. All he does is whine about how you won't talk to him."

"He should have thought of that before he—" I bit my tongue. She would only defend him. "Can we talk about something else?" If she said any more, I might break down and cry. Or actually call him. And I wasn't sure which was worse.

"Fine," she said through a long exhale. "How's school?"

"Fine. How about for you?"

"Good," she said.

"Good."

"Great."

"Fabulous."

I could hear her drumming her nails against the receiver. "Is there anything else you want to talk about?" she asked.

Like how someone had broken in to my house and was stalking people I knew, and I was pretty sure it was Reggie Wiles even though no one would ever believe me. How someone had burned down my friend's store less than a day after I'd been there looking at security footage that no one else knew existed. How a girl from my neighborhood had been murdered, and I was blowing my internship to prove Lonny Johnson wasn't a killer. How my father might have been dug out of a hole on the ninth green of the Belle View Country Club golf course. It all sounded ridiculous, even to me. "Not really."

"How's Spanish class?"

"I can count to ten and say *good-bye*. Want to hear?" I asked flatly.

She muttered something in Spanish under her breath. "I get it. Call me later, when you're not as cranky as Reece." She hung up.

When I got to the lab, I found Raj in the mailroom, packaging evidence returns. He lifted his head from a bin.

"Hey, I was going to call you a few hours ago, but then I remembered you were in class. I've got good news."

"Good news?" I asked skeptically. I'd had nothing but terrible news for the last few weeks.

"We got the DNA results back on the golf course bones. It wasn't your dad." A relieved breath rushed out of me. He handed me the report. "It was some dude named Karl Miller."

Karl Miller. From Belle Green. Eric Miller's father.

I'd seen Eric in computer class that morning, but then I hadn't noticed him in the halls the entire rest of the day. I wondered if he already knew. Maybe someone from the lab had broken the news to his family while I'd been at school.

"Are you okay? I thought you'd be happy." Raj's voice shook me from my thoughts. He looked concerned. And I couldn't afford to set off any alarms. This was the second body in less than a month that I had some kind of connection to. Karl had been in the poker club; he had been a friend of my parents. My mom had called him a good person. A loyal one. I smiled, trying to make it convincing.

"I am happy. Thanks for letting me know." I gave him back the report.

"I'm just packaging up the personal effects to be returned to the detective on the case. The guy was buried with his wedding ring, but his wife doesn't want it. She said we can burn it for all she cares. I guess she didn't like him very much."

Something didn't add up. My mom said Karl Miller had left his family for another woman. It was the same story Eric had been telling everyone since middle school. So why was Karl still wearing his wedding ring when he died? And what was he doing on a missing persons list?

"Here." Raj tossed me the bag containing Karl's ring. "Box this up and get it ready for the courier. He'll be here in an hour."

I turned it over in my hands, remembering the day my own mother had tossed my father's bag in the trash.

How was it possible that Karl Miller and my father both disappeared at the same time, and one of them turned up dead? Who would have wanted to kill him?

When Raj left the mailroom, I put the bag in my pocket. Instead of going home, I took the bus to Belle Green.

Eric and I had never had much in common. But standing on his front stoop, I almost felt connected to him. We'd both lost a father five years ago, had both stayed up nights wondering if we were somehow the reason he'd gone, or worse . . . if maybe we weren't enough of a reason to return.

I pressed the doorbell. Listened to his mother's high heels click on the hard floors as she came to the door. When it opened, her eyes were red-rimmed and her makeup was smudged, her expression hard and impatient.

"I don't want whatever it is you're selling."

"I'm not selling anything," I said quickly as she began to shut the door. Her eyes drifted to the lanyard around my neck. I'd forgotten to take it off and she stiffened—either at the words *forensics lab* or at the sight of my name, I couldn't tell.

"What do you want?" she asked through the narrow opening.

"I came to see Eric."

I fingered the ring in my pocket, reminding myself why I was here. She shut the door in my face. From inside came the muffled sound of an argument, followed by the snap of her high heels as they retreated from the door.

I turned and started down the steps. The door clicked softly open.

Eric looked cautiously up and down the street, like he

was checking to see who'd dumped me there. The way I had when someone had left a burning bag of shit on my porch.

My face felt hot. It was hard to look in his eyes, but I made myself do it anyway. "I heard about your dad," I said, gesturing to my lanyard. "I wanted to tell you I'm sorry." I squeezed my eyes shut, wishing I could eat my words. I'd always hated it when people said they were sorry that my dad was gone. They weren't sorry. It wasn't their fault. They just didn't know what else to say. I shook my head. Started over. "What I mean to say is that I think I know how you feel right now, and that sucks, and . . ."

And what? We weren't friends. We never talked outside of class. I didn't really know him, and I didn't really know how he felt because *my* father might still be alive. How could all this not sound totally disingenuous, even if I meant every word? I shut my mouth and pulled the bag from my pocket. I held it up so Eric could see the ring inside. "Your mom said she didn't want it, but I thought you might want to have it." He stayed where he was, wedged in the open the door, staring at me with narrowed eyes as if an ocean existed in the space between us.

I set the bag gently at his feet and walked away.

"What am I supposed to do with this?" Eric's breath hitched and when I turned, he kicked the bag with the dirt-caked toe of his sneaker. A long tear slid down his cheek and he brushed it away.

I didn't know how to answer that. What had I done with mine, except hope? And there was no hope of finding Eric's father alive. Maybe it had been a mistake, to think he would want it. But it was too late to take it back. Too late not to be standing in his front yard with nothing to say.

I shrugged. "I keep mine under my mattress. Sometimes, when I miss my dad, it helps."

Eric came out onto the porch, closing the door behind him. He bent slowly and picked the bag off the porch floor. Head down, he mumbled, "She lied about him. My mom thought he left us for another woman. That's what she told me." He shook loose another tear with the gentle shake of his head. "I hated him for it. All this time, I hated him. And I can't take it back."

"Maybe you can't take it back," I said, thinking of all the anger I'd felt toward my father since I discovered who he really was. What he'd done. "But maybe it's not too late to stop hating him."

Eric went back inside, and I walked to the foot of his driveway and looked down the street toward Jeremy's house. He hadn't been in school for the last two days. I'd assumed he'd ditched class to be with Anh at the hospital, but his car was parked in his driveway and it left me feeling uneasy. Jeremy was always *somewhere* after school, photographing a sports game or school event, or working on the school paper. I walked closer, shielding my eyes from the sun and finding the window to Jeremy's room. His blinds were closed. I peeked inside the garage window, but his parents' cars were gone.

Six months ago, I would have found the key under the rock in his flowerbed and let myself in, but the key he used to keep there for me was probably long gone now, and it felt strange knocking on Jeremy's front door. No one answered. He probably didn't want to see me. It had been stupid to think he would let me in anyway. I was almost at the end of the driveway when Jeremy's bedroom window slid open.

"You're the last person I expected to see."

"You weren't in school, and I . . ." I wasn't really sure what else to say. I didn't want to tell him about Eric's father, it wasn't my news to tell. "I guess I wanted to make sure you were okay."

Jeremy was quiet for a moment. "Use the key in the flowerbed."

"The flowerbed? But I thought—" The window slammed shut. Before he could change his mind, I dug the fake rock out from under the shrubbery. The key inside it was old and scratched. It looked like the same one I'd always used.

I climbed the stairs to Jeremy's room and found him staring out the window.

"I thought we agreed to change our locks. I even gave you a copy of my key. Why haven't you changed yours?"

Jeremy's voice sounded strange. Like he hadn't used it for days. "I wasn't going to. I knew he'd be angry. Instead,

I stopped putting the key in the flowerbed, and I thought maybe that would be enough. But I wasn't sleeping. I started worrying. What if someone had made a copy of my house key? Maybe that's how he got in to your trailer? By coming in and swiping your key from my dad's office? And if that's what happened, what's to stop him from doing it again? And I was worried about . . ." He took a deep tremulous breath. "I was worried. So a couple days ago I told my dad about the key in the flowerbed. I told him I thought someone was using it to get into the house."

I didn't like that Jeremy wouldn't look at me. That he wouldn't turn around. "What happened?"

"He was furious."

I walked slowly to Jeremy's side. Green and golden bruises covered his arms. The bridge of his nose was scratched and swollen. There was a dent in his glasses.

Anger boiled up inside me. "Why do you let him do this to you, Jeremy? Why don't you stand up for yourself!"

"What do you want me to do?"

"I want you to hit him back! I want you to defend yourself!"

Jeremy grew quiet and lowered his eyes to the floor. "Do you remember that day back in June, in the hallway at school when we were arguing?"

"I remember," I said. Jeremy had stopped taking his prescription medications, and had been experimenting with street drugs. It had been the only time in my life I had ever been afraid of him.

"I said terrible things to hurt you. I shoved you. I wanted to hit you. And I've never forgiven myself for that."

I cringed at the memory of his face and the tone of his voice. I'd hardly recognized him that day. "It wasn't your fault," I said. "You weren't yourself."

"Because I was him!" There were tears in Jeremy's eyes. "I was my dad! There's a piece of him inside me. It's always been inside me! And I have to keep pushing it away so I don't become someone like him!"

I wanted to tell him that would never happen. That he would never be like his father. But I wasn't so sure either of us had a choice.

He stared out the window. "I can suck it up and take it for one more year. Then I'll be gone and I can forget he ever existed."

"I'm sorry," I whispered, wanting to touch him, but too afraid of what I might feel.

"It's not your fault," he said quietly.

A tear welled in my eye and I blinked it away, certain that if I let one escape, the rest would all follow. I held out his old house key. Our fingers brushed, and it wasn't so bad. Sweet and familiar. Like maybe we were finally okay.

"I don't get it," I said, wiping my eyes. "If your dad knows about the break-in, why is the key outside again?"

"He refuses to change the locks. He's determined to catch the guy and turn him in." Jeremy picked a box off his bed and tossed it to me.

Do-It-Yourself Home Security Kit? "This is his answer? A nanny spy cam?"

Jeremy shrugged. "He wants me to install it in the foyer. He made me put the key back in the flowerbed. You know, to make it easier for someone to sneak in during the night and rob us blind. Or hack us to pieces and harvest our organs so they can sell them on the black market." He rolled his eyes. "Hey, at least we'll get it all on film."

Jeremy pitched the box on the bed. He cocked his head to look at me. "I've been cooped up in here since Sunday. My parents won't be home for a couple hours. Want to get out of here?"

I smiled the first real smiled I'd felt in days. "Absolutely."

17

I FIDGETED IN THE PASSENGER SEAT of Jeremy's Civic. The seat had been adjusted differently, the seat base pulled farther forward, far enough that it didn't fit my backpack between my feet. Probably because Anh liked to put hers in the backseat. It was like coming home after a long trip and finding all the furniture had been rearranged. But it wasn't my fur-

niture anymore. I reached under the seat and slid it backward as gently as I could manage. Jeremy raised an eyebrow,
but didn't say anything as I settled my backpack between
my feet.

"How's Bao doing? Have you heard from Anh today?" I
asked.

Jeremy gave a wan smile. "Bao's doing a little better this
week. They kicked him out of ICU when he was well enough
to make a pass at one of the nurses during his sponge bath.
The doctors say he'll be fine. It'll just take time."

I pressed my lips tight, staring out the window.

"Are you going to tell me what's wrong, or do I have to
employ my top-secret-and-most-deadly ninja-journalist skills?"

"I'm fine," I said.

"No, you're not. Is it Reece?" I couldn't help but hear the
hopeful quality in his voice.

"No. Maybe." I sighed as tears pinched my eyes for the second time. "I don't want to talk about him. But there's something else. I just have this weird feeling . . ."

Jeremy snuck glances at me as he drove. "Weird like how?"

I took a deep breath. "I have this weird feeling that the fire
at Bui's had something to do with me." There. I said it. There
was no taking it back.

Jeremy laughed. "You're being a dork. The police know
exactly how it started. The same way that pyro-kid from
North Hampton set those three fires in Burke last year. Any-

one can start a slow burn with a matchbook and a pack of cigarettes and walk out of a place without being seen." His smile faded. He darted quick looks at me, and I turned to face the window.

"You can't seriously think this had anything to do with you?"

I didn't answer.

"Look," he said, tapping the steering wheel thoughtfully. "I know the things that happened in June. . . the things TJ did . . . they weren't your fault. And I know we were hard on you. We blamed you for things we shouldn't have. I'm sorry. Maybe . . ." He gripped the wheel like he was bracing to say something difficult. "Maybe you're internalizing too much. Maybe all that blame is making you feel guilty for things you shouldn't feel guilty for."

I laid my head against the glass and looked at him sideways. "You sound like a shrink."

His lip quirked up. "Yeah, well, I've had a lot of practice listening to them."

Jeremy had spent more time than usual with shrinks lately, which was also my fault. The police were the ones who figured out Jeremy had bought street drugs with the intent of killing himself. But it should have been me. I should have been a good enough friend to see how badly he was hurting inside and stopped him. And some days, that's all I could think about when I looked at him.

"Want to hit the Baskin-Robbins? My treat. Maybe a double scoop will make you feel better," Jeremy said.

Maybe Jeremy was right. Maybe I was internalizing too much. Getting ice cream with him sounded great. Normal even. But somehow, I didn't think it would make me feel better. I had too many questions. And the only thing that I really wanted was answers. It may not have been my father's body on the golf course, but it raised the question of exactly what my father had been doing five years ago around that time, or worse, the possibility that he was dead too.

"Remember when you said you would help me find my dad?" I chewed my nail, wondering how to tell him where I wanted to go. And what I wanted to do.

"Why do I get the feeling I'm not taking you out for ice cream?"

"Because I'd like you to take me to the police station instead."

Jeremy braked and a car honked behind us. He swore and cut over a lane to let the pissed-off people pass us. "The police station? It's not like the police know where he is, or they would have arrested him already!"

"There are answers inside that building that we won't find on Google. It will only take a few minutes."

He pushed his glasses up his nose, and muttered under his breath as he pulled to a stoplight.

"Please," I asked, resting my hand on his sleeve.

He turned to me, and something in his face softened.

"So are you with me?" I asked.

"Yeah," he sighed through a smile. "I'm with you."

I pointed at the green light in front of us, feeling eager and hopeful. "Then let's go."

• • •

We sat in the parked car, watching the front door of the station. "So, what exactly are we doing here?"

"We're borrowing Nicholson's computer."

Jeremy's face crunched up. "I have a computer. Why do we need to borrow Lieutenant Nicholson's?"

I bit my lip. Maybe *borrowing* was a poor choice of words.

Jeremy took one look at my face and his eyebrows shot toward the ceiling. "No. No way in hell am I stealing Lieutenant Nicholson's computer! Are you out of your mind?" He reached for the gearshift and I grabbed his hand to stop him. He probably thought I was crazy. I could taste the sharp, peppery bite of astonishment the minute I touched him.

"Just listen for a minute. We're not stealing his computer. We're just borrowing his account."

His face was a mask of disbelief. "You're asking me to hack Nicholson's computer."

I waited, still holding on to him, hoping to pick up on some shift in his feelings. A hint of something cool and confident that suggested he was still with me. That he believed we could do this.

His gaze lingered on our hands. "Why are you doing this?"

I let go of him, and turned to the window. I had to tell him about Karl Miller.

"Eric's dad is dead. He disappeared around the same time mine did. They were friends. What if all those Google alerts we found weren't my father? What if we were wrong, and he's lying in a hole somewhere just like Karl Miller? What if he's been dead all this time, and I didn't know?"

Jeremy sighed, and I looked over hopefully. "How is getting Nicholson's computer going to help with that?"

"They've had an outstanding arrest warrant for my father for five years. Which means they've been looking for him. And they have a lot more resources than we do. Maybe they know something I don't know. Maybe he's been spotted somewhere. The police must have information on those computers they don't share with the public. I just want to see his records."

"Then why not just ask Nicholson for them?"

Have you had any contact with your father in the last five years?

"Because if he knows I'm looking for him, I'll lose my internship."

"If we get caught, your internship will be the least of your worries. Maybe . . ." He hesitated, tiptoeing over the words. "Did you ever think maybe it's better to not know?"

Of course it would be better. But I couldn't turn away now.

"We're not going to get caught," I said. "Lieutenant Nicholson won't even know we were here. He's in a meeting from four thirty to five on the other side of the building. I know because Gena and Alex are in the same one with him every week."

Jeremy pushed his glasses up the bridge of his nose and stared at the door of the police station. I waited, half hoping he'd put the car in reverse. That he'd be strong enough to keep us from doing something stupid.

He took the keys from the ignition and got out of the car. "Come on," he said. "It's almost four thirty. We don't have much time."

• • •

Jeremy stood to the side as I presented my lanyard to the desk attendant behind the window. When she put her call on hold, I told her I was there to drop off some lab reports. She buzzed me through, and when she turned to her phone to resume her call, I held the door open to let Jeremy sneak in with me. Nicholson's office was empty, but the lights were on. He was probably coming back after his meeting, before he left for the day. I closed the door behind us.

Wringing his hands, Jeremy stepped cautiously behind the desk.

"It's okay if you can't do this. You don't have to. I shouldn't have asked you to. Let's just go—"

Jeremy held up a hand, silencing me. His gaze lingered on an old CD player in the corner, and the battered classic rock jewel cases beside it. Then slid to the leather day planner on the desk and the newly sharpened pencil that held open today's page. A slow smile crept over his face when he spotted the plastic Rolodex beside the phone.

He picked the folded issue of The *Washington Post* off Nicholson's desk chair and set it aside. Then he sat down in front of the computer. "I can totally do this."

"But the security on the computers here—"

"Isn't much different than anywhere else."

"How will you hack in? Don't you have to be a programmer or something?" A fact I hadn't given much thought to before we came here. I hadn't thought this all the way through. Not until Jeremy put his bare hands on the keyboard and began typing. His fingerprints would be everywhere. What the hell was I thinking, bringing him here?

"Ninety percent of hacking has nothing to do with technology," he said softly, as if to himself. His hands were steady as they guided the mouse. "Hacking is mostly just social engineering."

He clicked open windows and closed them behind him. Then he paused at a blue screen. A curser flashed in the user name and password fields under a police insignia.

"Social engineering?" The term sounded dissonant to me. Like two notes that didn't belong together. "I don't understand."

Jeremy pointed to the Rolodex. The stereo. "Look around. Nicholson's a total neophyte." He tapped the open page of the day planner. "Clearly, the lieutenant is uncomfortable with modern technology or he wouldn't be listening to twenty-year-old CDs and keeping his contact list in a plastic box that's too big for his pocket. Security is only as good as the people who use it. And Nicholson is the kind of user who will want to keep it simple. Simple is easy. But it's also predictable." Jeremy studied the items on Nicholson's desk. He opened a drawer and carefully sifted inside. He pushed up his glasses, thinking. "He's the kind of guy who probably uses the same password for everything. Less to remember. See here?" He flipped through the day planner. "To-do lists, grocery lists, lists of meetings . . . he's got everything written down so he won't forget. I'll bet you a case of Twinkies that his password is written down somewhere in this book." I watched, fascinated and terrified, as Jeremy touched every page, leaving his fingerprints all over Nicholson's things. I couldn't even think about Twinkies. Every footstep in the hall outside made me jump. But I'd never seen Jeremy so focused. He flipped the last page of the planner. Nothing. He opened the Rolodex and flipped to the letter *N*, leaving oily smudges on the dark plastic cover, a nonporous surface that would yield a snowy surface of white crystals if we ever got caught. I reached to stop him from touching anything else. This was a stupid idea.

"This is it," he said, freezing my hand. Inside the Rolodex

was a card with Nicholson's name on it. And a user ID and password, written in the lieutenant's own block print. Jeremy's face broke in a wide grin.

He typed quickly. We were in. A cursor blinked in a search field.

He entered my father's name, David Boswell. The search returned more than one.

"Which one is he?" Jeremy turned to where I leaned over his shoulder. Close enough that his nose brushed my cheek, leaving the cool burn of peppermint adrenaline on my breath.

My face warmed. I pointed to a birth date.

"This one," I said, certain it was my father, remembering the way his candles sagged in his ice cream cakes in the July heat. The birth dates on his phony driver's licenses had all been fall or winter or spring. They were wrong.

But this . . . This was my father. Deep in the belly of the beast.

Jeremy scrolled through my father's record. And kept scrolling. It was too much to take in.

"Can you print it?" I asked through a lump in my throat.

Jeremy checked the small printer for paper, noting the model number. Careful to select the right one so we didn't print to some other machine on the network in another room. The printer came to life, spitting out far too many pages. I looked anxiously between the printer and the door. Finally, the machine went silent.

Jeremy stood and handed me the stack. He didn't let go.

"I'm sorry," he said in a broken voice. "For everything. I never wanted to hurt you. I never wanted to hurt *us*. I know I said some terrible things. I blamed you for things that weren't your fault. I just . . . I just want us to be okay."

He let the pages go. I wanted to put my arms around him. To tell him it was my fault too. But I was too afraid to say the wrong thing. To do the wrong thing, and break us again. I held the pages to my chest. "We're okay."

Three quick raps shook the door.

"Lieutenant?" It opened, and Reece leaned inside. My breath caught in my chest, and for a moment, all I could do was look at him. At the rings under his eyes and the dark stubble on his jaw. At the turned down corners of his lips.

He paled, his eyes darting between me and Jeremy. Then to the papers in my hand. He swallowed. "Leigh? What's going on?" His voice was thick with emotion.

"I needed something," I said through a trembling breath. "Please don't ask me what." The less he knew, the less trouble he'd be in if he tried to cover for me.

"What's he doing here?" he asked quietly, almost as if he was afraid of the answer.

"I asked him to drive me." I stood so close to Jeremy, our shoulders and hips touched. Instinct told me to step away, so Reece wouldn't get the wrong idea, but I stayed exactly where I was. Maybe then he'd know how it felt to see him with someone else.

Jeremy eased slowly out from behind the desk.

Reece shut his eyes, like he was searching for the right words. When he opened them, they looked anguished. "I've been trying to reach you."

"I know."

"Please, can we talk about this?"

A hand appeared on Reece's shoulder.

My heart climbed into my throat.

"Hey, Whelan. What's going on in here?" An officer I didn't recognize looked us all over, then at Nicholson's empty desk, then at me, on the wrong side of it. "Is the lieutenant around?"

Jeremy and Reece exchanged nervous glances.

"I was just delivering some lab reports," I said quickly. "He must be in a meeting. I'll leave them on his chair." I held the stack of papers at my side, and fidgeted with the lanyard around my neck making sure the officer noticed it.

Reece cleared his throat. "Hey, Walker," he said, drawing the officer's attention. "I heard you're good with a bike? I got this weird thing going on with my brakes. Got about *five minutes* to look them over for me?" Reece stepped into the hall, glancing at me one last time as he led the officer away.

I quietly shut the door, blocking Jeremy's exit.

"What are you doing? We should get out of here." He sounded panicked.

I looked around the office. At the Rolodex. The keyboard.

The printer. I plucked a Kleenex from the box, ready to wipe down everything we'd touched. Reece had bought us five minutes to cover our tracks, but there was no erasing the fact that we'd been here. If I'd learned anything from Lonny's case, I knew that assigning guilt was about more than just fingerprints. More than hair and fibers and things left out of place. It was about who we were, and what people expected us to be. My father's report was heavy in my hand. I crumpled the tissue and tossed it in the wastebasket.

"Nothing."

18

JEREMY PARKED IN FRONT of my trailer and killed the engine. I knew he wanted to come in, but I needed to be alone.

"I'll let you know if I find anything," I said, holding the police records to my chest. "And Jeremy? Thank you for helping me." I opened the door.

"I just want all of this to be behind us. You want that too, right?" he asked.

The police records were hot in my hands. I remembered what Anh had said. That sometimes you have to get through something before you can put it behind you. "Yeah, I want that too."

I went to my bedroom and fanned the police records over

my comforter. The list of my father's Known Associates seemed like a logical place to start. My mother, Butch, and I were first on the list, but below that was a list of other names. Jason Fowler, denoted as our landlord. Reginald Wiles, cross-referenced with his own case number. Then Anthony DiMorello, Karl Miller, and Craig Reinnert. My mind skipped over the old photograph of the poker club.

I flipped the page. According to Nicholson's files, an arrest warrant was issued for my father on June 28, 2009. A day earlier, an anonymous call had been placed to the police department, disclosing the details of a several counts of extortion and an illegal gambling ring being run by my father, in connection with a money laundering operation that used Reggie Wiles's brokerage firm as a front. The call had been traced to a phone in the lobby of the Belle Green Country Club. June 28 was the date Reggie Wiles had been arrested, according to the article in my bag. The same anonymous call—originating from the Belle Green Country Club—had incriminated both of them.

My stomach roiled. The anonymous call, the warrant for my father, the murder of Karl Miller, who was buried in the same golf course where the call was made. What if Karl Miller had been the one who'd made the anonymous call and turned my father in?

Or worse . . . What if my father killed him for it?

I dug the plastic bag out from under my bed. Carefully, I

removed the faded photo of my father and his friends. Karl Miller had his arm around Reggie Wiles. Reggie Wiles had his arm around my dad. They were all smiling.

I thought about Jeremy and Anh. The long stretch of days when we didn't speak. But even when Jeremy and I were angriest with each other, like the day we'd argued in the hall at school, or when Anh and I were at our most competitive, fighting for a life-changing chemistry scholarship, I could never have imagined killing them. The idea of my father—the man who'd gently placed Band-Aids on my knee, who'd never touched my mother when they argued—murdering anyone didn't sit right. This had to be wrong. I had to be wrong. There had to be another explanation.

Maybe Lonny was right. Maybe I shouldn't blindly believe. Maybe some latent piece of the puzzle was missing, something I couldn't see because I didn't have all the facts, letting a long rap sheet of other crimes sway me into thinking my father could be capable of something like this. But Lonny had also once told me that it all boiled down to motive—if I could identify a motive, I'd find the person behind the crime.

My father had opportunity. My father had a motive. And if the motive wasn't convincing enough, he'd run.

I dropped the photo and cursed every pushpin I'd stuck back in my wall until my eyes burned with tears. I stormed to the bathroom and splashed handfuls of cold water on my face.

Then I stopped. The bathroom smelled strange. I flipped on the light.

A stray drop of water trailed down the mirror. Over the letters written in bold, blue ink.

THE ENEMY HIDES BENEATH A FALSE FRONT. THE CLUB WILL ILLUMINATE ITS SECRETS.

A chill spread down the wet neck of my shirt, then through me. The smell of permanent marker lingered in the room.

Someone had been here. Hands shaking, I ran from room to room, checking locks, looking for anything unusual. Any clue to who had been here or how they'd gotten in. The deadbolts were intact, the screens and glass secure on every window. Nothing was missing. Nothing left behind but the message on my mirror.

I used my cell phone to photograph the message. Then I dialed Gena's number.

"Gena," I said, trying to keep my voice steady when she answered. "I need a favor."

I numbly half listened as she griped about all the favors I'd asked for lately. I held my phone in place between my ear and my shoulder, clutched an old rag my mother wouldn't miss and a bottle of her nail polish remover. I smeared it in circles, harder and harder over the letters, determined to wipe out every trace. My mother shouldn't see this. It would only scare her. But I needed to be sure we were safe. "I need to know if Reggie Wiles left the halfway house today. Can you find out if he's still there?"

Gena grew quiet. Then she asked, "Are you okay? Is everything all right?"

"I'm fine," I answered too quickly.

"I can come over. I'll bring dinner—"

"No," I said. "I have a test tomorrow. I need to study."

"Is there something you want to talk about? Did something happen?"

I swallowed hard. What could I tell her? If I told her someone had been inside my trailer, I'd have to tell her about Jeremy father's key to our trailer, and if the police involved Jeremy's parents, then Jeremy would take the brunt of his father's temper. He'd already risked too much for me. All I needed was proof that Reggie wasn't where he was supposed to be. "I just need to know."

"I talked to Reece a little while ago. He's really worried about you. He thinks the internship might not have been such a good idea. I'm starting to think maybe he's right."

"No!" I tried to hold down my panic. "The internship is fine. Everything's fine. Why would he say that?" Because he'd seen me in Nicholson's office and knew I was doing something I shouldn't be? Had he told her about that too?

"He also said you guys still haven't worked things out. You can't keep putting him off like this."

I didn't answer.

"I know you've been through a lot, Leigh, and your head's probably in a tough place right now. I still have the number for that counselor I told you about over the summer. Maybe you should talk to someone."

Great, she thought I was crazy. If I wasn't careful, she'd pull the internship out from under me and put me in therapy twice a week.

"Dammit, Gena! I told you I'm fine. I don't want to talk to anyone!"

"Maybe you shouldn't be alone right now."

It's what I used to say to Jeremy when things were bad at home. It might as well be code for "Intervention: I'm coming right over."

"Look," I said, deliberately smoothing my voice. "I'm sorry that I yelled. I'm fine, Gena, I swear. I know I'm probably worrying for nothing. Just please . . . will you check for me?"

Gena sighed. "Okay. Fine. I'll call Alex and see what he can find out. I'll call you back in an hour."

I hung up the phone and checked the bathroom for ink stains before putting the rag in the Dumpster at the end of my street. Then I rechecked the doors and windows and took the baseball bat to my room.

The faces of my father's friends stared at me from the photo. Their matching shirts and smiles.

The enemy hides beneath a false front.

Eric's dad had been buried under a false front. But the media didn't know that. They only knew the body had been buried under the golf course. The police hadn't released the precise location, keeping the exact details of the crime scene and the code on the bones confidential. No one should know this except the police, the people who worked in the lab, the groundskeeper at the golf course . . . and the person who'd buried the body.

. . . the message wasn't intended for just anyone to read. It was intended for someone specific.

I tore open my backpack, ripped a piece of paper from a spiral notebook, and grabbed a pencil from my desk. I closed my eyes, recalling the scratches in the bone. I wrote down the numbers in order by memory, fighting to keep the pencil steady in my hand.

90179257433275. If it was intended for me, like the message on the photograph and on the mirror were, then I should be able to decipher it. I should already know the key. I should already know the significance of these numbers.

A cold knot formed in the pit of my stomach. I tore open my closet door and dug frantically under a pile of loose clothes, scattering old textbooks across the floor. I snatched up last year's chemistry book and turned to the periodic table. Making furious notations, I paired the numbers together, over and over in different combinations, until I knew I had it right. Until the message was clear.

90179257433275 became 90-17-92-5-74-33-2-75.

Th-Cl-U-B-W-As-He-Re.

The Club Was Here.

My phone rang, flashing Gena's name. I picked it up and put it to my ear, the textbook still balanced on my knees.

"I talked to Alex. He called a friend, who called a friend, who confirmed with Reggie Wiles's parole officer. He's been accounted for all day. He left the halfway house once, for work release. He signed in on time, and came home immediately after."

How was that possible?

"Leigh, are you there?"

"Are you sure? Gena, I feel like I've seen him."

"Where?"

My mind wandered back to the slouching shoulders of the man who'd bumped me in the intersection. To the man reading the missing person flyer in Sunny View. To the man watching the crowd at Lonny's trailer. Nowhere I could prove.

"Just around. Everywhere. I feel like he's following me."

"Did he approach you? Did you clearly see his face?"

"Yes. Maybe . . ." I sighed, my breath still shaky. I'd only thought I'd recognized his face from a grainy black-and-white image in the paper. I couldn't even be sure they were all the same man. "No, he didn't approach me. But he's out there. I know it."

"Leigh, honey. I'm really worried about you. You need to talk to someone. Try to get whatever's eating you off your chest. Maybe find some closure. TJ's gone, Leigh. He can't hurt you anymore."

But it wasn't TJ I was worried about. And I wasn't imagining things.

"I'll think about it," I said, knowing that was the only thing she wanted to hear.

I disconnected and picked up the photo. I brought it close to my face, examining the logo on their shirts, a puzzle piece sliding into place. The Belle Green Poker Club.

The club will illuminate its secrets.

The club.

The poker club. That was the key. The key to figuring out who killed Karl Miller. And the key to figuring out who wanted me to know.

19

GENA WAS RIGHT. I did need to talk to someone. I'd been up all night checking the locks on my trailer and staring at the ceiling with my phone in my hand, thinking about calling Reece. I knew he would come if I called. That he would stay the night if I asked him to, so I wouldn't have to be alone. He'd covered for me at the station, and I wanted to be able to trust him with this too. I wanted to be able to tell him everything—about the break-ins and the message on my mirror. But he'd already

told Gena he was worried about me. And now she was worried too. And I couldn't risk Gena snooping around because
I'd been acting strangely. Not now, when I had a stolen bottle
of luminol in my backpack, a report hacked from a police
department computer, and an evidence bag hidden in a stack
of fingerprint cards I wasn't authorized to process. I had a lot
more than just the internship to lose.

But I couldn't figure this out on my own.

The next morning, I reserved the computer lab at school
for an after-school group project. In reality, it felt more like
an experiment. What would happen when I put four dispa-
rate elements together in a room, expecting us to yield some
solution?

Vince was first to arrive. He crushed a piece of paper and
tossed it at me. It was the note I'd left in his locker:

> I know who broke into your car, meet me in
> the computer lab after school if you want
> to know too.

He dropped into a chair. "You'd better not be playing
games, trailer trash."

I stood by the door, wondering who else would show up,
dreading the possibility that Vince might be the only one.

"Sorry I'm late." Jeremy burst into the room, red-faced
and panting. "I got your note." He smiled, trying to catch
his breath. "Yesterday was awesome, by the way. Haven't

been able to stop thinking about it. I still can't believe we—"
Jeremy paled when he noticed Vince across the room.

Vince laced his fingers behind his head, watching with a
salacious smile. "I always figured there was something going
on between the two of you."

The blood raced back into Jeremy's cheeks. "Why's he here?"

"I invited him."

Vince chuckled to himself. "If two geeks get busy in the
woods and no one is there to see it, do they still make a
sound?"

Jeremy took me by the elbow and pulled me into a corner,
his back to Vince. His irritation was sharp and metallic and it
set my teeth on edge. "You didn't tell him anything, did you?"

"Not yet," I said, jerking out of his grip.

"What's that supposed to mean!"

"Uh-oh," Vince sang. "Shit's about to get real. I got my
money on the hooker's kid."

"My mother's not a hooker!"

"Whatever," he said, standing up. "But someone better
fucking tell me who broke into my car, or I'm out of here."

Jeremy's gaze shot expectantly to me. I opened my mouth
to explain why I'd brought them here. That I couldn't yet
prove who'd broken into Jeremy's house or into Vince's car,
but I had a theory.

"Sorry," a quiet voice interrupted from the hall. "I must
have the wrong room." All three of us turned to see Eric Miller

standing in the doorway, holding the pink slip I'd left in his locker. The room fell awkwardly silent.

"You're in the right room," I said.

"Oh." He looked confused. "I was supposed to be meeting Mr. Hurley. Are you meeting with him too?"

I'd taken the blank pink slip from an unlocked supply cupboard between classes and signed Hurley's name. "The note in your locker was from me." I cast a warning glance at Vince to keep his big mouth shut, but Eric's presence was sobering. Jeremy and Vince pressed their lips tightly closed. I gestured to the empty seat beside Vince. Eric cast a wary glance at him before easing into it. I pulled two chairs out for Jeremy and me, nudging Jeremy into one.

Eric looked around the room. "So Mr. Hurley isn't here? I don't understand."

"Join the club," Vince muttered.

The words stopped me cold. We were all members of a club, our places handed down to us through our parents, without any of us realizing what kind of baggage we carried. And if my theory was right, the messages we'd received had been a warning meant for us. Someone who knew our parents had dug up their secrets.

I passed the picture of our fathers around the circle. Watched the shift in their body language as they recognized their own dads in it. "I'm sorry, man," Vince whispered to Eric as he handed the photo to him.

"This is the Belle Green Poker Club," I explained. "The photo was taken six years ago. The man whose face is torn away is Reggie Wiles—TJ's dad. Our dads were friends with each other, before . . ." I paused when Eric's eyes lifted to mine. I didn't know how to finish that sentence without making it sound like an admission of guilt. Before what? Before my dad and TJ's dad had conspired to rip off their friends? Before one club member was murdered and another one ran?

"What does this have to do with us?" Jeremy asked, glancing at Eric. Karl Miller loomed like a presence in the room.

I walked to the whiteboard and wrote the formulas for all three of Newton's Laws of Motion. Then translated them in layman's terms.

"The first law was left inside Jeremy's bedroom. The second was left inside Vince's car. The messages were meant to look like the ones TJ sent me last year. They're written in the same blue ink with similar lettering. But TJ is in prison. We know these messages couldn't possibly be from him."

Vince was halfway out of his seat. "You're not telling us anything we don't already know. This is a total waste of my time."

I ignored Vince. The backstory was for Eric's benefit. I pointed to the third law. "This one was left in my trailer three weeks ago. Someone broke in and left it in my room."

Vince eased back in his chair. "You never said. What does it mean?"

I set the dry erase marker on the rack. "Out of context, it means nothing. I figured it was a prank. Someone's idea of a joke. Everyone who followed TJ's case knew his MO.

"But there's more," I continued. Eric sat silent, staring at what may have been the last photo taken of his father. His finger traced the torn edges. There was no tactful way to say what needed to be said.

"For five years, Karl Miller was buried under a false front by the ninth green of the Belle Green Golf Course. Only, last week someone dug him up. Which means someone knew Karl Miller's body was there. And they wanted him found."

Eric curled in on himself. Vince's chair groaned as he shifted uncomfortably. "Hey, Boswell. Aren't you being a little fucking insensitive?"

"As much as I don't want to, I think we have to talk about this. It involves Eric too."

"How? I don't understand," Jeremy asked.

"There was another message. Last night. In my trailer."

"But you changed your locks."

"I did."

Jeremy paled. As long as his house was still vulnerable, mine was too.

"Someone wrote a message on my bathroom mirror."

Vince fidgeted and Eric scowled, picking at the edges of his backpack. I was losing them. In another minute, Vince would walk out. Maybe Eric too.

I talked fast, hating the urgency in my voice that sounded more like a plea. "It said, *The club will illuminate its secrets*. It can only mean one thing. The Belle Green Poker Club."

"I still don't understand what this has to do with Eric's dad," Jeremy argued.

I grabbed a marker and lifted it to the whiteboard.

"This is getting stupider by the minute." Vince erupted from his chair. "I'm out of here."

I furiously wrote all fourteen numbers on the board.

I turned in time to see Vince reach the open door. "There's more!" I said, already regretting what I was about to do. But they'd given me no choice. They weren't listening. "There was also a message—a number—carved in Eric's dad's bone. After the bones were dug up." Vince froze. Jeremy's mouth hung open. "This number."

90179257433275.

Vince looked disgusted. "You're nuts, Boswell. I'm going home."

I took up the marker. Added hyphens. Then slammed a copy of last year's chemistry textbook on the desk, startling them all. I stood aside, giving them all a better view. It was open to the periodic table, and I watched their faces fall as they gathered around it, their eyes moving back and forth between the numbers and the book.

90-17-92-5-74-33-2-75.

Th-CL-U-B-W-As-He-Re.

A thick and heavy silence filled the room. Vince slid into a chair by the door. Jeremy looked like he might be sick. Eric stared at the floor.

"Eric's father was a member of the poker club with our parents," I explained. "Someone knows what happened to him. *The club will illuminate its secrets.* I think one of our fathers knows the secret. I think one of our fathers knows who killed him."

Vince darted a nervous look around the group. "What are you trying to say?"

"The medical examiner and the detectives investigating Karl Miller's death think the body was buried in late June five years ago, while the false front of the golf course was under construction. It would have been an easy time to conceal the body. The dates coincide with the same week an anonymous tipster made a call incriminating Reggie Wiles and my father. The call that led to their arrest warrants was traced to the Belle Green Country Club."

Vince leaned forward in his chair. "Let me get this straight. You're telling us that your dad murdered Eric's dad because Mr. Miller ratted him out to the cops?"

"I'm not saying my dad killed anyone."

"But that's what you're implying," Jeremy said.

"I'm not implying anything." My cheeks burned, and I wondered if he could read the lie on my face. "We don't know who killed Eric's dad, but someone thinks the poker club is involved. And they want us to figure it out."

"No," Vince said, pointing a finger at me. "They want YOU to figure out. I don't want anything to do with this shit."

"Like it or not, we're all involved." And they were all I had left.

Jeremy and Vince started talking at once, their faces reddening with their raised voices. Both of them arguing about all the reasons this had nothing to do with them. All the reasons none of this made any sense. Panic fluttered in my chest.

"It makes perfect sense," Eric said. Vince and Jeremy fell silent, mouths still half-open. They turned to face the one who'd been so quiet we'd all forgotten he was there. "Think about it. Your dad kills my dad, and leaves town. Reggie Wiles goes to prison and your dad gets away." Eric's eyes creased at the corners, his brow furrowed, in anger or pain. "Meanwhile, no one said a word. Our families are all complicit. They all let Reggie Wiles take the fall. They all let David Boswell get away. Not a single one of them came forward to find my dad. Instead, they all bought into some bullshit story that he'd run off with some woman. Why? Probably because all their hands were dirty. Now they're all calling each other in a panic because Reggie Wiles is out on parole. And if I was him, I'd probably be pissed off at every single one of you."

"Wait a minute." Jeremy stiffened. "What do you mean, Reggie Wiles is out on parole?"

Eric looked surprised. "My mom got a call from Vince's mom. Vince's mom said she heard it from Jeremy's mom. I thought everyone already knew."

Jeremy looked to Vince. Vince shook his head. "How long has he been out?"

"About six weeks," I said.

Jeremy turned to me with a stunned expression. "You knew? Why didn't you say anything?"

"Because up until a couple of weeks ago, you weren't even speaking to me!'"

"Shut up!" Vince shouted at us. He turned to Eric. "So you think Boswell's dad killed your dad, and now Reggie Wiles is out of prison and wants to expose him. Just to get revenge?" Vince nodded to himself. "You're right, Miller. It makes perfect sense. And clearly, this has nothing to do with me and Fowler, so we're leaving. No offense, man. Real sorry about your dad and all. Come on, Fowler. Let's go."

Jeremy didn't move. His stare bored into me. "You should talk to the police."

"I did. I called Gena and Alex and asked them to check if Reggie ever left the halfway house. According to his parole officer, he didn't."

"Did you tell them about the break-ins? About the messages?" There was a cold, clear challenge in his eyes.

I didn't answer.

"You didn't, did you?" He shook his head, his disgust clear

on his face. "You're making the same damn mistake you made before. Reggie Wiles is out there, breaking into our houses and digging up bodies, and you're not going to say a word to anyone? You're putting us all at risk!"

"Even if I did tell them, they'd never believe me, Jeremy! Reggie Wiles is in a halfway house under twenty-four-hour supervision. If he did get out long enough to do these things, somebody was either asleep on the job, or they helped him do it. I'm going to need concrete proof. Before I go to the police, I have to figure out who's helping him and how he's getting away with this."

"Are you sure that's it?" he sneered. "Or are you just scared that if you tell Nicholson what's really going on, you'll give the police a more compelling reason to find your dad and arrest him for murder?"

A hot flush raced over my face.

"That's it, isn't it? That's why you wanted my help yesterday? So you could find him before they do?"

"No! If I were covering for my father, I never would have brought you here. Or told you what I know about the club."

He leaned in close and whispered harshly, "I can't believe you let me break into Nicholson's computer to do your dirty work, and you didn't tell me why you were really looking for him!"

"That's not why I asked for your help, I swear! I'm not

trying to hide anything. I just need time to figure this out."

"Figure it out yourself. I'm going home." Jeremy followed Vince out the door. Eric slipped out after them with his head down.

I slumped into Hurley's chair. Picked up the eraser from his desk and spun to face the numbers on the board. I had hoped we would work together. Hoped one of us would know more of our parents' story. If we could put the pieces together, we'd have some solid evidence to take to the police. And all I'd managed to do was make Jeremy distrust me, and spill the details of a case that were supposed to be confidential. That, and tell a grieving kid that his father's body was mutilated for the purpose of communicating a message intended for me. I wouldn't blame him if Eric hated me for the rest of his life, even if none of this was my fault.

The door clicked shut. I whirled around. Reece leaned against it, his head tipped back. Like he'd been out there, listening the whole time. My heart skipped at the sight of him and I hated myself for it.

"We need to talk," he said.

I closed the textbook. "How did you know I was here?"

"I was planning to find you at your locker after school, but I was running late. I saw you go upstairs, and I figured I'd wait for you—"

"So you followed me?"

He pushed himself off the door toward me, his face

pinched with anger. "What is it with you that you expect the worst of me? I didn't follow you! I followed Fowler." Reece clenched his jaw, like he'd said more than he'd intended.

"Why were you following Jeremy?"

"Because clearly you two have been hanging out a lot together and I wanted to make sure . . ." His voice trailed off, and he swallowed. "I wanted to make sure it wasn't anything more."

I resisted the urge to touch him, to taste the jealousy I saw on his face. "I thought we were over all the sneaking around."

"If you would talk to me, maybe I wouldn't have to." He looked away, as if ashamed, his gaze coming to rest on the whiteboard. "Were you ever going to tell me?"

I turned my back to him and tried wiping away the numbers, but the shadows of the message stuck stubbornly to the board. I sprayed it with the bottle of cleaning solution and told myself it was the isopropyl that made my eyes burn. "I could ask you the same."

"This isn't the same thing and you know it. This is about your safety, Leigh. This is about you not getting hurt."

"Bullshit!" I threw the eraser at him, making him duck as it sailed past his head. "If you didn't want me to get hurt, you would have told me about her! You would have told me you had feelings for someone else! I don't owe you anything!"

"This isn't about me, Nearly! It's about you! I've been

standing outside that door the entire time. I heard every-thing! Reggie Wiles is out on parole. Someone's broken into your trailer. Twice! You're being threatened. And now some-one's dug a body out of the ground and carved it up like a goddamn Christmas goose, gift-wrapped with a message for you, and you think there's anything more important to me than that?" His eyes flashed icy blue, his mouth close to mine. So close, I thought my heart would break.

"Are you finished?" I asked through a thin breath.

He shut his eyes and reached for my hand, but I pulled away. He was right when he'd warned me that there are some things you just can't un-see. And now, every time I looked at him, I'd see her face behind his shoulder. Every time he reached for my hand, I'd know she'd held it too. She'd held it, without ever having to feel what he made me feel. "You can't fix this," I said.

"Maybe not," he whispered. "But I can keep you safe." I could smell the sweet mint gum on his breath. The one he used to cover the smell of cigarettes and beer that followed him home when he'd been narcing. Because he knew how much I hated them. I looked up, secretly checking the smooth planes of his neck as I did, looking for a trail of hickeys, then berating myself for the relief I felt when there weren't any there. I hated myself for still wanting him. For wanting to forgive him. Maybe he could keep me safe, but safe wasn't the same as unharmed.

"How?" I said, forcing my gaze from his lips. "You can't possibly know Reggie's next move."

Reece thought for a minute, staring at the hazy numbers on the whiteboard behind me. "No, but there may be one person who does."

20

MY MOTHER WAS STILL SLEEPING when Alex's Charger pulled up in front of my trailer that Saturday morning. I'd spent the last three days trying to work up the nerve to tell her where I was going. Instead, I made up a lie about spending the weekend at Gena's place.

I grabbed my backpack, containing a change of clothes and a toothbrush, opened the back door of Alex's car and slung it in. Reece glowered with his arm stretched across the seat back. I wedged my backpack in the space between us and rolled my eyes at Gena. I had made it very clear I didn't want him to come, even if it had been his idea. She wore a sly smile in the visor mirror.

"Don't be like that," she scolded me. "He's worried about you, Leigh. He insisted on coming."

I leaned against the car door, as far from Reece as possible. He smelled cool and confident, like shower gel and shaving cream, and his T-shirt looked soft, as if it was fresh from the dryer. I rested my head against the window, trying not to breathe him in, resisting the urge to curl under his arm until all of this was over.

Gena craned her neck to look at me as Alex pulled out of Sunny View. She pushed her sunglasses down and stared at me over the rims. "Are you sure you want to do this?" Her smooth forehead was pinched with worry, making her look much closer to her real age than she usually did.

"You're the one who said I should talk to someone," I said.

Alex's gray eyes watched me in the rearview mirror. Reece had agreed not to tell them about the notes and the break-ins. If they knew the truth—any of it—they never would have agreed to this. As far as they were concerned, I needed this trip to put TJ's crimes behind me. To look him in the eyes, find closure, and move on. Gena had been concerned enough about my mental state to agree. And Alex had pulled strings to get us a pass into Powell Ridge.

"I need to do this," I said, more to myself than the rest of them. As much as I hated to admit it, Reece was right. No one would know Reggie Wiles like his own son. And if anyone was helping Reggie, TJ might be the only person to know who, and how they were pulling it off.

Reece frowned out the window. "I don't like this," he grumbled. "The guy is a sociopath. He tried to kill you. This is a bad idea."

"She'll be monitored the whole time. He won't be able to hurt her," Gena reassured him.

"If he does, I'm holding both of you responsible."

"Hey, don't take it out on Gena. This was your idea," I said.

His arm slid off the seat back and folded over his chest. "Don't remind me."

The rest of the six-hour drive to Powell Ridge was mostly silent. Reece's phone buzzed repeatedly, and he cursed under his breath every time he took it from his pocket, before sending the caller to voicemail. I wanted to pitch it out the window. I pretended not to care.

Alex pulled off the highway and into the parking lot of a small country diner with an adjacent motel, just south of Blacksburg, where we planned to stop for the night. Gena got out of the car and stretched. Alex leaned on the roof, watching the slope of her arched back with a content smile.

"You go get us a table," she said, batting her lashes. "I'm going next door to get us a couple of rooms."

A couple of rooms? Meaning two? Reece raised an eyebrow.

"Don't get any ideas, Romeo." Gena shook a finger at him. "One room for the girls, and one for the guys. And if you're lucky, they'll have two double beds, so you don't have to share."

Alex's and Reece's faces fell.

"I'd rather sleep on the floor," Reece muttered.

"That can be arranged." Alex locked the car and walked into the diner. Gena headed across the parking lot to the motel.

I started toward the diner, but Reece pulled me up short. "I was hoping we'd have some time alone. To talk. I know what it looked like . . . what you think you saw . . . but that's not how it was." I looked through the windows into the diner. Then at the motel. Gena would be back any minute with the room keys and Alex was waiting inside.

"Later? Please?" he asked.

I nodded, too tired from the long trip and from carrying around all of our unspoken words to argue. "Later," I agreed.

• • •

That night, Gena and I sat propped up on pillows on an oversized bed. She pointed the remote at the TV, clicking absently through the channels with the sound muted.

"Sorry," she said. "They only had one room left with doubles. I thought about making the boys take the king." She smiled wickedly. "But then I figured someone would probably be dead by morning. And that wouldn't be good. Don't worry, I don't snore. But Alex says sometimes I hog the covers." She paused at a reality TV show I'd never seen before, skipped past it, and settled on a cooking program. Then she rolled her pants cuffs to her calves, spread a hand towel over the comforter, opened a bottle of deep red nail polish, and began carefully stroking on a first coat.

"Okay, girlie," she said when she was finished. She put the wand back in the bottle and capped it. "Alex told me what happened at the station with that chick in lockup." Gena wiped a spot of paint from her cuticle. "You want to talk about it?"

"Not really."

"Great, let's talk anyway." She grabbed the remote and turned off the TV.

I picked at the comforter. "When you and Alex were working undercover, did you ever see him do something that made you doubt him?"

Gena bit her lip. "I thought we were talking about you."

"We are."

"What did you see?"

I tucked my knees to my chest. "Reece and that girl. They were holding hands."

I was taken aback by the abrupt shift in Gena's tone. "No. That's an oversimplification. You saw more than that."

I pulled at a thread. "It was only a minute. We didn't even talk."

"Think, Leigh. You're smart. You're aware. Close your eyes. Put yourself back in that place. Focus on the details."

"The details suck." I didn't want to dig them up. If I let them stay buried, I could forget they ever happened. I shut my eyes, mostly because I didn't want Gena to see me cry.

"Start simple. What were they wearing?" she asked, as if she were sitting on the other side of an interrogation room rather than the other side of a hotel bed.

I described Reece's worn gray T-shirt. I told Gena about the girl. How her hair clung to his cheek when she rested her chin on his shoulder. The slinky way she twined her fingers with his and wrapped herself around him, entirely too comfortable and familiar. The way he took her hand, a little too hard, and led her away.

"So what you're saying is that you saw her put her arms around him?"

I cracked an eye open. "Yes, but—"

Gena held up a finger and I closed it again. "Answer the question."

"Yes."

"And you saw her hold his hand?"

"Yes."

"And you saw him forcefully take hers for the purpose of dragging her pathetic clingy ass out the door?"

"Yes."

"So what you didn't see is Reece touch her in any affectionate manner?"

"No."

"And you didn't see him looking like he enjoyed having her all pressed up against his shit?"

I wanted to say yes so badly. If only to validate my feelings, but I couldn't. "No, but—"

"No buts," Gena said, taking me gently by chin. Her touch

was cool and certain, sprinkled with compassion. It soothed the lump in my throat. I opened my eyes.

"Sometimes, the things we don't see are more important than the ones we do. You're looking for evil everywhere, and I get it. I do. Your father betrayed you. Your mother wasn't honest with you. Your best friends turned their back on you. Your neighbor tried to kill you. None of us, not even me and Alex and Reece, turned out to be the people you thought we were. After everything you've been through, you don't want to be blindsided again, so you're looking for reasons not to trust people. But you're seeing things that aren't there. All those times you called me and thought you saw Reggie? That's your fear taking hold of you, making you see terrible things. Not everyone is a monster. Not everyone is out to hurt you. And all these doubts you're having about Reece? That's just your fear talking too." The room was quiet as she let that sink in. "He loves you. Try to remember that when you talk to him." She looked at her watch. I started at a soft rap on the door.

Gena leaped to her feet and pulled her cuffs back to her ankles. "We have a long day tomorrow. Don't let him stay too late," she said with a cautionary expression that said more than she did. She opened the door and walked barefoot past Reece to the adjacent room.

Reece stood in the doorway, looking awkward and uncertain. "Can I come in?"

I nodded, pulling a pillow into my lap. He sat down gently on the edge of the bed with his shoulders hunched, his long, dark lashes lowered toward the floor. The winding thistle tattoo tensed over the lean muscles of his forearm, his hands gripping the mattress as if he were afraid I might change my mind and ask him to go.

I squeezed the pillow. Watched his lips part, and then close again while he struggled to find words. It had been so long since we'd talked like this, alone in a bedroom. His dark hair had begun to grow in, full and soft at the nape of his neck and around the curl of his ear. I took a long, thin breath, and breathed in the citrus and sandalwood smell of his cologne.

"I know what you think you saw," he said again. The words were gravelly and deep. He closed his eyes and the muscles moved in his throat, like he was swallowing something painful.

"And I know it must have looked really bad. But you have to know, I would trade the eight hours I spent in that holding cell with her for one minute . . ." He took a deep, trembling breath. "One minute just to hold you."

His eyes misted over. I wanted so badly to believe him.

I swung my feet over the edge of the bed and stood in front of him. Before I could think, I laid my hand on the back of his neck. His sadness was a rush of salt water around something small and granular and sweet. His arm circled my waist. He held me to him, pressing his head to my chest.

"You were right about one thing." He lifted his head, and my heart tightened. "I should have told you from the beginning—before the school year started—that you might . . . see things that might make you doubt the way I feel about you. But you were wrong about everything else. I don't have feelings for her. And I never *did* anything . . . would never *do* anything . . . with her or anyone else, that would compromise what I have with you."

I felt a tear slide down my cheek.

"Tell me how to fix this," he pleaded, brushing it away with his thumb. "I need you. I need *us*. I can't do this anymore without you."

He pulled me onto his lap and pressed his forehead to mine, his nose lightly grazing my chin, then my lips. His eyes closed as his mouth brushed mine, warm and sweet and wanting. He held me closer, his mouth opening, his lips tugging at mine. I kissed him slowly.

"Say the word," he whispered into my neck, "and I'll call Nicholson right now and tell him I'm out."

I pulled away and stood up. "No! You can't do that. He'll put you back in jail for obstruction of justice." Going back to jail would kill him. It would kill us both. "We'll find another way to fix this."

"How? I'd rather do my time and hope you'll take me back when it's over than keep doing things that hurt you."

"What if—what if you tell me everything next time?" I said. "Even the things you think I don't want to hear. And when you're working, you try to stay out of places where I might be. I'm not trying to think the worst of you. But you and Mom and Gena . . . you all need to stop trying to protect my feelings. You need to be honest with me."

"Can you trust me?" he asked.

"I promise to try." Reece's arm circled my waist and he drew me close again.

"I love you," he murmured. I pressed my lips to his hair and whispered that I loved him too. He pulled me back onto his lap, his breath warm against my neck.

I shivered when his hands slipped under the hem of my shirt, sliding over my shoulder blades, holding me closer. He brushed his lips softly against mine. Then his tongue slowly traced the edges until I thought I would break in two.

I knotted my fingers in his shirt and I drew it up over his head. His brother's pendant fell back in place between us, heavy against his chest. His back was warm and smooth, his arms strong around me. I dipped to kiss the smooth pink scar on his shoulder, dotting a slow trail over the silver chain at his collarbone, then over his neck. Reece moaned softly, his hands sliding up my sides and easing off my shirt.

Clutching it in his hand, he sank back onto the mattress. Then he rolled me beneath him, so the warm length of his body molded against my own. Our eyes held. He stroked the hair from my face, his finger caressing my cheek, then my neck, pausing only to trace the bare skin over my heart.

Every touch was deliberate, careful and sweet. Filled with all the truth inside him.

I closed my eyes and pulled his mouth to mine. His fingers closed around my hair. His kiss was hot salt water, sadness, and need. I kissed him until the lines blurred between us. I touched him until I believed.

• • •

We lay together on top of the comforter in the dark, my head against his chest and my legs tangled up with his, Reece's thumb stroking the length of my arm. My eyelids were heavy and the red numbers on the clock on the nightstand glowed too brightly.

"Gena will be back soon," I said quietly.

His lips were soft against my forehead. "Let me stay," he whispered. "Just for a while longer. I'll let you sleep. I just . . ." My head gently rose and fell with the swell of emotion in his chest.

"Okay," I whispered, my eyes drifting shut and my breath slowing to the beat of his heart. "Just until Gena comes back."

21

In the morning, Reece was gone, and despite her saying she didn't, Gena snored quietly on her side of the bed. I got dressed before the alarm went off and waited for her outside.

The short drive to Powell Ridge was somber. Quiet. I held Reece's hand in the backseat, and I tasted the shift in his emotions, suffocating and sour when we rounded the final turn and the prison came into view.

Alex spoke to some guards at the gate, and then we were inside.

At the entrance, a correctional officer shook Alex's hand and clapped him on the back.

"Finally grew enough facial hair to graduate kiddie patrol, huh?" He leaned into Gena and gave her a peck on the cheek. "Congrats, doll. I heard about the upcoming nuptials. When's the big day?"

"Not soon enough," Alex answered for her. "Thanks for helping us out, Simms. We appreciate all you did to get us in here."

Simms shrugged it off. "I didn't have to do much. Only one of you is going in with me, right? Last name Boswell?"

Alex pointed to me. "This is Nearly Boswell. Like I told you on the phone, she'd like to speak with Thomas Wiles. Thanks so much for pulling the strings for us."

Simms looked confused. "No strings to pull, really. I'm not saying it isn't great seeing you both, but she's already on the list of approved visitors."

"What do you mean, she's already on a list?" Reece stepped forward. "What the hell does that mean, Petrenko?"

Alex and Gena exchanged wary glances.

Simms looked down his nose at Reece, directing his reply to Alex. "Certain inmates can request a short list of approved family and friends for regular visitation. The names are screened, and if the warden feels it's appropriate, he'll grant the request. After you called, I checked to see if Miss Boswell needed special approval, but she was already on Mr. Wiles's list."

A chill rippled over me. Reece stiffened.

TJ knew I would come. He wanted me here.

"He'll be awful glad to see you," Simms went on, oblivious to the sudden heaviness in the air. "He only put two people on that list, but his father's an ex-con and doesn't qualify. You're the first visitor he's had since he came here. The kid sent out a few letters when he got here, but I don't recall him getting a single one back."

"I don't like this," Reece muttered. "Come on, Gena. You know something smells all wrong about this. Let's just go. He doesn't have to know she was here."

But he already knew. He had to know I would come eventually, or he wouldn't have put my name on that list.

I was the only other person TJ Wiles had any desire to see. Not his ex-girlfriend, Emily Reinnert. Not Vince, his best friend since kindergarten. Not the uncle who'd practically raised him. TJ wanted to see me.

"Can I see him now?" I asked. The officer nodded.

I squeezed Reece's hand, and he pulled me into an embrace. He whispered into my hair, "When it's over, I'll be here."

• • •

Simms waited while I emptied my pockets before patting me down. Then he led me to the visitation area while he reviewed the rules. TJ would be shackled, he said. There would be no bars or Plexiglass between us. Simms caught the falter in my step and looked at me out of the corner of his eye. "Don't worry," he said. "I'll be watching. Just don't try to touch him during the visit, and don't try to hand him anything across the table. You'll be permitted contact twice, once at the beginning of your visit and once at the end, to hug or shake hands. If you want to, that is."

"No, no I don't want to." My hands went cold and clammy at the memory of TJ dragging me through the cemetery. Covering my mouth, suffocating me. Pressing a gun to my head.

We were buzzed into a room with two rows of metal tables. One row for visitors and one for inmates, Simms explained. The rows were separated by nothing more than a four-inch ledge. Nothing to keep TJ from crossing the divide, except Simms.

He led me to an empty chair. Families chattered quietly over the small partition, their palms pressed flat to the tables to avoid the temptation to reach across and touch each other. Minutes passed. I sat on my hands.

A few heads turned when the door buzzed open. An inmate in a green jumpsuit walked in slowly, shackles rattling at his ankles. If it weren't for the subtle limp, for the calculating gleam in those piercing eyes when they found me, I wouldn't have recognized him.

Simms directed TJ to the bench across from mine. He leaned close to TJ's ear and said, "You've done real good so far. You've only got a few weeks left in Level 5. Keep up with the good behavior, and you'll earn a spot in a privilege pod." To both of us he cautioned, "Now remember, you may not make contact over the partition. If you need to pass anything to him, set it on the ledge first. When you're ready to go, raise your hand and I'll come help you say your good-byes."

Then Simms melted into the background, and all I could see were the hard planes of TJ's face.

"You finally made it. What took you so long?" He folded his hands on the table. They looked strong, thick with callouses. If there had ever been anything soft about TJ, there wasn't anymore.

"How did you know I would come?"

"Because you have questions." He smiled. "And I have answers."

"What kind of answers?"

"The kind that make you do stupid things. The kind that make you drive six hours through the middle of nowhere to sit across a table from the person who wants to kill you."

"Then why don't you?"

TJ's knuckles were white where his fingers laced together. My breath held when his eyes darted to Simms.

"I could," he whispered. "I could reach over this partition and crush your fucking throat. But then it would all be over too quickly. What would I do without you, Boswell? What would I do with the eighteen hours a day I spend staring at the walls in this place, dreaming of the day I get out, planning ways to break you?"

Goose bumps crept across my skin.

"Oh," he said, narrowing his eyes at me. "Don't bother feeling sorry for me. This place is a step up from where you come from." I dug my nails into my palms, hating the way he said *you*, like Sunny View hadn't been his home for the last five years. "I get three square meals a day, health care, and plenty of exercise. I'm even getting my GED—I get cyber-tutoring three times a week. Of course, they won't let me meet with a tutor in person, given my history." His shoulders shook and his eyes shone with silent laughter. He thought this was funny. He'd killed the students I tutored. Marcia, Posie, Teddy, and Kylie.

"So, let me guess," he said, his gaze drifting to the ceiling. "My daddy is out of prison, and bad, bad things are happening."

"How do you know?"

TJ laughed. "Think about it, Boswell. Bad people don't stop doing bad things. You can stick them in a cage and make them behave when you're watching. You can make them earn their freedoms—their TV privileges, their visitations, their parole—but you can't change them. Bad can't be fixed. And a little freedom—that little bit of room to maneuver without people crawling all over your back, watching your every move—is all it takes to stretch that muscle." TJ tapped his temple.

So I was right. Reggie Wiles wasn't as tightly watched as Gena thought. And he was using it to his advantage. Which means he probably dug up Karl Miller's body. But how?

TJ leaned in, close enough to get Simms's attention. "But you didn't come here to ask me that, did you? Why don't you tell me why you're really here?"

"Tell me what you know about the Belle Green Poker Club."

TJ eased back. "Only as much as you do. Friday nights in Fowler's living room. Eating cookies and watching cartoons while our dads gambled away our college funds. They were into something dirty. One of them got spooked and called the police. And your dad ditched his best friend and left him to take the fall." TJ studied my face—my eyes, my nose, my mouth. But it felt like he was looking straight through me. "You look so much like him. You both have that same damn smile. I see it all the time. Sometimes, when it gets really bad, I daydream about knocking your teeth in—"

"Who killed Karl Miller?" I asked quickly, hoping he'd answer without thinking.

TJ's face split with a wide grin. He shook his head in disbelief. "You think because you're sitting over there and I'm over here—that because I'm the one in shackles—I'm that stupid?

Come on, Boswell. I'm in prison, I'm not incompetent."

"But you knew Karl Miller was dead. You knew he was murdered."

"Everybody does. It was on the news."

"But you know who killed him. Don't you?"

TJ licked his upper lip, thinking. I sat forward in my seat, waiting for his answer.

"You didn't have to drive all this way. The answer to that is pretty close to home. Look in the mirror, Boswell."

The implication sank like a stone in my heart. "You think my dad killed Karl Miller?"

TJ smiled. "The simplest explanation is often correct."

"You're a bastard!" I whispered harshly.

TJ set his jaw. He inched forward like he was ready to come out of his seat.

Simms's shadow appeared beside me. "Maybe it's time we wrap this up. We don't want anyone to get carried away and do something they'll regret."

"But—!"

"Thomas can earn weekly access to video-visitation. If you all want to try this again, maybe that would be best. Come on, Mr. Wiles. Let's get you back to your cell."

TJ didn't stand up. His eyes locked on mine. "I'd like a hug good-bye."

"That's Miss Boswell's prerogative, and based on what I just saw, I don't think—"

I stood and slowly stepped out from the bench.

TJ leered, like a heeled dog, careful not to pull on his leash. He waited until I nodded my consent to Simms. When TJ stood, I had to crane my neck to see the hatred in his eyes. He could kill me. Right here and now. I took a trembling breath, inching up on my toes as his arms came around me. There was too much fabric. No place to reach his skin through his jumpsuit. Reaching up to his neck seemed too risky a thing to do. But I had to know if there was any truth to what he'd said.

"Did my father really kill Karl Miller?" I whispered into his shoulder, softly enough to draw his head closer to mine.

His lips grazed my ear and I shuddered at the iron-hot rush of his hatred for me. It left a dry burn that felt like it would never be quenched, and I looked to be sure Simms was close.

"The secrets are in the club," TJ whispered back, "but you don't have all the players. One is still missing—the one with all the answers. Find the missing player, and the truth will come to light." As crazy and elusive as his answer sounded, TJ tasted like he believed every word.

His palms pressed tightly against my spine, crushing the air from my lungs. I pushed him away, and Simms took his elbow with a cautionary warning.

"Thank you for coming to see me, Nearly Boswell. I'd almost forgotten how it feels to hold you. And now . . . now I remember." Simms marched him toward the door while I stood there, my legs watery and my spine numb. "You're all I think about, Nearly," TJ called over his shoulder. "My reason for waking up in the morning. We will see each other again. I promise." His voice was sweet, juxtaposed against a sinister smile. He would have killed me if no one had been watching, I was certain of it.

Simms handed him off to another guard and escorted me back to where Gena and Alex and Reece were waiting. When he saw me, Reece leaped to his feet. He pulled me into his arms, flooding both of us with relief. But the taste of fear was slow to recede, and we were both reluctant to let go.

Gena took my hand. Her touch was like warm milk and honey, and it soothed the tightness in my throat. "How did it go? Did you find the closure you needed?"

I let go of her hand, even though she couldn't taste the lies. "It went fine. I think I found what I came for. Thank you for bringing me."

22

ON MONDAY MORNING, I had no choice. I put pink slips in Eric's, Jeremy's, and Vince's lockers after third period, checking the box marked "Urgent," and requesting their presence in the computer lab after school.

Reece hadn't let me out of his sight after Gena and Alex dropped us off at my trailer on Sunday afternoon, only leaving when my mother finally pushed him out the door at ten so I could get enough sleep for school. In the morning, he'd shown up early to give me a ride, then he'd texted me during lunch to make sure I was okay. When I'd texted him back to tell him I was staying to meet with Eric, Jeremy, and Vince, he'd insisted on being there too.

He perched on a lab table at the back of the room. We waited, the clock quietly ticking off the minutes while I prepared myself for the very real possibility that nobody would bother to come, even if I had told them I had new information about each of their parents. I wasn't surprised to see Eric arrive first. If it had been my father, I'd be hungry too. He slid into the same chair, looking curious and alert, like some of the fog of bereavement had lifted.

"I'm missing practice for this, trailer trash. This had better be—" Vince stopped.

Reece stood. My breath held. For a long moment, they stared at each other. Vince peeled off his sunglasses and took a seat. "This had better be good, Boswell."

Reece sat behind him.

Jeremy was next to arrive. "What's he doing here?" He jerked his chin at Reece, as if reading the thoughts of the rest of the room.

"Yeah," Vince piped up. "This meeting is supposed to be private."

Eric, Vince, and Jeremy angled their chairs toward one

another, as if they'd come here together. They whispered to each other, careful not to let Reece overhear. I watched, surprised, as something began to take shape. Not an organized or cohesive one, but something that loosely resembled a club. Maybe having Reece here was the right move.

"I went to Powell Ridge this weekend." The whispering quieted. "I talked to TJ. He didn't exactly come out and say it, but he also didn't deny that his dad could be behind the messages, which means Reggie is probably the one who dug up Mr. Miller's body. One thing's certain: TJ definitely knows more than he's saying."

Eric shifted in his seat. "What *did* he say?"

I knew what Eric really wanted to know. Because it's the same question I would have wanted the answer to. "He didn't tell me who killed your dad." It was the truth. TJ hadn't come out and said my father killed Karl Miller. "But he gave me a clue."

"A clue?" Vince blurted. "What does he think this is? Some kind of game?"

"It's always been a game to him." That's why he'd always dealt in riddles. Why he'd always framed his clues to have more than one right answer. Because he liked to watch me struggle to figure them out. He liked to see me fall off course. It made him feel in control. This was no different.

"What was the clue?" Jeremy asked.

I closed my eyes, recalling TJ's whispered advice. "He said,

'The secrets are in the club, but you don't have all the players. One is still missing—the one with all the answers. Find the missing player, and the truth will come to light.'"

"Great, so you go find your daddy, and then all this twisted shit will be solved." Vince said it as if the answer were obvious.

I shook my head. TJ's meaning wouldn't be so simple. It would be buried deeper. Closer to the bone.

"Emily," Reece said. "Emily is the missing player." We all turned to him. "She's the one with all the answers."

Vince glared at Reece over his shoulder. "Who invited you to have an opinion?"

Jeremy leaned forward in his chair. I could see the wheels turning in his head. "Of course. Emily and TJ were conspirators. She knew him better than anyone. She would know Reggie too. And her father was in the club, which makes her one of us. She's the one. The one of us who's missing."

"No way," Vince said with a hard shake of his head. "She doesn't have anything to do with Wiles or his fucked-up family anymore."

"You know where she lives?" Reece goaded him. It was a rhetorical question. We all knew where she lived.

"Better than you."

"Then you know her McMansion backs up to the ninth green. You could probably throw a rock from her window into the hole where they found Miller's dad."

"That doesn't mean anything. We all live on the green," Vince argued, gesturing at everyone but Reece and me. "Even Eric."

"Think about it." Reece leaned forward, getting in Vince's face. "If anyone's capable of sneaking around, planting letters, and marking up dead bodies, it's Emily Reinnert."

Vince shook his head. "No."

"She aided and abetted a serial killer."

"She's got nothing to do with this!"

"You don't know that," Reece said.

"She's on house arrest, jackass! You, out of everyone, ought to know she can't even take a piss without telling the police where she's going." Frustration colored Vince's cheeks an angry red. "There's no way she's involved with TJ. She's moved on." He slouched in his chair, his arms crossed defiantly.

"And Reggie is in the custody of a halfway house, but maybe that didn't keep him from stirring shit up. I'm not saying Emily's guilty of anything. I'm just saying, she might know who is."

"So we talk to her," Jeremy said. "That's easy enough. We'll just ask her."

"She doesn't talk to anybody," Vince said, his voice gravelly with some emotion I couldn't quite place. "She doesn't want to see anyone. She never leaves her house."

"Then we have to go to her," I said. "Jeremy and I can't go.

The restraining order won't let her within one hundred feet of us."

"Vince should go," Eric said.

"No, not Vince." Reece had his work face on. All method and strategy. The same face he used to talk to Gena about cases while he was narcing. "He's too close to her. We can't trust him with this."

Vince flew to his feet. Reece followed. They stood eye to eye.

"Reece should do it." We all turned to stare at Jeremy. "Reece should be the one to talk to her."

I shook my head as the group continued to argue. Last time Emily and Reece saw each other, her boyfriend shot Reece in the shoulder. Definitely a stupid idea.

"Hear me out," Jeremy interrupted. "Emily is a felon. She killed people, maybe not willingly, or by her own hand, but in a lot of ways, she was responsible. She's been in jail. She's being watched all the time. And she's not going to trust any of us. But she might trust someone who's walked in her shoes."

Reece stiffened.

There was a challenge in the lift of Jeremy's chin. "What? I'm not saying anything we don't all already know. Everyone knows Reece spent time in juvie. It's no secret that he was involved in that shooting in North Hampton last year." But it was a secret that Reece was a narc. I held my breath, hoping this was the extent of what Jeremy knew. That Reece's secret was still safe.

"So, I'm assuming he's probably got some kind of probation officer checking up on him all the time. Am I right?"

Reece gritted his teeth and nodded.

"All I'm suggesting is that Reece and Emily can probably relate to each other on some deep, morally ambiguous level." My hand curled into a fist. Part of me wanted to deck Jeremy for cutting open the scars of Reece's old wounds. The other part of me knew he was right. If anyone could lure Emily into spilling her secrets, it was Reece.

"I'm not doing it." Reece looked at me, almost apologetically.

But the more I thought about it, the more it made sense. "We could record everything. If she is involved and confesses anything, we'll have it on video."

"Think about this, Leigh. Think about what you're asking me to do."

"I have. It's our only option."

"That's fucked up," Vince said. "No way am I letting this asshole sneak around in Emily's bedroom."

"Who says I have to sneak around. Ten bucks says she invites me—"

Vince threw a punch. It grazed the side of Reece's face. Reece let it ride, wiping any traces of Vince away with his sleeve. He didn't look apologetic anymore.

"Fine. I'll do it. But remember," Reece said to no one in particular, "you wanted this." Then he walked out.

• • •

On Friday night, we all stood outside Emily's house, hidden from view behind her backyard fence. Reece held open his button-down shirt, exposing his chest while I floundered with the camera. He cringed as I used a strip of duct tape to fix the thin, short cable flat against his sternum, and narrowed his eyes at Jeremy. "Where'd you say you got the wire?"

"It's not a wire. It's a spy cam. From a highly reputable online vendor." Jeremy unpacked a receiver from the box and flipped up the antennae.

"It's a fucking nanny cam, is what it is," Vince mumbled.

Reece shook his head. "You've got to be kidding me."

"This thing is no different than the surveillance equipment government spooks use," Jeremy said. "If you make it into Emily's room, this thing will transmit full video up to three hundred feet away."

"*If* he makes it into her room, I'll eat my shorts," Vince muttered.

Jeremy ignored him, carefully connecting adapters and cables to his laptop. "The camera will do its job. You just worry about doing yours."

The evening air held an early autumn chill and my hands were shaking from the cold.

"Hurry up, will you?" Reece clenched his abs against a

breeze as my icy fingers pressed the adhesive to his skin.

"I have absolutely no idea what I'm doing," I muttered. All I knew is that if Emily touched Reece's chest, she'd know he was wired. And I wasn't sure if that thought was terrifying or some form of consolation. "There, that should do it." I snapped the tiny camera in place on his shirt and slowly fastened each button, letting my fingers graze his skin on the way down, tasting the exact moment when his irritation turned to longing.

When I got to the top of his jeans, I slipped my fingers around his waist, warming them against his bare skin. He shivered, bending his head to give me a slow, hot kiss. I don't know why I returned it so fiercely. Maybe because Jeremy was standing behind me. Maybe because Reece was about to stand under Emily's bedroom window and ask her to let him up. Maybe because I wanted to make a point, that he was mine, if only to prove something to myself. I leaned up on my toes, crushing his mouth to mine, careful to avoid the wire as I pressed him up against Emily's fence.

"Jeez," Jeremy whined in a loud whisper while he adjusted his laptop. "Is this absolutely necessary? Like, right now?"

I pulled back, but Reece held me in place and kissed me some more. Maybe because he wanted to make a point too. He tugged gently at the silver chain around my neck, freeing the pendant from my shirt. Then he brushed his nose gently against mine, and whispered, "This is who I am. Right now.

This. Promise me you'll remember that. Okay?"

It sounded like a disclaimer. Tasted like an omen. And the feathery lightness in my chest became a lead weight as I watched him walk through Emily Reinnert's gate.

• • •

"Are you sure you're up for this?" Jeremy asked when Reece was out of sight. He and Eric hunched down behind the fence, facing out onto the darkened line of trees that shielded us from the golf course.

"I'm fine." I snuggled into my jacket and hood and scooted close to Jeremy so I could see the video on his screen. Eric leaned over his other shoulder. Vince stood on the edge of the tree line, with his back to us.

"Sit down, Vince! She's going to see your big dumb head!" Jeremy barked. Vince flipped Jeremy off and dropped to the ground, refusing to look at the screen. But I didn't have a choice. I needed to see this, to hear it for myself. If anyone's secrets were being revealed tonight, I wanted to know.

A brick wall came into view, and then the white-painted wood trellis that climbed to Emily's second-floor bedroom window. It was bare, stripped of any dying vines, and I could imagine Reece standing in front of it, placing the best footholds in his mind. Planning his next move.

"Emily!" Reece's whispered shout came from both directions, one real, the other recorded. "Emily, down here!"

We heard the snap of a window lock.

"Reece! What are you doing down there?"

Vince glanced at the screen.

"I've been thinking about you," Reece said, deep and slow and flypaper sweet.

"Me?" Emily sounded nervous. Maybe a little suspicious.

"I mean, you know . . . your situation," Reece corrected.

I chewed my lip. It hadn't been an innocent slip-up. Reece didn't make those kinds of mistakes. "I know how lonely it can be. I thought maybe you could use some company."

"What would you know about it?" she snapped back.

"More than you might think."

She was quiet. I could picture him standing there, looking up at her with his thumbs hitched in his pockets. Could imagine the suggestive tilt of his head.

"Then tell me."

The camera panned left, then right, as if Reece were checking his surroundings. "More than I want to admit from down here. Besides, it's cold out here. My hands are going numb."

Another pause. "Fine. Come up then. If you want to, I mean."

Vince grumbled to himself, inching closer to the laptop. There was a scrabbling of noise and a blur of movement on the screen. The trellis came into focus. Then the open window. Then Emily's bedroom, her hand reaching to pull him inside.

He held it too long, not long enough to be an obvious

come-on, but long enough to make me bristle inside.

The camera panned slowly around the room. Over the bookcase full of cheer trophies and ribbons and yearbooks. A desk and mirror that looked more like the cosmetics counter at a fancy department store. A bed piled high with pillows.

Emily appeared in front of him. Her hair was long and loose around her shoulders, over a snug Hello Kitty sleep tee and a pair of plaid pajama bottoms tied low enough to leave a swatch of bare skin above her hips. I hardly recognized her. She wasn't wearing makeup, but then again, she'd never really needed any. She was still beautiful, but in a tragic sort of way. She raked her hair back from her eyes and I cringed looking into them. It was the first time I'd seen them this closely since she stood before me, crying and pinning a suicide note to my chest while she'd apologized for her role in TJ's plan to murder me.

"You look good," Reece said.

Emily shrugged like she didn't quite know how to respond. Like she wasn't comfortable with compliments anymore.

"Sorry," she said, wrapping her arms around herself. "I don't get much company."

"No one's come to see you?" asked Reece casually.

"No one who isn't too embarrassed to admit to it."

Vince pitched a pebble into the trees.

Emily sat on the edge of her bed and tucked her legs to her chest. An ankle bracelet peeked out from under the hem of her pajama pants and she tugged the fabric to conceal it. She turned away from Reece, like she was embarrassed. Like maybe he'd been staring at it.

Because it wasn't a bracelet. It was a tracker.

Jeremy's head snapped to Vince. "Why didn't you tell us she was LoJacked!"

"I told you she couldn't go anywhere without the cops knowing! It's the same damn thing."

But no. It wasn't the same thing at all. She couldn't have been the one who'd left the notes. This was a game-changer. Reece knew it too.

"So why'd you come to see me?" Emily asked.

Reece hesitated.

"I thought you and Leigh were, like, a couple or something."

I held a breath.

"We are," Reece said.

"But I thought she hated me."

"With good reason," I muttered.

Reece exhaled. He sounded frustrated. "No one hates you. TJ manipulated you, just like he manipulated everyone else."

She brushed her hair back roughly from her face. "I could have said no. I could have walked away, but I didn't."

"Do you think any of them would still be alive if you had? He would have killed you too. And after he was done, he would have found someone else to do his dirty work."

Emily was quiet. She twisted her pant leg around her finger. "You still haven't told me why you're here."

"Truthfully?" He did a slow turn around the room, pausing long enough for the camera to capture each of her framed photos. He traced a finger down the spine of her yearbooks. Then trailed it over her desk. With his back to her, he shifted a small stack of loose papers—a newspaper article and some letters and envelopes, just enough to let the camera catch their reflection in the mirror.

"Do you see that?" Jeremy asked, zooming to focus on the headline. *Local Teen Testifies Against Boyfriend Accused of Multiple Murders in Exchange for Leniency.* It was a clipping from a local paper back in June, with perfect creases where it had once been folded. I wondered if Emily saved pieces of her past, the same way I saved mine.

"Zoom out again," Eric said. "We don't want to miss anything." Jeremy adjusted the focus. Reece was still standing in front of Emily's desk mirror. He scratched his head.

"Now that I'm here, I don't really know why I came. I guess I just wanted to talk."

"Why not talk to your girlfriend? Why come here? You don't even know me."

Reece frowned, fingering the edges of the clipping. "Leigh's a good person. A really good person. Sometimes I feel like . . ." His eyes lifted to the mirror, deep into the camera. "Sometimes I feel like she expects me to be someone different. Someone more like her. Sometimes I think she can't understand how it feels, to spend your whole life apologizing."

My heart clenched.

"Apologizing for what?" Emily asked.

"You don't want to know," he muttered.

"I do." Her voice was gentle, curious now. It pulled Reece's attention from the mirror. From me.

He sat on the edge of her desk to look at her. "You remember the shooting at North Hampton last year?"

"The one where the narc got killed?"

"The narc was my brother."

Emily untwined her fingers from her hem. She slowly lowered her feet to the floor. "Were you the one who . . . ?"

"I was the dealer who set the whole thing up. I scheduled the drop, knowing he would be there. I knew what he was, and I ratted him out. I didn't know . . ." His voice grew jagged and thick. "I didn't know the cops would be there. I didn't expect it to get out of control, or for my brother to end up caught in the crossfire. I didn't pull the trigger, but I may as well have. And I'll live with that for the rest of my life."

Out of the corner of my eye, I saw Jeremy, Eric, and Vince exchange looks.

Emily bit her lip. "What happened?"

"I was arrested. Did six months in juvie."

She laughed coldly. "At least *you* don't have to wear a bracelet. You can come and go, hang out with your friends, go to school . . ."

"Yeah, sure. With my parole officer breathing down my neck." Reece laughed too, but it was a hopeless sound.

"What?" Emily asked. "What aren't you saying?"

"Nothing." Reece turned away. He fidgeted with something on her desk.

"But it gets better, doesn't it? I mean, once you do your time, it's not so bad, right?" Her throat sounded tight, her voice high and urgent.

Reece didn't answer.

In the mirror, Emily's eyes welled with tears. She curled in on herself, drawing her knees back to her chest. "So it's always going to be like this?"

Reece went to her. He eased down close beside her. Close enough that there was hardly any space between them reflected in the mirror across the room. "This thing," he said, hooking a finger in her tracker, his knuckle brushing her ankle. "It isn't permanent."

"Damn, he's good," whispered Jeremy. Eric nodded, his eyes glued to the screen.

Vince punched Jeremy in the shoulder.

"I know it's not permanent." A tear slipped down Emily's cheek. "But maybe it should be."

In the mirror, I could see something shift in Reece's expression, the crinkle of concern as it took root. "What do you mean?"

"Those days I spent in jail, before my dad's lawyers got me out. I felt like I was where I deserved to be. I knew exactly who I was. I knew what I had done to get there. I knew how to feel inside." Emily's voice was shaky. "But here. This thing—" She pulled at her ankle tracker. "I don't know what this makes me. They tell me I'm free to go home, but this doesn't feel like home. And I'm not free to go anywhere. They tell me I didn't kill anyone. But that's not how it feels when the people I love look at me." She started to cry then. Really cry. The deep silent kind that shakes everything loose inside you. Tentatively, Reece opened his arms and she fell against him, sobbing into his shoulder.

Vince swore. Jeremy and Eric bumped knuckles.

Reece whispered to her. I watched as he stroked her hair, rested his lips against her forehead. A gnawing burn crept up from my heart, because everything I was seeing was sincere. This common ground he shared with Emily felt solid and important. As big as the ocean of differences that divided Reece and me. Lately, I had been the one who'd been looking at him like he was a stranger. Like he'd done something wrong. I had been the one who'd made him feel the way Emily was feeling now.

"I have to go," I said, scrambling to my feet. I cut through the trees behind Emily's house, fighting the brush and low branches that reached for my arms and grabbed at my face.

I emerged on the edge of the golf course, skidding to a halt before I could trip over the yellow perimeter of sagging police tape restricting access to the ninth green where Karl Miller's body had been found. I stood over it, breathing hard, looking back through the cluster of trees I'd just run through. Emily's house lights burned brightly, less than a hundred feet away, through the gaps between branches of dying autumn leaves.

Remember, you asked for this.

I put Reece in this position. Because Emily might know something that could prove my father wasn't the one who put Karl Miller inside this hole. Maybe something that could prove a killer's DNA didn't run in my own blood. So I wouldn't have to spend the rest of my life feeling guilty for something I didn't do. So I wouldn't have to spend the rest of my life apologizing for being someone I didn't choose to be.

In that moment, I realized that I understood Reece Whelan better than he thought. And I didn't want to be the person who treated him like a criminal. I didn't want to be the one who made him feel guilty anymore. If I did, I would only manage to push him away. I marched back toward the lights of Emily's bedroom window.

• • •

When I emerged through the trees, someone pulled me back into the shadows. I opened my mouth to shout, but Reece put a finger to my lips. He tasted like apologies, painful dry lumps that were hard to swallow. But not entirely like regret.

"I'm fine," I said, trying to smile.

Jeremy cradled his laptop and the receiver in his arms. Eric stood beside him, clutching Jeremy's laptop bag, cords and cables hanging from its open zipper as if they'd left Emily's house in a hurry. Vince stood behind them, looking pissed off at everyone.

"What did you find out?" I asked.

Reece winced as he plucked the tape from his chest. He handed Jeremy the camera. "Nothing yet."

Vince threw up his hands and headed back toward Emily's street. "See, I told you. This was a complete waste of time. I'm going home."

We all watched as Vince stormed off.

Jeremy and Eric knelt to wind up the cables and pack up the gear, leaves and brush crackling under their knees.

"You saw the ankle bracelet?" Reece asked, brushing a pine needle from my hair. His thumb stroked my jaw, and his touch smelled sweetly of concern. But I didn't know if it was for me.

I nodded, trying to make sense of what he was feeling. "So she couldn't have been the one to deliver the notes or dig up the body, but that doesn't mean she wasn't involved."

"I'm not so sure. What if we're coming at this from the wrong angle? Emily's a member of the poker kids club, the same as all of you. Who's to say she hasn't gotten some kind of a message too? Maybe that's what TJ meant when he said she had the answers." Reece had that sharp, determined look in his eyes. I reached for his hand, to talk him out of whatever goose chase he was considering. His curiosity was warm, plucking at my tongue like cinnamon candies.

"Yes, but—"

"I'm coming back tomorrow night," Reece said.

I took a step back, letting go of his hand. "I don't think that's a good idea."

He looked surprised. "Why not?"

"Because Emily's sneaky and manipulative and really good at pretending she's not. There has to be another way to figure out what she knows. She didn't tell you anything tonight. What makes you think she's going to tell you anything tomorrow?"

"She's not going to just spill her guts to me the first time we talk."

"Why not? You spilled all of yours."

He cupped my cheek in his hand, dropping his head to look me in the eyes, until all I could taste was his sympathy. "I had to. This isn't going to work unless she trusts me."

"Maybe you're trusting her a little more than she's earned. Whose side were you on up there, Reece?"

His eyes clouded. "It wasn't like that."

I fought to keep my voice from shaking. "Then what was it like, Reece? Because it sure looked like you were connecting back there."

"Of course we connected. What kind of creep do you

think I am, Leigh? You think I can just use someone and not feel anything?"

"Isn't that what you told me? Isn't that how you said it was, with that girl I saw you with in lockup?"

He stepped back as if I'd slapped him. The rustling of cords stopped. Jeremy and Eric looked up with curious expressions. Reece's eyes darted to Jeremy. "I wasn't the one who wanted this." Then he disappeared through the brush.

Jeremy and Eric zipped their packs without a word. I watched them crunch their way through the trees after Reece.

I buried my face in my hands, furious with myself for feeling this way. For doing exactly what I'd told myself I wouldn't do again.

A twig snapped behind me. Dead leaves rustled in the breeze, like the trees were breathing. I looked over my shoulder, disquieted by the cloaking darkness and the odd feeling that we hadn't been alone.

23

I WAS CLINICAL THE NEXT NIGHT as I taped up Reece's wires. Careful not to touch his skin.

His brow was furrowed as he held his shirt open. "Do we really need to record this? It's not like we're looking for some kind of confession anymore. Maybe I should go without the camera this time." I gritted my teeth and stuck the tape hard to his chest, letting him button his own shirt when I was finished. I'd spent all day in my room, waiting for him to call or text me. When he finally did, it was to tell me he had to work. But his hands didn't smell like garlic or pizza cheese, and his shirt didn't smell like oregano. Where he'd actually been working all day, I wasn't really sure.

He leaned down to kiss me, but I moved before he could get close. I slid down the fence beside Eric and Jeremy, and stared at the screen, pretending to be engrossed in the business of spying. Reece threw his arms up as he walked away, and I had to bite my lip to keep from calling his name.

"Brilliant idea, trailer trash." Vince sauntered up and sat in protest a few feet away.

"I didn't hear you come up with a better one," I mumbled. "Probably because you couldn't be bothered to get here on time."

"I had better things to do than hang out with you losers."

"Charitable of you to finally join us."

Jeremy swatted the air and shushed us. I turned back to the screen. The camera swayed dizzyingly with Reece's stride. Then focused on the familiar crisscross of the trellis beneath Emily's window.

"Emily?" he called quietly. He paced the side of her house, trying to see into darkened windows, but the shades were drawn for the night. He called her name again.

"She's not answering. I'm going up," he whispered into the microphone. Her window came into view, then the lace curtains inside. A cool suspicion trickled into my veins. Reece paused, as if he felt it too. The curtains rustled, billowing into the room. The window was already open.

Reece said Emily's name. He waited a moment, then crawled inside.

"She's not here," he whispered. Vince stiffened, craning his neck to see.

The camera panned the room. Paused over Emily's unmade bed. Over the tracker nestled in the blankets.

"I knew it," I whispered. I felt a rush of righteous indignation, until Reece took Emily's ankle bracelet in his hand. "No, don't touch it!" I said, even though he couldn't hear me. He turned it around slowly, then carried it to the lamp on her desk and held it under the light. He scraped it with a fingernail.

"Blood," he said softly. "She must have hurt herself trying to rip the damn thing off."

"That's impossible." Vince scrambled over the grass to narrow his eyes at the screen. The tracker appeared to be intact. Slipping out of it couldn't have been easy, but probably not impossible.

Reece turned a slow circle, letting the camera capture the room. Nothing out of place but the rumpled sheets. "I'm coming down." He pulled a Kleenex from the box on Emily's desk and wiped down the ankle bracelet. Then he carefully set it back in place on the bed.

I held my breath as Reece paused, straddling the window-sill. There would be no way to wipe away the handprints he was about to leave without jumping, and a jump from this height could break both his legs. He swore quietly, gripped the sill with both hands and lowered himself down the trellis.

When he hit the ground, I leaped up to my feet, brushing dirt from the back of my legs.

"I knew it," I said as he came over the fence. "She was involved. She wouldn't have run if she wasn't." Emily was guilty of something. She had to be.

"I don't like it." Reece shook his head, staring off into the trees. "Why would she run? It doesn't make sense."

It did make sense, because she was guilty, but clearly Reece thought . . . I took a step back, sick at the thought. "You still think she's innocent? Reece, she helped TJ kill four people! She stood there and watched while he tried to kill me! Now she's ditched her ankle bracelet and you still believe she didn't have anything to do with this?"

"I never said that." He reached under his shirt and tugged at the wire, tossing the camera to Jeremy. "But I never gave her a reason to run. I never even had a chance to ask her about the notes, or the club." He put his hands on his hips and turned to her open window. "If she did run, then some-one tipped her off."

We all turned to Vince.

"Don't look at me! I didn't tell her anything!"

"Well, someone must have," Jeremy said.

"What do you think I said to her? Hey, Emily. I was stalking your house last night with a druggie and a couple of dorks to see if you've been violating your house arrest—"

"The question is," Reece said, silencing him, "where the hell is she?"

Vince's jaw rocked back and forth. He stared defiantly at Reece.

"Come on. You know her best. Where would she go to get away if she thought she was in trouble? Where would she go if she didn't want to be found?"

Vince lowered his head. He kicked the dirt. "There is one place she might go. We used to sneak out there to smoke weed sometimes."

"Where?"

"Dyke Marsh Trail," Vince said.

The marsh wasn't far. A couple miles maybe. And it would be an easy place to hide.

"Okay, say we go, and she's actually there. What are we supposed to do once we find her?" Jeremy asked.

"We turn her in," I said.

"No," Reece and Vince said in unison. They eyed each other. "We don't know that she's done anything wrong," Reece added. "She's probably just scared. I'll convince her to come home before she does something stupid."

"Like violating her house arrest?" I asked, incredulous. "Reece, you said it yourself, she hasn't spent enough time with you to trust you. What makes you think she'll listen?"

Reece ignored me. "Take Jeremy's car."

"I can drive myself," Vince said.

"No, the pipes on the Camaro are too loud. She'll hear it coming a mile away. We don't want to spook her any more than she already is. Grab a couple flashlights. Park by the marina and walk to the trailhead. I'll meet you there."

"I'll ride with . . ." I started to say. But Reece disappeared into the trees before I could finish. ". . . you."

"Guess you're riding with us," Jeremy said.

I followed Jeremy, Eric, and Vince to Jeremy's house. We all watched as Jeremy punched in the code to the garage. It was neatly organized, like everything else inside their home. All the tools mounted on pegs in descending order by size, garden rakes and golf clubs and expensive bicycles mounted on hooks.

"Wait here," Jeremy said quietly. His father's car was parked in the driveway. Cautiously, he opened the interior door and set his computer bag down on the floor of the mud-room. He disappeared into the kitchen. A moment later, he emerged carrying two flashlights. "Take this. Let's go, before my dad realizes we're here." He gave one of the flashlights to Eric, and we all loaded into his Civic, Eric claiming shotgun and leaving me stuck with Vince in the backseat.

"Why do you think she ran?" I asked Vince.

"Couldn't tell you." He stared out the window. He was uncharacteristically quiet, but his fingers tapped a steady, anxious rhythm in the small space between us, and I let my hand graze his as if by accident. He tasted smoky and elusive, like he was hiding something. The taste of secrets was almost strong enough to disguise a lemon-sour twist of remorse.

• • •

Reece's bike wasn't in the parking lot of the marina.

Vince slammed the car door. "Where's your boyfriend?"

"He said to meet him at the trailhead. Maybe he parked there." I began walking that way. Reece might think Emily was innocent, but I didn't, and I didn't want to miss anything she said.

I walked faster.

Behind me, Jeremy and Vince bickered, their voices growing farther away.

The sign for the trail came into view. Reece's bike was parked along the road beside it. I took the footpath to an elevated walkway of wooden planks. Reece wasn't there. I kept going, following the trail to the end. Vince, Jeremy, and Eric thumped over the boards behind me. We rounded the turns, marsh grasses swaying in the breeze and licking up over the sides.

Reece leaned against a piling at the end of the point, waiting.

"She's not anywhere on the trail. Where would she be?" Reece asked Vince.

Vince jerked his chin. "There's a clearing, a few feet off the trail that way."

Reece stepped off the boards, into the muddy grass.

"That's where we stashed the boat."

Reece stopped and looked over his shoulder at Vince. "What boat?"

"The one we used to get to the island." Vince pointed out toward the water.

Reece shook his head, swearing quietly to himself, and swatted his way through the weeds. He emerged a minute later.

"The boat's gone. Looks like someone dragged it to the water's edge. She probably took it across." Reece dropped his coat to the ground. He kicked off his boots and unbuttoned his shirt.

"What are you doing?" I sputtered as he peeled off his socks.

"It's not far. It can't be more than a hundred yards." He stripped down to his boxer briefs and walked into the shallows.

"You'll freeze to death! Don't be stupid."

"The water's warmer than the air tonight. I'll be fine." He waded out to his waist, and dove in. "I'm going to try to talk some sense into her," he said. Then he sliced through the river in smooth, cutting strokes toward the island.

Oh, hell no. This was not happening.

"What are you waiting for?" I shoved Vince toward the edge of the walkway. "Go with him!"

"Are you crazy?"

The sound of Reece's kicks began to fade. I couldn't make him out in the darkness anymore.

"Fine," I said, ripping off my coat and shoes. I tossed my jeans to the ground and stripped down to my undershirt. I didn't care who was watching. Then I stepped off the edge and splashed into the shallows.

The chill of the wind needled my skin, but Reece was right. The water was warmer, and I bit my lip and trudged in.

Jeremy ran toward the edge of the walkway. "Leigh, what are you doing? You're a terrible swimmer!"

I made it out to my waist, my toes pressing into the thick marsh bottom. I sucked in an anxious breath and stepped out a few more feet, but the depth of the water held just below my chest. "It's just a marsh. I can walk it. It's not deep. Reece said it's not far. I can make it." I'd be damned if I'd leave him mostly naked and hypothermic on a deserted island in the middle of the river with Emily Reinnert.

My steps came down firmly in the mud—three steps, then five—until the bottom fell away. The water pulled at me, dragging me under. I fought my way to the surface, sucked in a breath. Felt my toes stretch for the bottom and then I was under again. Under water as dark as the sky. An arm grabbed my waist, pulling me up. My face broke the surface, and I gasped, taking in a lungful of burning cold air.

"You're an idiot!" Vince said, slinging me onto his back. I wrapped my legs around his waist and coughed, spitting water as Vince swam toward the island in uneven strokes, hindered by my weight. The beach came into shadowy view. Vince stopped swimming and stood in the waist-deep water.

A few feet ahead of us, Reece stood in the shallows, staring at the shore.

At the boat.

The river lapped at its hull, and the moonlight cast a blue glow on the worn wood. Over the white arms and legs draped over its sides. Over the silvery mop of wet hair that hung over Emily's shoulders, and the dark empty space where her foot should have been.

Vince's breathing became ragged and I scrambled off his back to Reece's side. He was shaking, his chest heaving from exertion. I pulled at his shoulders. "Reece, we have to go!" The touch of his skin was choking. It left my tongue numb with terror. "We have to go now!"

I pulled him backward into the deeper water, until he finally turned toward the opposite shore and started swimming. I held on to his shoulders, letting him pull me through the water. Behind us, I could hear the splash of Vince's strokes.

We all scrambled up the riverbank at the end of the trail.

Vince sat in the mud, his face pale and his lips trembling.

"Get up, Vince," I said, frantically tugging on my jeans and shoes. "We need to get out of here." My mind raced through the last two days, over every surface in Emily's room Reece had touched. The tire marks in the gravel where he'd parked his bike. Impressions in the mud where he'd walked when he'd searched the clearing. I grabbed on to the fact that he hadn't touched her body. He hadn't even walked on shore at the island. The most they could do was trace him here. To the marsh. "Get up!" I shouted at Vince, desperate to shake him.

"Where's Emily?" Jeremy asked.

"She's dead." Icy water trickled down my face, and I wiped it on my sleeve. My nose was numb, my fingers and toes tingling cold. "We have to get out of here now."

Reece dressed quickly, and pulled Vince to his feet. He half carried him back to the trailhead. When we reached Reece's bike, I took the flashlights and ordered Jeremy and Eric to help Vince to the car. "You have to leave," I told Reece. "Just go. We'll be fine."

He reached for me, his body trembling. He started to ask me to come with him, then stopped at the calculating look he must have seen in my eyes. It was the only thing holding the tears back. He nodded.

"Take the bike somewhere," I told him, remembering the

advice he'd once given me. "Go somewhere with cameras. Someplace public. Then go to Gena's. Don't go home alone."

"What are you going to do?" He gripped the handlebars to keep his hands from shaking. He was freezing and wet, and the wind was bitter. If he didn't go now, he might not make it.

"I'll check the tide tables," I said. "I'll wait until high tide to report it. The water will cover some of our tracks. I'll make an anonymous call. Tomorrow, I'll go to the crime lab to see if they know anything. Then we can all meet at—"

Reece took me by the shoulder. His whole body shivered and his teeth clattered against the words. "There's something you should know. Something I didn't tell you."

"You should go, before you're too cold to ride."

"I was there. At Emily's. Earlier tonight."

I pulled out of his grip. "What are you saying?"

"I needed time with her. Time alone. To get her to confide in me. Without the cameras and bugs. Without . . . everyone hearing us." He said "everyone," but he was focused on me.

"You were with her? Alone in her room?"

"No." He shook his head. "She was gone. The tracker wasn't on her bed when I was there. I figured she was just downstairs with her family, having dinner or watching TV. I didn't think . . . I didn't know . . . ." He wiped a shaking hand across his lips.

"I don't understand."

"I don't expect you to. It was stupid. I shouldn't have done it. But I need you to know, because someone might figure out I was there. In her room. Before someone did this to her."

He wanted me to cover for him. He wanted me to cover for the fact that he was in another girl's bedroom before she was murdered. He reached for my face, taking my cheek in his hand, choking me with his emotions.

"Oh, Reece." His prints and fibers and hair. It was all there, a latent trail leading back to him. How could we have been so stupid?

He looked down at the ground. Kicked the bike off its stand and flipped on the headlights. "I'm sorry," he said. Then he tore off, and all I could do was stare at the invisible trail he left behind him.

24

I RAN TO CATCH UP with the others. When I got to Jeremy's car, they were crouched inside in the dark with the heater blasting. Vince rested his head on Jeremy's seatback with his arms wrapped around his knees. After a moment, he cracked open his door, and was quietly sick.

"Can we go now?" he asked, his voice unsteady.

Jeremy put the car in gear and pulled out onto the parkway, heading home.

"Thank you," I said to Vince, "for coming after me back

there. The water . . . it was deeper than I thought. I wasn't thinking." He didn't move. I touched his arm, and recoiled. He tasted guilty, and reeked so badly of it that I felt nauseated too.

"I didn't do anything," he whispered.

We drove in silence for several miles.

The car slowed to a stop. Brake lights in front of us illuminated Jeremy's face red in the rearview mirror. He swore to himself.

"Why are we stopping?" I asked.

"Looks like an accident." Eric sat up taller in his seat, straining to look over the cars.

We moved forward at a crawl. Sirens wailed in the distance.

"Get us out of here!" Vince snapped.

"I can't. We're boxed in." Jeremy's knuckles were white where they gripped the wheel. The tension in the car was palpable. So thick and pungent I could practically taste it.

I opened my door.

"What are you doing?" Jeremy shouted. "Get back in the car!"

"I'll go see what's blocking the road. Maybe there's a way around it."

I jogged past the long rows of idling cars. Blue lights flashed so brightly, I almost didn't see the motorcycle, flat against the black pavement. Or the dark silhouette of the body in the road.

"Reece." I ran toward the lights. "Reece!"

Paramedics knelt around him, blocking my view.

"Reece!" I scrambled toward him. Someone grabbed me, holding me back.

There was blood on his face, but his eyes were open and alert. He lifted his head at the sound of my voice. "It's just road rash!" he told the paramedics. "I can walk. Let me up!" One paramedic held his shoulder to the pavement, while another cut open the shredded remains of his jeans. I never should have let him drive. "Leigh," he shouted. "It was the brakes. Check the brakes! Then get out of here! I'll be okay."

The brakes. I jerked loose of the person holding me and ran toward Reece's bike where it lay scraped up and dented a few yards away.

Brakes. I wouldn't even know where to look, except for the hand lever he used to slow down.

"Leigh, we have to go." Eric tugged at my sleeve. He looked anxiously over his shoulder toward the Civic.

"Give me your flashlight." I knelt down by the front tire and studied the handlebars, though I wasn't really sure what I was looking for. Eric handed me his light.

"What are you doing?" he asked impatiently. "Everyone's freaking out back there. We should go back."

The brake lever seemed fine, as far as I could tell. "Where's the brake line on this thing?"

"No clue," he said. "Come on, let's go."

I shined the light down, following the narrow cable connecting the handlebars to the front tire, looking for anything out of place. But with fluid and metal everywhere, everything seemed out of place. I pulled my wet hair from my face and stared at the wreckage.

Eric put a hand on my shoulder. "Just leave it. We need to go!"

I shook him off and reached to unbuckle Reece's leather saddlebag from the bike. I tucked it under my arm. If there was anything of value in it, he'd want to know it was safe. And if there was anything incriminating in it . . . well, I didn't want to think about that.

Reluctantly, with one last look at Reece, I let Eric pull me away. As we ran, Eric bent to snatch Reece's helmet off the ground and shoved it into my hands. It was scraped up, but salvageable.

We dropped into the Civic, breathing hard.

"What happened?" Jeremy asked, looking for a way out of the traffic.

"It was Reece. He's okay."

Cradling his helmet in my lap, I traced a finger over the scratches in the black enamel, reading it like a relief map of his accident. One side of the helmet had dragged against the road, but the rest of it was perfect and smooth. Or rather, it should have been. But it wasn't. My fingernail caught on a deep scratch. I held the helmet up against the headlights of the cars behind me, and a chill raced through my veins.

$$\sum F = 0 \Leftrightarrow \frac{dv}{dt} = 0$$

"What is it?" Vince asked, leaning over to see.

"An object at rest remains at rest, but an object in motion . . ." I whispered.

It was the brakes.

This wasn't an accident. Someone wanted him dead.

I looked down at the saddlebag between my feet and peeled the buckles open, rifling through the contents—Reece's favorite wool cap and spare set of riding gloves, a bag of beef jerky, a small set of lock picks and pocket tools . . .

And a plastic garbage bag, rolled into a cold, tight bundle.

I pulled it into my lap. It felt all wrong.

Reece never kept trash on his bike.

I handed the helmet to Vince without taking my eyes off the bag.

Unrolled it.

Switched on the flashlight and aimed it inside.

I clapped a hand over my mouth to keep from screaming. It was Emily Reinnert's foot.

• • •

Jeremy pulled to a stop in front of my trailer, but left the car running. My body was stiff with marsh mud and my hair was matted and thick. Beside me, Vince's teeth chattered from shock and the cold. The air in the car smelled like vomit, and something else I couldn't place, but probably tasted like fear.

"Why would Reggie do this?" Jeremy's voice was shaky. "I mean, taking house keys and leaving messages in our bedroom is one thing. And digging up a body to use as a note pad is pretty freaking crazy. But Emily was alive! And he cut off her foot, Leigh! Who's doing this? What does he want?"

I wasn't sure anymore. I'd been certain it was Reggie. "It made sense that he would want revenge against our families. Because of the club. But . . ." I looked at the helmet in Vince's lap. At the bag in my hands.

Jeremy smacked the steering wheel. "Reece isn't in the poker kids' club and that wreck was no accident! So why's someone trying to kill him?"

"I don't know. Maybe to hurt me?"

"If that was the case, why not just kill you?" Vince asked.

"I don't know." I pressed my fingers to my temples, but I was too rattled to think. "None of this makes any sense." Everything about this reeked of TJ, but there was no possible way he could have done these things. Unless he was working with someone. He had only wanted to communicate with one other person while he was in prison, and that person was his father.

Bad people don't stop doing bad things.

"I still think Reggie is behind this. The timing is too conspicuous. All of this started when he was released."

"We all know when it started. But when does it end?" Eric asked. "Who's next?"

We all fell silent.

"What do you mean?" asked Vince.

"First Emily, then Reece . . ." Eric said, letting us all fill in the blanks.

"He means this is far from over," I said.

Vince, Jeremy, and Eric . . . they all looked to me. "So what do we do?" Vince asked.

I took a breath. "First thing we do is find a safe place for Emily's foot."

"We should bury it," Vince said, rocking slightly with his hands around his knees.

I thought about Karl Miller's body in the golf course green, how it had gone undetected and undisturbed for five full years before someone dug it up. Maybe, if we buried the foot carefully, no one would ever find it. But that's what a guilty person would do. Destroy evidence. Try to cover a trail.

We were not guilty.

"Does anyone have a freezer?" I asked. "Someplace where we can keep it cold for a while where no one would look?"

Jeremy paled like he might be sick. Vince just looked angry. "We should get rid of it."

"I'll take it," Eric said, craning around in his seat. "We have a chest freezer in our basement."

"What if your mom finds it?" Jeremy asked. "Maybe Vince is right."

Eric reached for the bag. "My mom doesn't cook. She's the

take-out queen. It's full of Lean Cuisines that expired in the late 90s, because she's too lazy to clean it out. It'll be fine."

I handed him the bag, relieved to be rid of it. "Fine. It's settled. Eric will hide the foot until we can figure this out. Obviously someone is trying to frame Reece for Emily's murder. Which means they know he was in her room." I thought back to the twig that snapped in the woods behind her house. The feeling of being watched, like we weren't alone. Someone had been there. Which meant they knew we were recording those meetings. "Jeremy, we need to destroy the recordings."

He nodded. "They're on my laptop. I'll delete them when I get home."

"High tide should still be a few hours away. I'll wait until then to call the tip line about Emily. I'll go to the lab tomorrow morning and watch the investigation from that end. Reece didn't kill her, but he was in her room, and it won't take them long to figure that out." The thought of Reece behind bars for murder turned my stomach. I couldn't let him go to jail for this. "Go home. Try to get some sleep. I need time to figure out what to do."

Jeremy and Eric waited in the car with the headlights aimed at my door. Vince walked me up the steps and hovered, shivering, while I unlocked the deadbolt. I reached for the knob, but he stopped me. Cautiously, he pushed the door open and poked his head around it before letting me inside.

"I didn't know you played ball." Vince gestured to the baseball bat as he shut the door.

"I don't. It's my mom's."

He raised an eyebrow.

"High-tech home security system," I explained, feeling my cheeks warm with embarrassment.

Vince stood on the small square of curling linoleum by the door. His nose wrinkled up when I flipped on the living room light. "This is your house?"

I wiped tangles of hair from my eyes. I was spent. Too exhausted to throw around insults with him. "Sorry," I said, with as much sarcasm as I could muster. "It's not exactly Belle Green or anything."

He looked around, at our thin throw pillows and worn-out carpets. At the lamp in the corner with the yellowing shade. "It's not so bad."

It was a lie. But I didn't know if he was lying about my house, or the implication that he'd never seen it. One thing was certain. He was hiding something. Something to do with Emily.

"It's after two." I nodded to the door. "My mother will be home from work soon, and we all need some rest. Tell Eric and Jeremy we'll meet in front of the school tomorrow afternoon at four."

Vince looked down at his shoes. He nodded once, then left without a word.

I locked the door and pulled out my phone to call Reece. He answered on the first ring.

"Where are you? Are you okay?" He sounded frantic.

"I'm home. I'm safe." I heard him sigh with relief. "What about you?"

"I'm okay. Just a couple scrapes and bruises, but they dragged me to the ER anyway. They're working on my discharge papers and Gena's on her way to pick me up."

I leaned against the wall and slid to the floor, exhausted. Good. He'd be safe with Gena. "What are you going to tell her?"

"As little as possible."

That wouldn't be easy for him. It would be better to wait and tell him about the foot in his saddlebag tomorrow. And even though I still had doubts and questions—about him and Emily and why he'd hidden his visit from me—for now, he was safe. And that was all that mattered.

"Okay, I told the others to meet tomorrow at four in front of the school. And Reece," I said through a lump in my throat. "You were right. It wasn't an accident."

"I know," he said softly. "Try to get some sleep."

25

I SLEPT, but it was a fitful and restless three hours of mostly terrible dreams. Images of TJ woke me through the night, bits and pieces of our conversation in the prison coming back to me and the feel of his arms squeezing the air from my lungs. Only in the dreams, he was wearing his father's face.

My eyes burned with fatigue. I stepped off the bus, blinking against the early morning sun. High tide had come and gone before sunup. At my transfer stop, I found a pay phone behind a gas station, and dialed the police tip line to report Emily's body. I talked quickly, distorting my voice. Then hung up just as my next bus pulled into view, and climbed on.

"Whoa, totally didn't expect to see you here," Raj said when I opened the break room door at the lab.

I froze. "You too."

He dumped sugar into his coffee and stirred it with a finger. "Are you kidding? All kinds of crazy stuff goes down on Saturday nights. Drive-bys. Burglaries. Muggings. Sunday mornings in the crime lab are where we see the most action. What about you? Aren't you supposed to be sleeping or something? I read somewhere that teenagers need more sleep than the average human."

"Whatever." I plucked on the sleeve of his LEGO Batman T-shirt and pushed past him toward the coffeepot, struggling to act normal. "You should zip your fly. I think your Mutant Ninja Turtles are showing."

Raj dared a quick look at his crotch. "That's funny, Boswell. You know what's not funny? That huge stack of cards in the Latent Prints lab." Raj's face was stone-cold serious.

Coffee splashed over the side of my mug and I scrambled to clean it up. "What do you mean?" My breath held. Had they found Lonny's phone?

"There were about fifty new cards in my in-box on Friday." He sipped his coffee, raising an eyebrow over the brim of his mug.

"So what are you suggesting?"

He looked around conspiratorially. "It's Sunday morning. Which means the place will be quiet for another few hours. Things won't start hopping until noon. What do you say I log you in to the Latent Prints lab and you can feed The Monster for a couple hours. Might as well make yourself useful since you're here. And there might be a few performance-based donut holes in it for you."

I let out my breath. This couldn't be more perfect. My hands shook ever so slightly as I lifted the mug to my lips, and I hoped Raj wouldn't notice. "Fine. As long as you promise to come get me if anything exciting happens." By now, police would be swarming Dyke Marsh Trail. Emily's body would be here in a few hours, hopefully in time to shed light on the progress of the investigation before my meeting with the others.

Raj dropped me off in the Latent Prints lab and logged me in to AFIS. When I was sure he was gone, I dug my fingers into the box and felt around for Lonny's phone. Still there. I sat down in front of The Monster and typed a name in the search field.

Reece's fingerprints appeared on the screen, and I studied the records tied to them. All of them dated before his brother died. My finger twitched over the DELETE key. I clicked it.

"Are you sure you want to delete this record?" the computer prompted. But the flashing cursor felt like it was asking more.

"I'm sure." I closed my eyes. Clicked it again.

Reece's records were gone.

I scanned the rest of the cards as quickly as I could, feeding The Monster fifty new names to make up for the one I'd just taken. Then I kept going. Through the older stacks in the box.

Until I reached the bottom of the stack and my fingers found Lonny's phone.

Bad people don't stop doing bad things.

It was one thing to delete Reece's fingerprints, it was another thing to steal evidence. I unzipped my backpack and stuffed the phone inside. I'd return Lonny's phone to the evidence room on my way out of the lab.

The door opened and I jumped when Raj rushed in. He headed straight for the supply cabinet and began rummaging inside. His face was flushed, like he'd just run up the stairs.

"What's going on?" Raj never moved this fast, unless it involved a body.

He didn't answer as he withdrew containers of fingerprint powder and gloves. The hair on my neck stood on end. It was too early. There was no way Emily's body could be here so soon. Unless it had been discovered by someone else. Before I'd made the call. Before the tide came up and washed over the tracks on the shoreline. I turned off the monitor, my stomach in knots.

He drew on a lab coat, stuffing the supplies into the pockets. Then he grabbed a field test kit with a layer of dust on it, and pushed past me to the door.

"Where are you going?" Lab techs didn't go into the field. They weren't allowed.

"A dismembered body was called in this morning. And since I'm not on the clock, and Doc isn't here, there's no one to tell me I have to stick around and wait for the meat wagon to bring it in."

I followed after him. "Wait! I want to go too. It'll be like a field trip."

"No way," he said. "You can stay here and feed The Monster."

"But I finished the entire stack of cards!"

"Then you can wash dishes."

"I'll stay out of the way. I promise."

"Sorry, kid."

I couldn't let him leave without me. If he left me behind, it would be hours before I knew what they'd found at the crime scene, or if Reece was being considered a suspect.

"If you let me come, I'll tell you what Veronica said about you." I felt sick the moment the words were out of my mouth. This was exactly the kind of thing my father would do.

Raj almost tripped. He stopped at the end of the hall to look at me. "Veronica said something about me?"

I nodded.

"What did she say?" I didn't have to touch Raj to know how he felt about her. But Veronica had been good about hiding her emotions. And here I was, ready to leverage them to get what I wanted.

"I'll tell you everything, if you take me with you."

Raj stomped back into the lab, grumbling under his breath. He reached into a cabinet.

"I'm going to get in so much trouble if Doc finds out about this. Here, put this on." He handed me a lanyard, similar to the one I already wore around my neck. But this one said "Crime Scene Investigator." He tossed me a lab coat and I stuffed my arms into the sleeves while I chased him down the back stairs. As soon as he unlocked the door of his car, I jumped in and snapped on my seat belt. A Yoda bobblehead nodded at me from the dashboard.

"We shouldn't be doing this," he said. "I'm only taking you along because I'm your internship supervisor and I am responsible for . . . you know . . . supervising you, or whatever. So spill. What did Veronica say about me?"

"She told me she likes you."

"Like how?"

"Like, she really likes you. You should ask her out."

"What if she says no?"

"She won't say no."

"How do you know that? Did she tell you?"

I looked away, out the window. "In a manner of speaking. Can we please go?"

Raj's eyes lit, and I wasn't sure what he was more excited about—the possibility of a date with Veronica or the crime scene we were about to sneak into. He started the car and programmed his Garman. "Where are we headed?" I asked, even though I already knew.

"Belle Green. The body was found on the island off Dyke Marsh Trail. And get this . . . she's missing a foot." Raj peeled out of the lot.

"So why are we going to Belle Green?" I asked cautiously. I'd have to be careful. I knew things that Raj hadn't had time to figure out yet. Her identity, exactly where she'd been found, how the crime had been reported. And that her foot was in Eric Miller's basement freezer.

"Police reported a teenage girl missing early this morning.

She was on house arrest in her home in Belle Green. Apparently, her parents found her ankle bracelet in her bed, and her window was wide open. She fits the description of our Jane Doe. Doc's on his way to the island, and there's a small CSI team at the house already. Nobody we know. I already checked."

"Do you know who the girl is?"

"All I have is an address."

"What are we going to do there?" Raj had stuffed his pockets full of fingerprinting supplies. My heart skipped. My mind raced through every surface of Emily's bedroom, the trellis, the fence . . .

"Nothing," he said. "We're going to watch."

"Then what's all that stuff in your pockets for?"

"To make us look official, in case anyone asks questions."

I hadn't thought about that when I jumped into Raj's car. "What if someone sees us? What if they know we shouldn't be there?" I wasn't exactly a stranger in Belle Green, and Emily's parents were sure to recognize me.

"Most of the CSI teams are at Dyke Marsh. And the girl's parents were taken to the station to talk with investigators so police could secure the scene. They probably have one or two newbs in blue guarding the door. Maybe a couple of investigators." Raj smoothed the collar of his lab coat. "We look official enough to pass for the real deal. We'll get in, watch the crime scene photographers do their thing, practice pulling a few prints . . . Maybe we'll get lucky and be the ones to find the missing foot."

A nervous giggle escaped my throat.

Raj turned off the interstate and headed south on Route 1. We passed the burnt shell of the Buis' store and the road to my trailer. Then, a few miles farther, the site of Reece's bike accident. Sun glinted off scraps of metal that had been brushed to the side of the road. There was a note at every site. A message. Ink on my mirror. A number in bone. A formula on the helmet. A bread crumb drawing us further in. The night before, in the dark on the island, we'd all been too freaked out to look. But that didn't mean a message wasn't there, waiting for daylight to be discovered.

The club will illuminate its secrets.

I shifted in my seat.

Raj drove through the wrought iron gates into Belle Green and we wound through manicured streets of stately brick colonials. My phone buzzed and I pulled it from my pocket. Jeremy. Probably wanting to know if I'd heard anything about the investigation yet. I silenced it as the yellow tape perimeter around the Reinnerts' lawn came into view. We parked along the curb behind a police car.

"Stay close and follow me. Act like you belong here."

Raj got out of the car with his stolen field kit. He nodded once at the young-looking officer by the door and walked right past him into the house, while I stared at his heels and tried not to look guilty. A few photographers in CSI shirts descended the winding center stair, carrying armfuls of gear.

"We're all wrapped up in there. Scene's all yours." We stepped aside with our heads down to let them pass. Then we crept up the stairs. When we got to the top, Raj paused.

"Second door on the left," I said, remembering the placement of Emily's window from where I'd sat outside her fence.

"How do you know that?"

Stupid! I bit my lip and thought fast.

"I have a friend who lives on this street. Same floor plan," I said, trying to sound confident. "Lucky guess."

"Impressive." Raj poked his head into Emily's room. "You've got good instincts. You'd make a good investigator."

Or a great conman. I dug my nails into my palms. Clamped my mouth shut.

Inside the room, an investigator bent over Emily's wastebasket under her desk, picking through its contents with gloved fingers. We stood, silently watching.

My phone buzzed in my pocket. The investigator started. Raj jabbed me with an elbow and I rushed to shut it off.

"It's about time," the CSI guy said into the can without looking behind him. "You all were supposed to be here twenty minutes ago."

Raj coughed. "Sorry we're late. We got held up with the team at the marsh."

"There are booties by the door. Don't track any marsh crap on the carpets."

Raj and I exchanged what-the-hell-do-we-do-now looks. Then he handed me a set of blue booties and we slipped them over our shoes. A box of latex gloves sat on the edge of the bed, and we each took a pair.

At the sound of the snap of the gloves on our wrists, the CSI guy reached backward and held something out to Raj. "Bag this, will you?"

My breath caught. Pinched in his fingers was a pair of tweezers, and pinched inside those was a used condom, stretched out like a worn sock, opaque against the light of Emily's window.

Raj faltered a moment, then reached for a paper evidence bag from the collection kit.

"Use a cup. This one's still juicy," said CSI guy.

Raj made a face. He unscrewed a specimen cup and CSI guy dropped the condom in.

"You must be new." The guy rose to his feet. He pulled a marker from his pocket and yanked off the cap with his teeth, never once looking at us as he took the cup and labeled it. "Looks like this little scavenger hunt is just about over. The murder weapon was found in the trees behind her house—"

"What was it? A butcher knife? A saw?" Raj was entirely too eager, and I stepped hard on his toe.

"A rope. We can't sign off on it until Doc Benoit gives his

two cents. But the guys at the marsh say it looks like strangulation was the cause of death. The amputation was probably done post-mortem. The only thing missing now is the girl's foot." His phone rang. "Make sure this makes it to the freezer," he said, handing the cup to Raj and stepping out of the room to take the call.

Raj stared at the cup with a look of complete fascination. "Do you have any idea what this is? This is probably a DNA sample from the last person to see the victim alive. Probably the same person who killed her. Aside from the murder weapon, this is the single most damning piece of evidence in this case."

Raj crossed the room and examined the window. "No sign of forced entry. Nothing looks out of place. The murder didn't happen in her room. Which means she was alive when she climbed out that window. She probably knew her attacker. Maybe even trusted him." Raj stuck his head out and pointed toward the golf course. "She was probably killed where they found the weapon, in the trees right behind the house. Which is why the ankle bracelet never alerted police to the fact that she'd been missing. The killer must have climbed back in, to put it in her room. Then he moved her to the island to get rid of the body before anyone knew she was gone."

But who killed her? Who did she trust enough to let in her room? In her bed? Who would she trust enough to follow out into the woods in the dark?

A knot tightened in my throat.

I was there. At Emily's earlier tonight.

I had to believe that the contents of that cup didn't belong to Reece.

"Come on," Raj said, setting the cup on the bed to strip off his booties and gloves. "Another team is on their way. We shouldn't stick around."

I followed him outside. I told myself the cup was better off where it was. Jeremy, Vince, Reece, Eric, and I—we'd all been there, in those trees. In her yard. We'd all been complicit. The cup could be the one piece of evidence that saved us all.

So why did I have such a hard time turning my back on it?

"Are you going to take that?" Raj asked.

I jumped. But he wasn't talking about the cup. He looked annoyed. My phone buzzed insistently in my pocket.

Jeremy. Again.

I held the phone to my ear. "What?"

"Jeez, Nearly," he shouted. "I've been calling for an hour!"

"Can't this wait? Now's not exactly a good time."

"No, it can't wait." I heard his deep trembling breath through the phone. "The recordings. They're gone."

I sighed with relief. "Good. That's great, Jeremy."

"No, you don't understand. I didn't delete them."

I lowered my voice, turning my back to Raj. "What do you mean, you didn't delete them?"

"I couldn't. It's my laptop. Someone took it. It's gone."

"I can't talk now." I hung up the phone.

"Come on," Raj said. "We should get back to the lab." He was halfway across the lawn to his car.

"You go on without me." I handed Raj my lanyard and lab coat. "I forgot I have a study group meeting at my friend's house. He lives just down the street. I can catch a ride home with him."

Raj grinned. "Right. Study group. I'll see you at the lab on Tuesday." He unlocked his car and tossed me my backpack. "Hey, are you sure Veronica wants to go out with me?"

My backpack felt too heavy. I didn't feel sure of anything anymore. "Yes, I'm certain of it."

Raj's smile spread from ear to ear as he got into his car and drove away.

I turned toward Jeremy's house. His car was in the driveway, and I ran to his front door. I knocked loudly, looking up at his bedroom window. He peeled the curtain back and let it fall. I waited, anxiously bouncing on my toes, and when he didn't answer the door, I rang the bell, over and over until I heard his shoes lumber down the stairs inside.

He threw open the front door and blew past me, car keys in his hand.

"How'd you get here so fast?" he asked over his shoulder.

"I was at Emily's," I said, almost running to keep up. "Why didn't you call me last night? Those recordings put every single one of us at the crime scene. We have to find them!"

"I know. I'm sorry." He stood beside his car with his back to me. "I should have called as soon as I got home."

"Then why didn't you, Jeremy? Do you have any idea how much trouble we'll be in if those recordings end up in the wrong hands? For all we know, they could already be on You-Tube or something!"

Jeremy turned to face me. An angry red welt spread across the left side of his jaw and there was a small cut in the corner of his lip. "I said I know. And I'm sorry."

My breath caught. "What happened?"

"My dad caught me sneaking into the house at three a.m. and demanded to know where I'd been."

"What did you tell him?"

"I told him I'd been with Anh. After that, I didn't really have time to look for the recordings."

"Oh," I said. When he'd left so late last night, I hadn't even thought about the fact that he would have to go home and avoid being caught by his father. That he had to protect himself against more than just the monster that was trying to kill us. He had to protect himself against the one that lived under his own roof. "It's okay. We'll figure something out. It's almost four. We've got to meet the others."

The garage door groaned open. Jason Fowler stood inside it with a red face, angrier than I'd ever seen him. Jeremy stepped away from the car.

"I told you you're grounded," he said, stalking toward us.

"No," Jeremy said in a small voice. "You told me I couldn't see Anh."

Jason's hands were clenched at his side. He darted looks up and down the street. "This is my house!" he hissed. "I make the rules! I'm not just going to sit around and let you make a spectacle of this family while you run off and wet your dick with some cheap, foreign dollar store salesclerk!"

Jeremy gritted his teeth. "She's my girlfriend. And I won't let you talk about her like that."

"Don't you dare mouth off to me!"

Jeremy flinched.

My eyes flicked to Vince's house across the street. I thought about running and banging on his front door.

"And how many times do I have to tell you stay away from this one?" Jason's hand shot out and grabbed me by the shirt. "I raised you better than this. And you insult me by bringing this gold-digging tramp to my—"

Jeremy shoved his father. "Don't you touch her!"

His father's face contorted with rage and he lunged. Jeremy wound back and hit him hard in the jaw, knocking him back. There was a wild recklessness in Jeremy's eyes. His chest heaved with adrenaline.

Jason righted himself, wiping his mouth with the back of his hand while he stared coldly at his son.

A door slammed across the street. Vince stood on his front porch, watching intently, his hands loose and ready at his sides. Jason looked from him to me to Jeremy. "I'll deal with you later," he said, and stormed back into the house.

When he was gone, Jeremy stared at his hand.

"I'm sorry," he whispered.

I took his hand. He tasted confused and disappointed and scared.

I squeezed it tight and said, "You didn't do anything wrong."

26

WE DROVE TO THE SCHOOL in silence, Vince's car following close behind. As we neared West River, I spotted Reece getting out of Alex's Benz. He'd parked on the street a block away from the entrance, probably to make our presence here less obvious. Taking Reece's lead, Jeremy parked a few car lengths behind him. Vince rolled past us, pulling to a stop in the center of the lot.

Reece reclined against the Benz, waiting for Jeremy and me. Our eyes met as we walked toward him, and his smile was a little uncertain, like he wasn't quite sure where we stood. My smile felt awkward too.

"I could have given you a ride," he said, casting a sideways glance at Jeremy.

"It would have been out of your way." I shrugged. "Besides, I needed to talk to Jeremy anyway."

"About what? Did you hear something in the crime lab today?"

I bit my lip and started walking toward the school. Where would I even start? Emily's foot, the stolen recordings, the condom in Emily's room? "Come on. I'll fill everyone in when we're inside."

"Should we wait for Eric?" he asked, once we'd caught up with Vince.

"He just texted me. He's on his way," Jeremy said, looking up from his phone.

"Tell him to meet us in the computer lab," I said.

Jeremy started typing a message, then paused. "The computer lab isn't a good idea. It'll be locked."

"Not a problem," Reece said.

"There's a security system in the computer lab. Motion sensors and a silent alarm. Only the teachers and custodians know the code."

Vince looked anxious. "We're in enough deep shit. Let's just pick someplace else. My parents aren't home. We can go to my house," he said.

"We're already here," Jeremy said, pushing his glasses up over the bruise on the bridge of his nose. I didn't blame him for not wanting to go back to Belle Green so quickly. "We can sit outside and talk."

Vince hitched his thumbs in his jeans and shrugged. "The ball fields should be empty by now. We can grab one of the picnic tables behind the school. It should be private enough."

But I wasn't so sure. I couldn't shake the feeling that we were all being watched.

"Text Eric and tell him to meet us upstairs in the chemistry lab instead. Let's get inside, before someone sees us."

Reece was quiet while he picked the lock on the front door to get us in. I snuck glances at him while Jeremy filled him in about the helmet and Emily's foot. It was hard not to stare at the road rash on Reece's arm or the bandage on his wrist, or the way he took the stairs with a slight limp. Or to look at Jeremy's face without feeling like, somehow, I was responsible for all of it.

Once we were inside the lab, Reece leaned against a table, watching me pace the room. Jeremy scrolled through his phone while Vince rummaged in the supply closet. Once Eric arrived, the club—what was left of the club—would all be here, and we could figure out what the hell to do. But first, I would have to tell them all what CSI had discovered in Emily's bedroom.

"Ha!" Vince shouted from inside the closet. "I knew there would be booze in here!"

I rolled my eyes. "That's ethanol."

"It's grain," he argued.

"That cabinet's locked, Vince."

There was a shuffling, then the scrape of metal on metal. Then the unmistakable shudder of a locker being yanked open. "Not anymore."

I buried my head in my hands as I listened to the liquid pour in a slow, steady trickle from the tap of the ethyl alcohol dispenser.

"Whoa!" he choked out. "That shit burns going down."

The hazardous materials cabinet rattled shut. Vince emerged from the closet, sweating and red-cheeked, holding a silver flask.

"Where'd you get that?" I asked, hoping he hadn't stolen that from Rankin's closet too.

"It's mine," Vince said, turning the flask to prove it. His initials were engraved in the finish. "Just taking a little juice for the road. That's all."

"Isn't it a little early for that?" Reece asked.

Vince looked disgusted. "We found Emily's foot in the saddlebag of your bike last night, and you're asking me if it's too early to get numb?"

Reece's eyes darted to me.

I hadn't wanted him to find out this way. "I was going to tell you once everyone got here," I said.

He swore under his breath.

Vince plopped down into an empty chair, pulling his seat tight beside Jeremy's. Jeremy slumped in his, looking miserable. He checked the time on his phone.

"We might as well get started. Eric should be here soon. What did you find out?" he asked.

I shut the door and took a seat. Reece winced as he settled gingerly into the chair beside me.

"Investigators found the murder weapon in the trees behind Emily's house. A rope. She was strangled."

"Was there a number? A note?" Jeremy asked.

"I was in Emily's house earlier today while the CSI team was there. No one mentioned an obvious message at either of the crime scenes."

"Did you get rid of the recordings?" Reece asked Jeremy. Jeremy and I exchanged guilty looks.

"My laptop was stolen sometime last night. Probably while we were out looking for Emily. The recordings were on it."

Reece eased back in his chair, his face drawn with worry. "What about the foot you found in my saddlebag? Is that gone too?"

"It's safe," I said.

The lab door creaked open and Eric popped his head in, looking relieved to see us. He sank into an empty chair.

"So what did they find?" Eric asked, winded from his run up the two flights of stairs. "They had to have found something."

"They did find . . . something."

I couldn't tell if the flush in Vince's cheeks was the grain or something else. Reece stared stone-faced at the floor, like he was bracing himself for more bad news.

"It will take a few days for the lab to process the evidence. But the investigators think she knew her killer." I pressed my lips shut, chancing a glance at Reece. His eyes met mine.

"Emily had sex with someone the same night she was murdered. They found the condom in her bedroom." Reece didn't look away. Even when Jeremy turned in his chair to gape at him.

"What the hell were you thinking?" Jeremy shouted.

"It wasn't me," Reece answered, but he was looking at me.

"Relax, Jeremy," Eric piped up. "Reece wasn't in her room before we got there, right, Reece?"

Reece's jaw clenched.

"I knew it." Jeremy buried his head in his hands.

Eric looked around the group, like he was waiting for someone else to ask the obvious question. "What were you doing in her room?"

Reece gritted his teeth. "I went to her house to talk. She wasn't there." Eric raised an eyebrow. Reece looked disgusted. "I didn't sleep with her. I didn't touch her. And I sure as hell didn't kill her!"

"Then who did?" Eric asked. "I mean, there's no way Emily would have been sleeping with TJ's dad, right? That's kind of gross."

Jeremy rubbed his bloodshot eyes. He heaved a frustrated sigh. "Obviously, it was someone who didn't want her to talk to us. Someone she was close with. Someone who knew what we were up to." Jeremy's voice trailed off. The room fell quiet.

Eric turned to look at Vince. We all did.

Vince flew out of his chair and threw open the door. Reece and Jeremy scrambled to their feet and chased him to the stairs.

I grabbed Eric by the wrist and pulled him to the window, tasting a wild peppermint rush. "No," I said, certain he wanted to go after them. We'd never be fast enough to keep up. "Come on! We'll be able to see where he goes from here."

We cranked open a window and leaned out just in time to see Vince tear out of the front door at the far end of the building. He tripped off the curb, then made a beeline for his Camaro with Reece at his heels and Jeremy behind him. That's when I saw them.

The blue letters spray painted on the roof of Vince's car.

$$2\,C_8H_{18} + 25\,O_2 \rightarrow 16\,CO_2 + 18\,H_2O$$

Octane.

Combustion.

"Reece! Not the car! It's a trap!"

Reece skidded to a stop at the sound of my voice.

"It's going to blow up!"

Reece took off toward Vince. He pumped his feet faster while Vince dropped into the driver's seat and fumbled with his keys. He was slow, clumsy from the grain, but he slipped a key in the ignition. Then he reached for the door. Reece grabbed his arm and pulled, dragging Vince from his seat. They rolled over the pavement, swearing at each other. Vince threw a punch at Reece's face, but Reece dodged it and planted his knee under Vince's ribs, dropping him to the ground.

"Get away from the car!" I shouted.

Reece slung an arm under Vince and dragged him across the parking lot while Vince struggled to catch his breath.

The sound of the explosion rattled the windows and my teeth. It threw Vince and Reece to the ground in a tangled heap. The car began to flame, black smoke curling from the hood and spewing from the empty seat where Vince had been sitting. Eric and I raced down the stairs. He stopped to grab a fire extinguisher off the wall to douse the flames. Jeremy ran into the building for another one. Breathing heavily, Reece and Vince bent over their knees, staring at the smoke and white spray billowing around Vince's totaled car.

I ran to Reece, stopping myself an arm's length away. I knew better than to touch him after a fight. His eyes were a cold, cold blue, and he was looking at Vince like he wanted to kill him. He cradled his bandaged wrist.

"Are you okay?" I asked.

"I'm fine," he said, still winded.

Jeremy and Eric doused the last of the flames and ran to catch up with the rest of us.

Vince swiped blood from his lip and stared at his car, his hands clenched at his side.

Reece shoved him, getting his attention. "Why the hell did you run?"

"I didn't know what else to do!" He wavered a little on his feet, but his eyes were sober. "It was me. I was the one that was with her that night. But I didn't kill her."

I touched the sweat-slicked skin of Vince's arm, as if to reassure him. He tasted strong and clear. Truth, for me, was always crisply defined, no matter what emotion lay at its center. In Vince's case, that emotion was grief. I looked to Reece, gave a small nod.

"I swear I didn't kill her. She was fine when I left." He scrubbed a hand over his face. "I am so screwed. The only hope I had of getting out of this were those fucking recordings. If the police suspected Reece, maybe I'd be off the hook. You know, reasonable doubt and all that shit. But now the recordings are gone, and once the cops figure out the condom was mine, that's it."

"What do we do now?" Jeremy took off his glasses to wipe the sweat from his eyes.

Reece frowned at the smoldering car. "We get out of here before someone sends a patrol car. Jeremy, you take Eric and Vince." To me, he said, "If you want, you can ride with me." He sounded uncertain, like he wasn't sure I would accept. I didn't object. "Leigh's house is closest. Her mom's working tonight. We can talk there. Figure something out." He turned to Vince. "Give me your hootch."

Vince reached in his back pocket and withdrew an expensive-looking silver flask. Reece took it. Then he rummaged in a nearby trash can for an empty bottle. He poured an ounce of Vince's grain into it. Then he pulled a pocket-knife from his jeans, grabbed the front of Jeremy's T-shirt, and began cutting along the seam.

"What the hell are you doing?" Jeremy pulled away, but it only made Reece's job easier and the last of the fabric tore free. He put away the knife and stuffed the cloth strip in the bottle, leaving a piece to dangle over the lip. Then he wiped the glass clean and set the bottle in the middle of the parking lot.

"If the cops come, they'll think some neighborhood kids were messing around, setting off Molotov cocktails. You can tell them you left your car here while you went out with some friends."

"Yeah, right," Vince muttered. "Some friends."

Reece turned around fast and put his hand at Vince's throat. "You're lucky to be alive. Remember that."

Vince nodded. Swallowed. He looked at the healing road rash on Reece's face. "I know."

27

WE SAT ON THE FLOOR of my living room in the half dark, passing Vince's flask around the circle. When we'd gone back into the school to get our things and lock up the classroom,

Vince had refilled his flask. In the closet, he'd found an empty glass bottle with a rubber stopper and he'd filled that too.

Jeremy took a pull from the flask, his face crinkling and his eyes watering behind his glasses like they were on fire. He passed it to Eric. Eric took a drink, coughing into his hand as he offered it to me. I stared at it, remembering the last time I'd felt intoxicated, tempted to dull the fear I was feeling, even for a little while. But I'd been useless that night, when I'd bumped into TJ at the rave—so drunk on the highs of the people around me, I hadn't recognized TJ when I'd touched him. If I'd been clear-headed, maybe Kylie would still be alive. "No thanks," I said, handing the flask back to Vince.

Vince offered the flask to Reece. He looked at me and passed.

"What was the deal between you and Emily?" Reece asked.

"The deal?" Vince traced his initials in the side of the flask. "It's no secret that we started seeing each other back when she was still with TJ. I kept telling her she was too good for him."

I bristled. "Why? Because TJ wasn't Belle Green enough anymore? Was he just trailer trash to you?"

Vince scowled. "Don't get your undies in a bunch. It wasn't about the money. I mean . . . they were good for each other for a long time, even while he was living here in Sunny View. But after a while, he was just angry all the time. After he messed up his knee, I took him to three different doctors.

They all said the same thing, no more football. They could do surgery and try to repair the ligament, but TJ's uncle Billy wasn't working and they didn't have insurance. The trust fund Reggie had set up barely covered their expenses. Even if they could afford the surgery, TJ knew he'd never play again."

Vince took a long thoughtful breath. "I hadn't seen TJ that wrecked since his mom killed herself. He was mad at the whole fucking world, and I had a feeling he was taking some of it out on Emily. But she wouldn't break it off. I think she was scared. She'd come over, sometimes just to talk, but mostly we'd mess around, and she never wanted anyone to know."

He took a swig and winced. "So after she got out of jail, she called me, saying she missed me and she wanted me to come see her. I told her no. Too much had changed, you know? It's like she was going to be grounded for the rest of her life. No prom, no homecoming, no basketball games. It wasn't like we could really go out or anything." He shook his head, thinking. "But then when we were sitting there in her yard, and she let Whelan in her room . . . I don't know. Something just snapped. I hated that he was up there with her, and I wasn't. So the next day I went, and she let me come up, and well . . ." He looked uncomfortably at each of our faces and then at the flask in his hand. "You all know what happened after that."

We were quiet. It was hard to know what to say as Vince took another long pull from the flask.

Jeremy looked down at the floor and picked at the carpet, his blond bangs falling down to cover his glasses. "I owe you an apology, Vince. I was the one who told TJ that you and Emily were seeing each other behind his back. I was the one who took the picture of her kissing you." His throat sounded thick, like he was holding back tears. "I didn't like you, and I was angry, and I didn't know TJ had been hurting her, or that he would—"

"I know, Fowler." Vince cut him off, his words beginning to slur at the edges. "And I get why you did it. I was kind of an asshole to you, for like, you know . . . forever. But let's not get all sappy and shit." Vince's lip twitched with a hint of a smile. "Fucking lightweight," he muttered, shoving Jeremy in the shoulder. Jeremy smiled back with glassy eyes. I wondered how long it might take for the grain to burn out of their systems, or if I'd be stuck here babysitting them until morning.

I heaved a sigh. When I looked up, Eric was fiddling with the Rubik's cube I'd left on the sofa.

"I still can't believe my chem lab partner was really a cop," he said. "That big, scary Oleksa kid is really that Alex guy you keep talking about, right?"

I nodded. It's not like it was a secret anymore.

I looked at Vince and Jeremy, bent over with laughter on my living room floor. None of us felt like the same people we had been just a few weeks before. Or maybe we were, and we were only beginning to see each other from a different angle. "People can really surprise you sometimes."

"Maybe I should get them something to eat," Eric said, getting to his feet. "Mind if I raid your kitchen?"

"There's some bread and peanut butter in the cabinet next to the stove. And some jelly in the fridge. Knock yourself out."

I stood up, suddenly needing some air. Reece followed me outside. He propped his elbows on the porch rail, staring out at Sunny View. I shut the door and leaned against it, shivering from the cold. We were all tired, and scared.

We stood there, quiet, for a long time.

"I wasn't going to Emily's house to *be* with her," Reece finally said.

I came behind him, wrapping my arms around his chest and burying my face in the warmth of his neck. "I know," I said.

"Is that why you're touching me now?" he asked softly without turning around. "For the same reason you touched Vince? To make sure I'm not lying?"

I squeezed him gently through the soft, worn cotton. "I don't have to touch you. I know you're not lying."

His muscles tensed under my fingertips and he turned around, slowly. I slipped my hands under his shirt, and his skin rippled with goose bumps. I drew him to me and kissed him, tasting relief, feeling warm and drowsy and safe for the first time in weeks.

"Okay," I said, looking into his eyes. "Vince told us he was with Emily between six and seven. You said she was gone when you showed up around seven thirty. Which means between seven and ten, someone talked her out of her window and into the woods, strangled her, cut off her foot, put the bracelet on the bed, took her body to the island, left her foot in your saddlebag, messed with your brakes, and scratched a message on your helmet. Why?"

It all boils down to motive.

"Every other time something bad happened, there was a note. A message. Maybe we missed something."

Reece laced his hands around my waist.

I laid my cheek against his chest, exhaustion sucking the last of my energy as my eyes drifted up the street. So many bad things had happened. Too many. Like the dark void at the top of Sunny View Drive where the lights from Bui's Market used to be. Like the empty place where Lonny's car used to park in front of his trailer.

The fuzzy, tired feeling in my head began to clear. My heart quickened. Reece's arms tightened around me.

"What's wrong?" he asked, following the direction of my stare.

Lonny's trailer. Bui's Market. Bad things.

Things are already in motion . . .

Lonny'd been arrested for strangling a girl before we started getting the notes. Anh's family's market burned to the ground along with the security recordings. As far as I knew, Lonny had nothing to do with the poker club. And yet, I couldn't shake the feeling that these crimes weren't a coincidence.

I pulled out of Reece's arms and threw open my trailer door. Inside, Vince and Jeremy were sprawled over the floor, taking turns draining the last of the grain from the glass bottle, the flask empty beside their feet. Eric sat on the sofa eating sandwiches, barely noticing as I blew past them to my room. I opened my backpack. Dug deep inside. Pulled out Lonny's cell phone.

"That's not the one I gave you. Where'd you get it?" Reece asked, closing the door behind us.

"It's Lonny's," I said, scrolling through the photos of Adrienne's dead body. Searching for numbers in the shape of her limbs. In the twigs she'd been dumped on. In things that weren't there. Nothing. I tossed the phone onto my mattress, dragging my hands through my hair. I slumped to the floor. Reece eased down beside me. "There has to be a message. A number."

Our eyes met.

A message. A number. On a cell phone.

Reece reached for the phone. He toggled through the menu to recent calls.

To the last number dialed.

A number far too long to be a phone number.

I scrambled for a scrap of paper and my chemistry book.

"9875236839892287." Reece read the numbers aloud. It looked disturbingly similar in length to the number carved in Karl Miller's bone. Reece watched over my shoulder as I tested different combinations, scratching out the ones that didn't work.

Until they did.

Until the message was clear.

9-8-75-23-68-39-89-22-8-7

F O Re V Er Y Ac Ti O N

For every action, there is an equal and opposite reaction . . . Lonny wasn't in the poker kids club, and someone was trying to frame him. So what did this have to do with him?

What if this wasn't about the poker club after all.

There had to be something I wasn't seeing . . . something I'd missed. Something the killer wanted me to see.

What if the fire wasn't set to cover something up? What if the fire was set to reveal it?

I leaped to my feet. "Get the flashlights," I told Reece as I pulled on my sweatshirt. "And get those three sobered up. We're going to Bui's."

• • •

It was dark when we crossed Route 1, flashlights in our pockets and steam on our breath. Jeremy, Vince, and Eric reeked of grain alcohol, and I was grateful for the sobering chill in the air.

"Think we should call Anh?" Reece asked me. He looked over his shoulder. Behind him, Vince half carried Jeremy, making them both stumble. Eric took up the rear, tripping over a pothole.

"No!" Jeremy said. "You can't call Anh. If she finds out I've been hanging with you and I didn't tell her, she'll be pissed! I hate when she's pissed." He'd had the talkies since we left my trailer, and all I wanted was for him to shut up. But he was right. Anh would be pissed. And at this point, why put her through more than she'd already been?

"Let's see what's there first," I said. "If we find something, we can call her."

"What exactly are we looking for, anyway?" Vince adjusted his grip on Jeremy, shifting to balance his weight.

I didn't know exactly. Only that I'd know it if I saw it. Because if a message was there, it was intended for me.

Dull music pumped through the walls of Gentleman Jim's and the tattoo parlor, where all the cars in the lot seemed to cluster. It had never been unusual to see a patrol car at Bui's on a Sunday night, since they gave free coffee to the local police, but after Bui's shut down, the patrol cars started parking at the 7-Eleven down the street.

This end of the lot was empty and dark. Reece and I peered around the side of the building. No looters. Probably because there was nothing left inside to steal. We walked undetected to the back door, where Bao's office used to be. A section of yellow police tape brushed the ground. Low enough to be an invitation, or just a reasonable excuse if we got caught poking around. Reece stepped over it and popped the back door open with a quick hard jerk. The frame was damaged, the door only opening partway, forcing him to turn sideways to squeeze through.

I followed the glow of his flashlight. Debris shifted under my feet. Behind me, Vince whispered insults at Jeremy as they struggled to get over the tape. I turned to shush them, and almost jumped out of my skin. Eric stood behind me, his face strangely illuminated by the upturned light in his hands. His breath smelled strongly of peanut butter, and he looked clearheaded and alert. He grabbed my hand to steady me, and I braced for a rush of emotion. Some pile-on to the adrenaline already pumping through my veins, but it didn't come. His hands were warmly bundled in gloves, making me wish I'd been careful enough to do the same.

Vince's face crunched up as he squeezed through the door, widening the opening so he could pull Jeremy through it. Vince dropped him on the floor and clicked on his flashlight.

Jeremy shielded his eyes. "That hurts. I'm getting a headache. And I'm thirsty."

"Don't be such a pussy," Vince said.

"Both of you, shut up!" I hissed at them. This building had already been searched and cleared. And trespassing wasn't a felony. If we were quiet, no one would know we were here.

We took slow, cautious steps in the dark, broken glass

crackling under our feet. The air was thick with the smell of burnt plastic and chemicals, our lights illuminating smoke-stains that climbed up the walls. The interior office door was gone, burned right off its hinges, and when I stepped through it, my heart broke for Anh's family all over again. Reece cast his light low across the floor, throwing cautious rays over the remains of the store. Metal shelves stood empty, their con-tents melted away, except one that had been almost entirely destroyed. Here, the damage seemed much worse. I knew Bao's store as well as I knew my own trailer. This shelf had contained first aid supplies—Band-Aids, ointments, and rub-bing alcohol.

Rubbing alcohol. It was highly flammable. Harder to detect than most other accelerants. The hair on my neck stood on end. If this had been an accident, the point of origin would have been an electrical outlet, or an appliance—a cof-feepot, a hot dog grill, or a microwave.

If someone wanted to leave a message that could survive a fire and the ensuing investigation, where would he leave it?

My feet tapped through shallow pools of dirty water as I continued down the aisle. Reece's light illuminated the walk-in cooler at the end of the row. I peeled the door open and stepped into the refrigerated room. I flicked on my light. The air inside was marginally cooler and the floor was sticky and wet, glittering with glass shards.

I shined my light over the burst soda cans and broken juice

bottles, the empty spaces on the shelves where cartons of beer and wine coolers had been looted after the fire. Not a single bottle was left intact.

Except one. It rolled across the floor, wobbling toward the far wall where I'd accidentally kicked it, and coming to rest against a pile of empty cans and broken glass. It was clear and perfect, and empty of liquid.

It was corked.

I crouched down beside it, shining the light through the glass.

A single playing card had been curled to fit inside.

The door creaked open behind me. Beams of light spilled into the room, and the crackling of footsteps of the others as they circled behind me.

I set my light down. Withdrew the cork. Held the playing card in the light they shone over my shoulder. A nine of clubs. Written across it was a message in blue ink.

Are you clever enough . . .

I knew how the message was supposed to end. It was the exact same question TJ had asked me in a *Missed Connections* ad back in June. The ad had posed a challenge. To solve the riddle before something terrible happened.

Are you clever enough to find me in time?

Was this a challenge too? And in time for what?

Find the missing player, and the truth will come to light.

A terrible feeling took hold of me. I had already failed this test. The fire was weeks ago. Emily was the missing member of the club. And I was supposed to find her. Before he killed her. And I was too late.

Unless . . . I looked at the group, all of them hovering around me, their lights bright in my eyes. I counted us. All of us.

Wiles, Boswell, Miller, DiMorello, Fowler, Reinnert. There were only six members of the original group. But the card in my hand was a nine of clubs. Something didn't add up. There had to be something I was missing. I turned the card over and held it under the light.

The club, it said, *isn't what you think.*

28

THE NEXT DAY was Columbus Day, which meant school was closed. I paced the small interview room at the police station, waiting for Lonny's attorney to show up.

Alex opened the door and gave me a hard stare. I had called him every hour after sunup. Even had him paged several times while he was out shopping with Gena. I'd basically nagged him to the point of submission.

I looked past him into the hallway. "Where's Lonny's lawyer? You told me you'd arrange a meeting."

Every muscle tightened under the hard line of his jaw.

"Court-appointed public defenders don't like to work on federal holidays. And they don't get the luxury of charging their clients by the hour. He'll get here when he gets here."

"Court-appointed?"

Alex stared at me, his gunmetal eyes firing with both barrels. "Would you take his defense? Risk your career?" He knew as well as I did that I already had.

"I have information that might help Lonny's case."

His lip curled with a knowing smile. "Don't confidentiality disclosures mean anything to you?"

"I said I *have* information. I never said I was *sharing* it," I snapped. "I'm here on a fact-finding mission. That's it."

"The fact that you're here at all is a conflict of interest. If Nicholson or Benoit find out, game's over. All bets are off."

"I never anted. This is about finding the truth. I can't sit back and watch them gamble with Lonny's life. It isn't a game."

Alex laid a heavy hand on my shoulder. "Maybe the life you should be defending is the one that was taken." He pulled the door shut behind him, leaving the ghost of Adrienne Wilkerson in his place. I rubbed my eyes, pushing her pale face from my memory.

The door opened again, and a large man waddled in. His thin ivory dress shirt pulled tight around his middle and revealed the silhouette of an undershirt beneath. He wasn't wearing a tie. He looked around the confined spaces of the interview room while he blotted sweat from his forehead with a folded hanky. His puzzled expression settled on me. "I'm sorry, I must be in the wrong place," he said between labored breaths. "I was supposed to be meeting someone from the forensics lab?"

"You're Lonny's attorney?" I guess I had always imagined Lonny's lawyer as someone slick and formidable in a tailored suit. Someone who wore a Rolex and signed his name with a hundred-dollar pen. I hadn't yet wrapped my brain around the fact that Lonny's future rested in the hands of a public defender.

He raised his chin, as if to make himself taller. His beard was threaded with gray and needed trimming. "I'm Philip Vernon, Leonard Johnson's attorney. And you are?"

"Leigh Boswell. I'm a . . ." My brain scrambled for the right introduction. One that wouldn't make me look like a child. Or a flake. ". . . an acquaintance of Mr. Johnson's."

He looked me up and down, starting at the hole in my pocket tee and ending with the black powder stains on the tongue of my sneakers. "Detective Petrenko said I was meeting with a representative from the lab."

"I'm an intern." Philip Vernon arched an eyebrow. "But that has nothing to do with why I'm here," I added quickly.

He extended a tentative hand. I shook it firmly, the way I'd seen Alex and Lieutenant Nicholson do. It was hard not to be first to let go. Vernon tasted sour, skeptical enough to pucker my lips. I pulled out a chair and sat down. Under all that distaste, a dull, dry fatigue lingered. I gestured to the chair opposite me, certain he would take it.

The man stalled, drawing back his sleeve to check his Seiko. The chair legs creaked when he finally settled into it.

"Well, then, Ms. Boswell. Do you mind telling me why I'm here?" He pulled a yellow legal pad from his briefcase and uncapped a Bic pen.

"I need to know anything you can tell me about Lonny's whereabouts the night Adrienne Wilkerson was murdered," I said.

He blinked at me. Then he stood, put the cap on his pen, and began packing up.

I jerked to my feet, almost knocking my chair over. "Wait, you need to talk to me!"

"For what purpose, I have yet to make sense of." He picked up his briefcase and reached for the door.

"Because," I blurted, "I have information that might prove Lonny couldn't have been at the crime scene when Adrienne was murdered."

Vernon stilled.

"If I'm right, and if you can tell me where Lonny says he was the night Adrienne was murdered, then I will give you what you need—enough evidence to convince the police to drop the charges."

"You are undoubtedly aware that evidence tampering is a felony."

"What if I told you there wasn't any evidence to tamper with?" The most damning piece of evidence in the case, Lonny's phone containing the photos taken of Adrienne, was missing. Even if I couldn't find proof of Lonny's alibi, a missing piece of evidence had to be leverage for something.

Vernon turned. His eyes were razor-sharp, but there was something inside them. Something less cynical.

"Go on," he said hesitantly, still rooted by the door. It felt like a challenge. To say just the right thing to lure him back into that groaning chair.

"The photos—the ones of Adrienne—they were taken minutes after she died. They were time stamped, which is how the investigators knew almost exactly when she was killed. So all we need to do is prove that Lonny wasn't there at that time."

Philip Vernon laughed derisively and turned back to the door. "If it were that simple, he'd already be a free man. But Mr. Johnson has no verifiable alibi for the night Ms. Wilkerson was killed."

"Bullshit," I said without thinking. "Everyone has a verifiable alibi. Because everyone leaves a trail. It's the very principle forensic science is grounded in." I pointed a hard finger at his empty chair. "You left a trail without even knowing it. The DNA in your sweat, the fibers from your pants, your fingerprints on the seat back . . . it's all right there. Just because no one is looking doesn't mean it can't be found!"

Philip Vernon smiled. It was the same smile Alex wore. The one that said I was a sad, silly little girl who couldn't possibly understand. "You're right. We might find Mr. Johnson's DNA, or maybe even a fingerprint, at the empty pier he says he visited that night when his so-called business associate stood him up and left him conveniently without an alibi. So maybe he brushed a piling and left behind a hair or a shirt fiber. But none of those bits of trace evidence will tell us exactly *when* he was there. And that, my dear, is precisely what I need to know in order to convince the judge to release him."

I ignored Vernon's condescending tone. "So Lonny went to the pier to make a drug deal, and his customer didn't show up?"

Vernon stiffened, clearly surprised by my candor. I waited while he gathered himself. "The meeting had been prearranged," he said slowly, as if hesitant to say this much. "Mr. Johnson claims his phone and lighter went missing from his front porch that afternoon, not long before his meeting. He didn't notice them missing until it was time to leave. He was forced to leave home without them. According to Mr. Johnson, he arrived at the pier at ten p.m., on schedule, but his associate never arrived."

Because the whole thing had probably been a setup from the beginning. To guarantee Lonny would be alone in a remote place. So he wouldn't have an alibi.

"And he searched his house and car that night?"

"Several times, by his account."

Which meant he might have called his mobile service provider from his home number that very night. Those calls "were recorded for customer service." Which meant there might be a way to trace Lonny to his own trailer, or maybe a pay phone somewhere else. "When did Lonny order his replacement phone?"

Vernon's brow furrowed. "I'm sorry?" He looked lost. Like he'd never thought about the possibility that maybe Lonny wasn't guilty. All this crap about "Mr. Johnson claims" and "by Mr. Johnson's account" and "according to Mr. Johnson," like he'd completely bought in to the idea that Lonny was making all this up.

"His replacement cell phone," I said, dragging mine from my back pocket and slapping it on the table. "He would have ordered a new one the same night. He would have had the number immediately redirected. Hell, he probably paid extra for overnight shipping. Lonny's a dealer. His phone is his lifeline. It's how he conducts business. How he pays for his rent. Do you seriously think he'd just shrug it off, especially right after he'd thought he might have missed a critical meeting because he didn't have it with him?"

Vernon eased to the table, his face drawn and thoughtful. The chair whined as he sat down and pulled out his note pad. He began scribbling notes.

"Okay, so you're going to call his mobile service provider

and see if there are any recorded conversations or activity that can be traced to a specific location the night of the murder." I took a deep breath. Let it out slowly. It was a long shot. By the look on Vernon's face, he knew it too.

There was still time. I could change my mind and return the phone. No one would have to know.

"If the phone company doesn't turn anything up . . . if you can't find another way to prove Lonny is telling the truth . . . ask the prosecuting attorney to produce the cell phone. Tell them you want to see it. I have it on good authority that it's lost."

Vernon tipped his head. "Lost?"

Like my internship. Lost. Once Doc Benoit got the call, he and Raj would put it together and know that I was the last one to handle the evidence. That I was the one to steal it. "Use that as leverage to make them drop the charges."

Vernon tapped his pen on his notepad. "It's not enough," he said thoughtfully. "They wouldn't drop the charges for that."

"But—" I started to argue. He shushed me with a finger.

"But we can use something like this to try to negotiate bail."

"Bail? What good would that do? He'd still be charged. He'd have to come back for trial."

"True, but maybe if we can get Mr. Johnson some time at home, between the two of you, you can come up with something that might help his case. The question is, does

Mr. Johnson have an indemnitor—someone who would be willing to take the financial risk. If we're successful, the bail amount will be steep." And if Lonny skipped town, the loss would be unrecoverable. It was a gamble. A gamble on all I had left. But if I was right—if Adrienne's murder was connected to Emily's—a few days might be all I'd need to prove that the same person had killed them both. And I was sure that person was Reggie Wiles. I just had to convince Lonny that running wasn't an option. Because if he ran, his wasn't the only life he'd take with him.

"He has an indemnitor," I said. The words barely had enough breath to carry them.

We were both quiet for what felt like a long, long while.

"Why did you agree to talk to me?" I asked. He wasn't supposed to be discussing Lonny's case any more than I was. And yet here he was, divulging it all to a stranger on the unverified assumption that Lonny and I were nothing more than acquaintances, even though he'd thought Lonny was guilty.

Vernon flipped the page of his yellow pad and turned it toward me. The sprawling handwriting didn't match his. It was punctuated by deep, angry holes where the tip of the pen had jabbed in.

> Philip Vernon has my permission to disclose the details of my case to my friend Leigh Boswell, of the Joseph Bell Regional Forensic Lab. I authorize Leigh to represent my

interests as an expert witness, because she
is a badass brainiac and she knows her shit.
Please tell Leigh everything she wants to
know.

Signed,
Leonard Johnson III

My laugh was panicked and breathy, like someone had just dumped the weight of the world on my chest. Expert witness? I was nothing more than an office gopher. The intern who'd misplaced evidence from the mailroom of a lab and then blabbed about it. I might as well not even be an intern anymore. And here I was representing the interests of a drug dealer wanted for murder in a case I wasn't allowed to even discuss. What the hell was I doing here?

Vernon began packing up his briefcase. He paused to look at me, thoughtfully stroking his beard.

"You believe he's innocent, even in light of the evidence against him. Why?" He tilted his head, as though genuinely puzzled.

I thought back to the first moment I knew Lonny was innocent. To the way his hand felt when I'd touched him through the bars. I gave him the only answer that would make any sense.

"It just feels right in my gut."

29

WHEN I GOT TO THE FORENSICS LAB on Tuesday, something was different. The whole place seemed too quiet. The break room was empty and the halls felt like a ghost town, everyone silently working at their desks or tucked away in their labs, like someone had cracked a whip. A woman who worked at the desk in the receiving area stopped me on my way through the door.

"Are you Leigh?" she asked with an uncomfortable smile.

I nodded.

"Doc Benoit wants to see you in his office." My mouth was dry and my feet were heavy as I walked upstairs to Administration and knocked on Doc's door.

"Come in," he said in a gruff voice.

I poked my head inside. "You wanted to see me?"

Two men stood in front of Doc's desk, wearing badges around their necks and holsters around their shoulders. They were all looking at me. I came in and shut the door.

"Detectives, this is Leigh Boswell, one of our interns. She was working with Mr. Singh when he packaged the evidence in question." Lonny's cell phone. Vernon must have told the DA it was missing. And now they'd come looking for it. I clutched my backpack tight against my shoulder.

One of the detectives extended his hand to me. I shook it, holding on a moment longer than I'd planned to. I'd expected he would feel suspicious. Smoky with distrust. Or even angry. That he'd come looking for some kind of confession from me. But it was his pungent anxiety that turned my stomach and bit the back of my throat.

The detectives were worried.

"Leigh," Doc said, snapping me to attention. "A little over three weeks ago, Raj boxed up some items associated with a murder investigation involving the strangulation of a young woman: a cell phone, a lighter, a knife . . . Raj says you were with him when he packaged these pieces of evidence and shipped them back to the detectives. Do you recall the items I've mentioned?"

I nodded.

One of the detectives continued speaking for Doc. His voice was even and confident, but there was a sheen of sweat on his upper lip. "One of those items—a cell phone—has gone missing. The defendant's attorney has requested to see it, and our office has been unable to locate it. We believe Mr. Singh may have misplaced the phone. That it never made it into the box with the other evidence."

They were lying. If they believed that was true, they would be angry, or impatient, or suspicious. They wouldn't be so nervous unless they were concerned this might be their own department's fault. Unless there was a chance they had been the ones to misplace it. It could just as easily have been a mishandling in their evidence room. Which meant no one was on the hook yet. I just needed a little more time.

I looked both detectives in the eyes. "I was there. I saw Raj put the cell phone in the box. I watched him seal it up. The cell phone was never lost in the lab. I'm certain of it." It was the truth. Every word. I'd only omitted the part where I took it.

The first detective swore under his breath. The other scrubbed a hand over his face.

"May I be excused now?" I asked.

Doc smiled at me, but it felt thin. Like if I touched him, he would taste worried too. "Thank you, Leigh. You've been very helpful."

• • •

I raced to the Latent Prints lab to find Raj, but it was dark. And the break room was empty. I headed to Veronica's office, hoping to find him there, but she was alone.

"Is Raj out sick today?" I asked.

Veronica sighed. "He's here, hon. He's just having an off day. Try the Latent Prints lab."

"I was just there."

"Did you try the storage closet?"

I tipped my head, certain I misheard her. "The what?"

She nodded. "Trust me."

I went back upstairs. The lab was still dark and empty. This time, the soft blue glow under the closet door caught my eye. I rapped gently.

"Raj? Are you in there?"

"These aren't the droids you're looking for. Go away."

"Um . . . okay. Does that mean I can go home, then?"

I heard a deep sigh. Then the door cracked open. The storage room was pitch-black, except for the walls and the ceiling, which were dotted with fading neon blue lights. The effect was almost magical, despite the cloying smell of bleach. Raj sat in a corner, staring at the ceiling with a spray bottle in his hand.

"What are you doing in here?" I asked.

The blue lights on the walls began to fade. He picked up a brush, dipped it in a cup of bleach solution, and flicked it at the wall. Then he sprayed a fine mist of luminol over the area, lighting it up like the Milky Way.

"If I used blood, it would make a terrible mess and someone might try to have me committed. At least, with the bleach, there's no cleanup. Plus, the reaction's brighter. No sense in making a planetarium with dull stars." He rested his chin in his hand, looking defeated. "Here," he said, handing me the spray bottle. "You want to try?"

I chose a dark swath of concrete, and flicked some bleach at the wall. When I sprayed, the luminol revealed brilliant blue constellations. My breath caught, and for the next thirty seconds, while I watched the lights fade, so did everything else . . . the murders, the messages, Lonny's case. It was beautiful and mysterious, and suddenly I understood Bao's desire to have his own luminol. And Raj's choice of hiding places. When the lights were off, the spray illuminated a whole other world, a peaceful one. And when the lights were on, no one was the wiser. Raj's secret was hiding in plain sight.

"Raj," I asked quietly, "why are you in the closet?"

He cleared his throat. "Doc put me on probation, pending an internal investigation. The police think I lost a piece of evidence." He shook his head, his voice cracking. "I don't know what happened. I logged it out myself. But the detectives said it wasn't in the package with the rest of the evidence when they signed for it. I think Doc would have gone easier on me if the case wasn't such a sensitive one, but the detectives raised holy hell. They said the guy might walk if we can't find it. I turned this place upside down. I looked everywhere. It's not here."

My heart clenched. The stars and spots had all faded and we sat in silence in the dark. I'd thought I was risking my internship when I'd taken Lonny's phone. I'd never considered that I could implicate Raj too. And now there was no way to fix it. Not without getting in Philip Vernon's way. And I needed this plan to work.

"I know. I was just in Doc's office, talking with the detectives. I told them I saw you put the phone in the box. That I watched you seal it up. Doc can't keep you on probation forever."

"Thanks." He rested his head against the wall. "You know, I only remembered you were with me that day because that case really seemed important to you. I'd never seen you so upset before." He looked at me thoughtfully. "You didn't, by any chance . . . ?"

A knot tightened in my throat. A bright curiosity lit his eyes, then faded like a luminol star.

"Never mind. It was a ridiculous question."

"I'm sure the evidence will turn up," I reassured him.

If Raj had taught me anything, it was that nothing stayed hidden forever. And we were all running out of time.

• • •

On Wednesday after school, I shouldn't have been as surprised as I was to see Lonny standing in the open door of the chemistry lab. I let out a relieved breath. Vernon had done it. Lonny was out on bail, using the money my father had left me. It had taken every penny, but as long as Lonny stayed in town and showed up in court when he was due, I wouldn't lose it. When I'd met Vernon to sign the papers, making myself Lonny's indemnitor, I'd given him an envelope for Lonny, with cab fare and a firm directive to come here before returning to his trailer in Sunny View. Before he could pack a bag and run. Vince, Eric, and Jeremy turned in their chairs, and Anh scooted a little closer to Jeremy. Reece sat on the counter under the window on the far wall with his arms crossed.

"Someone mind telling me what I'm doing here?" Lonny asked, staring coldly at Reece.

"Have a seat," I said. Lonny turned slowly in my direction, tattooed knuckles curled into fists at his side. Then back to Reece, some stupid game of chicken playing out in the space between them. "Both of you," I added.

Reece kicked off the counter and sauntered to a chair, a small satisfied smile on his face.

"A word, Boswell?" Lonny glared at me. He waited for me to follow him into the hall.

"What the hell is this all about?" he asked when we were alone. He hovered over me, close enough for me to smell the jail cell he'd just been released from.

"I need your help if we're going to catch the guy who killed Adrienne."

A slow cynical smile stretched across his face. He scratched his jaw, where his scruff had filled the space between his long sideburns and his goatee. "That's funny. I'm pretty sure you just bailed him out."

"You've been charged. That doesn't mean you're guilty. We have time to figure this out."

"Ain't nothing to figure, Boswell. I told you. They're going to make this case stick."

"Not if we can solve it first."

He leaned against the wall, resting his head against it and looking at me with something that could almost be admiration. "You paid your dues, Boswell. We're even."

"We're nowhere close to even! You have no idea how much this is costing me!"

Lonny straightened, taking in every tensed muscle in my body. His eyes darkened and his brow furrowed deep, like he was watching me drown and it was too late to save me. "The lab didn't lose the phone, did they?"

I blinked hard, determined not to cry. "Reggie Wiles is out on parole. I'm willing to bet he was the one who killed Adrienne. I'm certain he burned down the Bui Mart. And I think he killed Emily Reinnert too. I won't let that monster take anyone else."

A slow fire lit behind Lonny's eyes. I brushed his arm as I left him standing in the hallway. He tasted like blood, and I was certain he would follow me.

He came into the lab a moment later, sliding into the last empty seat in the circle of chairs. Everyone was silent. Waiting. Looking at me.

"The club isn't what we thought," I said. "That's what the message in the bottle said."

"Obviously," said Jeremy. "I mean, look at us. The original poker club was my dad, Vince's, yours, TJ's, Eric's, and Emily's. I still don't understand why Anh's family got dragged into this. Or either of you, for that matter." Jeremy inclined his chin toward Lonny and Reece.

"There's a common thread connecting us all. I had thought it was the poker club, but it's bigger than that. We have to

look for the motive in order to figure out what the killer
wants, so we can stop this before someone else gets hurt.

"So let's start with what we know. First, Lonny was framed
for a murder he didn't commit. Then someone dug up Eric's
father's remains, in order to implicate mine in his murder.
Anh's store was burned down. Then Emily was killed and
someone tried to pin it on Reece. Someone blew up Vince's
car. We've all been made victims."

"Why?" Jeremy asked. "I still don't understand what we all
have in common."

"We all hurt Reggie's family. Reece, Lonny, Anh, Vince,
Emily, and I all came forward as witnesses against his son. We
helped put TJ behind bars."

Lonny jerked his chin toward Eric. "I don't remember him
being involved in TJ's conviction. What does he have to do
with this?"

"Eric's father was the one who reported Reggie to the police
five years ago. Karl Miller was the one responsible for Reggie's
arrest. I stand by my theory," I continued. "I think Reggie Wiles
is behind this. He and TJ are the only people who have a reason
to hurt all of us. And there's no way TJ could have done this.
Not alone. *For every action, there is an equal and opposite reaction.*
This is about revenge. And the only person capable of this, with
a strong enough motive to exact revenge, is Reggie Wiles."
Lonny made a subtle gesture, as if tipping his hat to me.

"But what about me?" Jeremy shifted in his seat. "I never

did anything to those people. I mean, sure, I was in the cemetery the night TJ was arrested, but I couldn't even provide a statement to police. I was knocked out cold. I wasn't awake for any of it. I never hurt anyone."

"You did hurt them," Eric said. "You said it yourself."

Jeremy looked confused.

"You were the one who took the photo of me and Emily," Vince said. "You were the one who told him she was being unfaithful."

"But he had a right to know," Jeremy argued.

"So you did it out of the goodness of your heart?" Vince narrowed his eyes. "Bullshit! Admit it, Fowler. You did it to get one over on him. You did it to hurt him. And it did hurt him! Believe me. Emily and I were there for the fallout. Hell, you're probably next on his hit list."

Jeremy sunk in his chair, looking stricken. That photograph had been the match that ignited a string of murders, and now it was coming back to burn him. "You think I'm next? You think Reggie will try to kill me?"

"Not if we can stop him first," I said.

"So what do we do?" Reece asked.

"What do you mean, what do we do?" Anh looked incredulous. "We go to the police!"

"No," Reece said firmly. "It's too risky."

"Risky for you, maybe," Jeremy said, pointing the finger back at Reece.

"Risky for all of us. They'll never believe us."

Lonny scratched his goatee. "Whelan's right. If it is Reggie Wiles, the only way he's getting away with it from inside a halfway house is with help. He's probably got a cop in his pocket. There has to be another way. Some way we can prove he's involved."

"We solve it."

They all turned to look at me with quizzical expressions.

"Reggie Wiles knows who killed Karl Miller. That's why he dug up the body. That's why he marked it with a code that I could decipher. He knows all the circumstantial evidence already points to my dad. But he wants me to find the proof."

"I don't get it," Jeremy said. "If he knows your dad killed Karl Miller, why doesn't he just go to the police and turn him in?" Jeremy looked hesitantly around the circle. "Is anyone else not understanding the logic here? How is finding Karl Miller's killer supposed to bring all this to an end? Presumably, Reggie wants to hurt all of us, Leigh. How is this supposed to hurt you?"

I flew to my feet. "You don't think it would kill me to have to turn my own father over to the police? If I'm right, that's exactly what Reggie wants!"

"But what if you're wrong." Lonny frowned, pushing and pulling the barbell through his lower lip. "As far as Reggie knows, you've been looking for your father all this time. He could be working on the assumption you'd try to cover for him. He might be expecting you to hide the evidence."

"Or counting on her to destroy it," Reece said.

Eric inched forward in his chair, his eyes wide with panic. "Why would Reggie want that? If Leigh destroys the evidence, no one will ever know who killed my father."

"Exactly." Reece looked at Lonny. "Are you thinking what I'm thinking?"

"That Reggie was the one who actually killed Karl Miller, and he's hoping to use our girl here to clean up his mess? It makes sense. He'd kill three birds with one stone. He'd be off the hook for Karl's murder and there's enough circumstantial evidence to make it look like David Boswell did the deed. The cops would be a lot more motivated to hunt him down. There would be more pressure on them to find him and prosecute him on murder charges, leaving Leigh to go to jail for obstruction of justice in a felony homicide investigation."

I sat down slowly as everything clicked into place.

Reece swore quietly and scrubbed a hand over his face. "We have no way to be sure."

But I was sure. This was the answer. The motive. This was the outcome Reggie wanted. It had to be.

"There's only one way to know." I said. "We solve this. And we end it now. We figure out the riddle of the club, and find proof that Reggie really killed Karl Miller."

"And if the evidence points to your father?" Eric asked.

"We find the evidence and expose it, no matter what it is." Eric deserved this much. If my father did murder Karl Miller, then his freedom was a price I was willing to pay. Not Reece's life. Not anyone's in this room.

Anh slipped her hand around Jeremy's arm. *"The club isn't what you think.* That's what the message said. So if it's not the poker club, then what is it?"

"When I went to visit TJ, he said the secret to finding out who killed Karl Miller was in the club," I said.

"Which means the club probably has something to do with Eric's dad," Reece said.

"So what do we know about Eric's dad?" Lonny asked. We'd all forgotten that Lonny had been in jail since all this started. There were pieces of the puzzle we'd have to fill in for him.

"Karl Miller was in a poker club with my dad," I said. "And TJ's. He made an anonymous call to the police five years ago, which resulted in arrest warrants for both of them. Then Mr. Miller disappeared. We know he was murdered and buried under a false front in the golf course at Belle Green."

"False front?" Lonny asked.

Vince rolled his eyes, looking impatient. "It's a slope built into the golf course, to make the game harder. The one they found the body in was being constructed when Eric's dad was brained—"

"Vince!" Anh shushed him. "That's an awful thing to say."

"Well, he was!"

"Brained with what?" Lonny pushed and pulled at his lip ring thoughtfully. No one answered. He raised an eyebrow, like he was surprised we didn't know. "You want to convict a man of murder, you need three things. Motive, opportunity, and a murder weapon. So what is it?"

"I don't know," I said, thinking back to the day I'd seen the bone fragments in the Fridge. "Doc Benoit's been tied up, waiting on some forensic anthropologist to finish the reconstruction of Karl Miller's skull." Eric's jaw clenched and he stared at the floor. I spoke delicately. "I saw the remains. There was evidence of blunt force trauma to the head. The skull was crushed in several places, but a lab tech I work with said the impacting object probably had a small surface area, suggesting multiple blows with a . . ." My voice trailed off.

The club isn't what you think.

"With what?" Vince muttered. "Your mom's baseball bat?"

Eric and I locked eyes across the circle.

The enemy hides beneath a false front. The club will illuminate its secrets.

"No," I said. "Like a golf club."

• • •

Jeremy, Anh, Eric, and Vince piled into Jeremy's Civic. Lonny's Lexus was still impounded for evidence, so he rode with me and Reece in the Benz. We headed to Eric's house. He punched in the garage door combination.

"Do you think they're still in here?" Anh asked.

"My dad's clubs?" Eric's voice was tinged with urgency as he darted under the opening door. "Yeah, they're here. My mom tried to sell them once, but they're lefties. Plus they're engraved. She was asking way too much for them."

Eric led us around the shiny gray Audi sedan parked inside. On the wall behind it hung two bicycles with thick, clean tires, some folding beach chairs, a dirt-grimed shovel with a bright red handle, and a leather carrier full of golf clubs, the heads coated in a thick layer of dust. Eric reached up.

"Careful!" I said. "Don't touch the clubs."

He threw me an irritated look, and lifted the bag off its hook.

"They look normal enough. Exactly the same as my dad's. Fourteen," Jeremy counted. "They're all there."

Vince pushed his way toward the bag. "I thought you said your dad was a lefty, Miller?"

"He was."

"So why'd he play with a right-handed nine iron?"

Eric scrunched up his face and studied the club heads. I didn't know the first thing about golf, but one of the bigger heads seemed to angle differently than the others. Eric shrugged. "I don't know. I don't really play."

Vince grabbed a rag from a car-care kit on a shelf. He raised an eyebrow, as if asking my permission. I nodded, curious.

Carefully, Vince wrapped the rag around the club and slid it from the bag. He handled it confidently, like he was comfortable with the weight and shape of it in his hands. Then he withdrew another. This one was almost identical, if not a bit smaller. "These aren't from the same set. See the engraving?"

We all circled close. The smaller club was left-handed, like the others, and engraved with the letters *K.M.*, just below the leather wrap. The larger one—the right-handed nine iron—was the only one that wasn't. "I think we just found the missing nine of clubs," Vince said.

The club will illuminate its secrets
The truth will come to light.

I threw off my backpack and dug my hands to the bottom. I'd taken the luminol kit to make good on my agreement with Bao, but after the fire, I'd forgotten to bring it back to the lab. I grabbed the bag of dry chemicals, and read the directions on the label on the bottle. Moving out into the open air of the driveway, I angled my face away while I poured the pale powder into the spray bottle of reagent.

"Shut the door," I instructed, still shaking the solution as I came back into the garage. If the luminol reacted with any latent blood on the club, it would be easier to see the reaction in the dark.

Eric punched in the code and the door lowered, plunging us into semi-darkness.

Vince set the club on the concrete, and we all gathered

around it. I knelt beside it and sprayed the head of the nine iron. A bright white luminescence flashed and gradually began to fade as I sprayed a fine mist over the shaft.

"Someone tried to clean it," I said aloud to myself, certain that's what I was seeing. "Probably with bleach." That would account for the brightness of the initial reaction. Curious, I moved to the carrying case. I sprayed the leather bag. Pale neon-blue spatters awakened on its surface. "That's blood. The nine iron is the murder weapon. It has to be. And the killer used bleach to clean the metal part of the club. But he didn't bleach the bag, or the grip. Why?"

"Because the bleach would have ruined the leather," Reece answered. "It would have discolored it. Made it obvious that something was wrong with it."

"And if the killer didn't bother to clean the grip—" Anh gave me a pointed look.

"He might have left fingerprints too."

Anh jumped to her feet. "I'll go home and get the coffee can and some glue. I'll be back in fifteen minutes, tops."

"The glue won't work," I said, stopping Anh. "The grip's made of leather, which means it's porous. We'd have to use iodine."

"We can't do it here." Eric checked the time on his phone. "Let's meet up in the chem lab at school in thirty minutes." He reached for the nine iron. Vince took a step back, using the rag to hold it just out of his reach.

Eric's face was flush with emotion. "That thing killed my father. It was in my garage. I should be the one to bring it."

Vince held it out to me. But one look at the hard set of Eric's jaw and I knew he wouldn't let me take it. Thirty minutes was more than enough time if I'd wanted to get rid of it, and he had no reason to trust me. Before I could say anything, Reece stepped forward and took the club from Vince, careful to grasp it through the cloth.

"But—"

"We can't afford to screw this up," he said. Then he handed the nine iron to me.

30

ERIC HAD INSISTED on riding with me and Reece, so he could keep an eye on the club. I guess I couldn't blame him. Lonny rode ahead with the others to pick up the coffee can, and we stayed behind to safely dispose of the luminol and return everything in the garage to its place. Eric excused himself and disappeared into his house. He was gone for a while, and I hoped he was checking to make sure Emily's foot was still safely hidden. When he emerged, he set the security system and closed up the garage, and we left to meet up with the others. When we finally arrived at the school, the front door was unlocked. We carried the club up the stairs to the science wing, and surfaced to the sounds of an argument. Vince was kneeling in front of the chem lab door, working a credit card between the latch and the frame.

"You're doing it wrong," Lonny growled.

"Says who?" Vince muttered.

"Says someone who knows what he's doing."

"What else did they teach you in prison?"

"Fuck you."

"You too, Leonard." Vince drew the card down too hard, snapping off the edge inside. "Screw this. It worked downstairs."

"Because the door was already unlocked, you idiot," Lonny growled.

Eric turned at the sound of our footsteps. His eyes darted from Reece to me, searching for the club. As soon as he saw it, his shoulders slumped with relief.

Reece reached inside his jacket and withdrew the sleeve of tools I'd salvaged from his saddlebag after the accident. He unrolled it, revealing a collection of slender metal implements. Lonny's dark eyes appraised the row of shiny picks and he stepped aside to let Reece through. Lonny and Vince hovered close, watching appreciatively.

The lock popped and we filtered in. Anh set the coffee canister on a lab table, then disappeared into the closet in search of iodine. Reece and Vince picked the locks on the supply cabinets, Eric put on a lab apron, and Jeremy hunched over the computer on the teacher's desk.

Lonny stood by the door with his hands in his pockets, looking uncomfortable—completely out of place.

"Anyone have a knife?" I asked.

Lonny lifted his head and reached in his pocket, producing a silver blade that made an elegant swish in his hands when he flicked it open, similar to the one I'd seen in the mailroom at the lab. It looked too long to be a utility knife, and I had no doubt it would light up like the Milky Way galaxy if I sprayed it with luminol. I gave Lonny a pair of gloves, instructing him to carefully cut the leather grip from the club.

Knife poised, he paused before making the long vertical incision. "You sure about this?"

The question sliced me all the way through.

If I did this—if I removed the grip from the murder weapon—it was destruction of evidence. Even if we did find the prints . . . even if we found a match and delivered the proof of the identity of Karl Miller's killer to the district attorney's front door . . . it would be inadmissible. And if the match was to my father, I'd be responsible for setting him free. But if the print belonged to Reggie, we would have solid proof that he killed Karl Miller. If we told Gena and Alex everything now—about the notes and the codes and how they tied to the golf club—they would have to believe us. With their help, we could prove he'd killed Emily and Adrienne too. Which would be enough to send Reggie back to prison for a long, long time.

My future balanced on the tip of the blade. But the decision wasn't only mine to make.

I searched the room for Eric. Found him, arms crossed and face severe, watching me.

"If it's Reggie, there'll be other evidence to convict him," I said.

He swallowed. "Do it," he said. "I have to know."

I nodded, feeling the pinch in my gut as the tip of the blade pierced the grip. In a few hours, Eric might know the identity of the person who'd killed his father. Lonny made the careful cut down the length of the grip, then carefully peeled back the curling leather.

As it fumed, I peered into the canister, waiting for some sublime reaction. Some confirmation that this choice—Eric's choice—hadn't been in vain. If we could find one print, if we could match it, maybe we could bring an end to the suffering Reggie Wiles had inflicted on all of us. Maybe just by knowing the truth, we could bring Eric some peace.

Anh checked the time on her phone. She pulled on a pair of gloves and opened the coffee can.

"We've got one!" Anh said triumphantly. "We have a print!"

Vince and Lonny slapped hands. Jeremy put a supportive arm around Eric's shoulder, and hugged Anh with the other. I looked at Eric. Neither of us smiled.

"Jeremy, can you get us back into the police network from here?"

He thought for a moment. "I'm pretty sure I can get in using Nicholson's user ID and password." It was already after five o'clock. Nicholson was probably off for the night. Once he was in, I could use Raj's password to access AFIS, and run a search based on the characteristics of the print for a list of possible matches.

"Then let's figure out who this print belongs to."

Anh and I carefully transferred the prints using the remaining black powder I'd stashed in my backpack the day I'd taken it from the Latent Prints lab. Then Jeremy used his smartphone and the lab's computer to create a digital image of the prints. My breath caught when he projected the partial thumb and full index finger on the overhead screen at the front of the room.

I stood before the killer. Close enough to trace the loops and whorls he had left on the world.

I began to count, measuring the space between them. Orienting myself against the slopes and angles of the peaks of what could be my father's hands.

Then I fed him to The Monster.

• • •

Hours passed. Anh and Jeremy sat on the floor against the wall, her head resting against his shoulder. Eric had collected all of our loose change and headed downstairs to the vending machines for sodas and chips. I listened to Vince complain about the new padlock on the ethyl alcohol cabinet while Reece paced the long line of windows, watching the darkness deepen.

"What's taking so long?" Lonny grumbled, head tipped back and eyes closed as if he'd been sleeping. His feet were propped on a lab table and crossed at the ankles.

"We're waiting on a list of possible matches."

"If we don't get out of here soon, someone will notice the lights." Reece was right. It was late. The school should be empty. We couldn't risk getting caught here. Not with the murder weapon that killed Eric's father.

Jeremy eased out from under Anh's sleeping head. He got up and bent low over low keyboard, checking the screen. "Leigh," he said. "I think it's done."

This was it. This was the answer I'd been searching for. Not the *where* of my father, but the *who*. This was the truth. "Search Completed" flashed on the screen. I clicked "Print Report," and the ink jet in the corner hummed to life. The cartridge slid too slowly, back and forth, less than a dozen times across the page, before spitting the printout to the floor. There it was. The black and white I'd been searching for.

And I couldn't make myself touch it.

Jeremy bent to pick it up. His eyes silently skimmed the page. Then they froze. He curled it in his hand as he backed away.

"What's wrong?" I reached for the report, but he put it behind himself, making me snatch it from his hands. What was he trying to protect me from? I already knew my father's name would be on it.

Only it wasn't.

There were less than ten names. I didn't recognize any of them.

Except one. Jason Fowler. Jeremy's dad.

"Oh, Jeremy, no." A wave of emotions crested inside me, burying any relief I should have felt.

The first slow tear fell down his face. He shook his head. "It's wrong. It has to be." He ripped his glasses from his face to wipe his eyes. Then he stared at the wire-frames, at the small dent near the hinge where his father had knocked them from his face. His eyes lingered at his wrist, over the fine white scar there. The first in a trail that disappeared up his sleeve. "I didn't know," he whispered.

Eric came through the door, struggling to balance an armful of soda cans, candy, and chips. "I brought dinner," he said, his voice fading as he looked at our faces. He set the food on a lab table without looking at it. Without shutting the door. A soda can rolled slowly over the edge to the floor.

"What's wrong?" he asked, looking like a cornered animal. We were all staring at him. At Jeremy. Unsure what to say.

I unrolled the report. Eric's eyes widened and he dashed toward me, ripping it from my hands. His eyes moved over the page, frantic. Desperate.

"I'm so sorry, Eric." Tears streamed down Jeremy's face, his voice thick with emotion. "I didn't know. I didn't know!" He pressed the heel of his palms into his face, like he was pushing back memories. "I mean, I know he gets angry. I know that. Sometimes he gets angry, but he doesn't hurt me . . . he wouldn't . . ."

Anh's eyes shone with tears. She reached for his hand, and he snatched it away, clutching it to his body. Because his father did hurt him. Over and over.

A strange expression passed over Eric's face. A collision of relief and rage. His hands balled at his side and he choked on something between laughter and a cry. Lonny rose slowly to his feet, maneuvering himself nearer to Jeremy, close enough to break up a fight. I caught the smell of Reece's jacket. The heat of his body at my back.

Eric's breathing became rapid and strained. His hand clenched into a fist and I grabbed it without thinking, making him look me in the eyes.

The taste of his anger was sharp and fast and metallic. It beaded like quicksilver off my tongue, revealing something deeper underneath. Gratification, I realized. Sweet and satisfying and complete.

Eric knew the truth. He'd found his father. He'd discovered the answers. He'd quenched his fire, the one I still felt burning inside me. He was not suffering. Not like Jeremy. Not like Anh, or Reece, or Lonny, or Vince. Or me. This moment, these answers, were a gift.

Wait. No, not a gift.

These had been earned.

This gratification was Eric's . . . reward.

Eric was the mole.

"He used you," I said to the broken, angry boy I saw crouched inside him. My mind raced back to Powell Ridge Penitentiary. I had asked TJ if his father was the one behind the bad things that had happened. He'd never really answered, only told me to think about it. That bad couldn't be fixed, but that small freedoms could be earned—like the cyber-tutoring and the video-visitation Simms had mentioned—and a little freedom was all that was needed to exercise that muscle. He'd pointed to *his head. His mind.*

He hadn't been talking about his father. He'd been talking about himself.

He had planned this. Orchestrated the whole thing behind bars.

"TJ used you." I gripped Eric's hand, the truth curling my tongue like a bitter pill. "He told you he'd help you find your father. You wanted the answers so badly, you were willing to dig him up yourself. And TJ promised you he would help you find the person who killed him. That he would help you get revenge if you agreed to do everything he asked. That's why you took the Google searches from my bedroom. Because he had you completely convinced that my father killed yours. You were going to help TJ get his revenge on me, and then TJ was going to help you find my dad."

The room fell silent. The others gaped at Eric. Reece

tensed behind me. Eric jerked his hand from mine. "I didn't do anything. I was only the messenger. I only delivered the notes. Passed along information." He backed toward the door. "I never hurt anyone."

Then he turned, and tried to sprint.

Just as the door snapped shut in his face.

The lock clicked.

"No!" He launched himself at it, clawing to get out. "No!" He banged it with his fists. "This wasn't the plan. I called you! I told you they were here! You're supposed to let me go!" Eric banged hard, again and again. Then his fist paused. His wide eyes drifted down to the corner of the room near the door. He scrambled backward, into a lab table, toppling chairs. The smell of sulfur followed him, and we all inched back, away from thin wisps of smoke spilling over the lip of a bucket of some kind of industrial grade cleanser.

Anh pulled her sleeve to her mouth and grabbed my shoulder. We pressed against the chalkboard behind the desk. Reece dashed over with a metal trash can, and slung it over the bucket, slowing the fumes.

"Hydrogen sulfide," Anh said through her cuff. She was right. The rotten egg odor was a giveaway, but it was already fading, overpowering our sense of smell as the gas spread through the lab. We didn't have much time. If we couldn't get out, we were all dead.

"Get on top of the tables!" I shouted. "Get as high as you

can." The gas was denser than the air. It would stay low to the floor, until it slowly filled the room. Until there was no air left to breathe.

Air. I looked to the windows.

I jumped from table to table and landed on the shelf beneath them. Anh and Reece, Jeremy, Vince, and Lonny were right behind me. The cranks were stubborn and slow, and when we finally got them open, we put our heads out, sucking gasping lungfuls of cold night air. Below, the front door of the school smacked open hard, and a man lunged onto the sidewalk, breathing loud and fast like he was already winded.

"Hey!" Reece shouted down. The man looked up, still running, his gait uneven and slow. TJ's uncle Billy was red-faced. He focused on the end of the sidewalk ahead of him, and ran faster, toward the ball fields and the trees. Home, toward Sunny View.

Reece threw off his jacket and squeezed his shoulders through the narrow window. He looked down the two stories, and swore. Lonny slipped through the window beside him. Vince struggled, sucking in and angling his chest, almost too wide to make it through. He was taking too long.

"Jump!" he yelled at them. "It's not that far." Lonny and Reece looked down and cringed, teetering on the edge and gripping the window frames. "Go! He's getting away! I'll be right behind you."

Lonny crossed himself, then leaped from the window, thudding to the ground with a loud curse. He scrambled to his feet, limping a little while he trained his eyes on TJ's uncle, already halfway across the practice fields. He took off after him.

Reece looked back at me. At the bucket by the door.

"Go," Vince said. "I'll make sure they get out!"

Reece leaned in, kissed the top of my head fast, then threw himself out the window. The bushes rustled and then he emerged, gripping one leg before he took off after Lonny, who was quickly closing in on Billy Wiles's diminishing shadow.

Jeremy, Anh, Vince, and I breathed in the chilled fresh air, heads stuck as far out the window as we dared. One at a time, Jeremy and I climbed onto the narrow brick ledge. Then we helped Vince through. Anh stayed stubbornly inside, her eyes pinched shut with tears.

"Come on, Anh." I reached for her with one hand, gripping the bricks with the other as I balanced on the ledge. I was trembling. My knees felt watery. I made myself steady. Made my voice strong. "It's not that far. They both made it down fine. We can too."

"No," she whimpered. "I can't. I can't do it."

"She's afraid of heights. We'll never get her out here," Jeremy said. "What do we do?"

A drawer slid closed in the lab. Where was Eric? I ducked

my head and shoulders back inside, seized by a cold dread. Eric stood in the middle of the lab, holding something behind his back. His eyes were pleading.

"What are you doing?" I asked, as calmly as I could manage.

He walked sideways toward the door, hands concealed. "We can't get out that way." He stood beside the overturned trash can, his eyes watering and clear streams of mucous sliding down his lip.

"Eric, please! Come to the window. The others jumped and they were just fine. We'll be fine too. It'll all be okay."

He shook his head, wiped furiously at his eyes. "Nothing will be okay. I'm going to jail. I don't want to go to jail."

Anh hugged her knees under the window and sobbed. Jeremy and Vince gripped the sills and watched through the glass, their knuckles white.

My eyes began to water. My throat burned. "You're wrong," I said. "You were manipulated. Just like Emily . . ." It was the wrong thing to say. I knew it the second it crossed my lips. The second Eric tipped his head to the side, his face smoothing over, like he'd come to some resolution. Like he'd let go of something.

Eric pulled his hand from behind his back. He clutched a striker, the kind we used to light Bunsen burners in chemistry class. His thumb poised over the trigger. He kicked the bucket over, letting the invisible gas spill into the room. He looked up at us then. His eyes wet and swollen, they found Jeremy's face pressed against the glass. Eric's lip trembled. Tears streamed down his cheeks. He held up the striker.

Vince shouted and grabbed Anh's hand, pulling her through the open window in one swift motion, barely letting her feet catch the bricks before he pushed her over the ledge. She screamed, and he shoved Jeremy after her.

"Jump!" he shouted, taking my hand. Searing cold peppermint flooded my cheeks and rushed through my veins. We were falling. Then we hit the ground hard. Vince scurried to his feet, pulling me with him. We ran after Jeremy and Anh, hand in hand, until I was drunk on adrenaline and the rush of our fear. Across the field, Reece and Lonny closed in on Billy Wiles. They dove, catching him across the back and slamming him to the ground.

Finally, when we reached a safe distance, I skidded to a stop. The lights were still on in the chemistry lab.

I braced myself for the explosion, huddled under Vince's shoulder, but the blast never came.

The windows were all shut. Eric had closed himself inside.

31

THERE HAD NEVER BEEN BLOOD on Jason Fowler's golf club. Only bleach. I stood across the gravel street and watched as the real murder weapon, Mr. Miller's own blood-crusted nine iron, was found and removed from under a floorboard in TJ's uncle's trailer, which is how TJ had first come to learn about the murder at all. TJ had found it by accident sometime last year, and his uncle, drunk and loose-tongued, had told him too much.

The search was still on for Reggie Wiles. His roommate in the halfway house said he'd gotten a call late last night, warning him to leave town. Police traced the call to Powell Ridge, to a phone TJ had been granted permission to use, around the same time Eric had gone downstairs to the vending machines. Reggie had fled before an arrest warrant could be issued for the murder of Karl Miller on the Belle Green golf course five years ago.

According to Billy Wiles's statement to the police, my father had warned Reggie five years ago that Karl was a mole. When my father refused to reveal how or why he knew, Reggie was reluctant to flee with him.

But on some level, Reggie must have believed his claim.

In the late afternoon on the day Karl Miller was murdered, Reggie and Billy Wiles parked down the street from Karl's house. They watched Karl argue with his wife in the driveway. She was angry because he was going to miss dinner. He was obviously distraught, and said he just needed time alone to think. Reggie and Billy watched Karl load his clubs and a small athletic bag into his car just before dusk. They watched him carry his clubs to the driving range. He hit balls until the country club was dark and most everyone had gone home.

Sometime after sunset, Billy and Reggie followed Karl to a dimly lit veranda behind the clubhouse. Listening from a close distance, they were the only witnesses when Karl placed the anonymous call to the police and told them everything. They listened as he named names. Reggie's name. And my father's.

Reggie was furious. When Karl hung up the phone, Reggie and Billy dragged him out onto the green and killed him with Karl's nine iron.

They buried him that night. Billy drove Reggie's car back to Sunny View and hid the bloody club in his trailer. Reggie drove Karl's, and left it in the parking lot of a cheap motel. He booked a room with Karl's credit card. Then left a forged note for Karl's wife beside the bed. After that, they returned Karl's golf clubs to his garage, but the set was conspicuously incomplete. So they took the nine iron from Jason Fowler's matching set, doused it in bleach, and left it in place of the murder weapon in Karl's golf bag, creating the perfect setup in case the body should ever be found.

But the whole thing had taken too long, and when Reggie returned home later that day, the police were in his driveway, waiting to arrest him for the crimes Karl Miller had reported in the moments before he died.

Now, just four days after we'd all jumped out a window together, we stood side by side in Respite Meadows cemetery, at the foot of Eric Miller's grave. His mother had held a small, private ceremony a few hours earlier. And even though we hadn't been invited, paying our respects—forgiving him for the things he couldn't forgive in himself—seemed like the right thing to do.

Jeremy slipped his hand in mine. Anh held his other. The taste of his sadness was hard to place. The kind that changes the more you chew on it. On one hand, his father wasn't a killer. And there was a small relief in knowing that. But on the other hand, Jason Fowler was no less a monster. He'd just been feeding it slowly, in smaller bites. I had to wonder if Jeremy's bittersweetness came from the burning wish I knew he held inside, that the bloody club had been his father's. That it was his father being taken away in cuffs, instead of Billy Wiles.

In the end, none of the faces of the men I'd seen had belonged to Reggie Wiles. He had never left the halfway house when he wasn't supposed to, and had never come to

Sunny View. I had let fear tunnel my vision, making it hard to see anything beyond the scope of my own suspicion. Making it impossible to see who was really behind the crimes.

The police found Emily's foot in Eric's freezer, and Jeremy's laptop under Eric's bed. In hindsight, I could see it all so clearly. All the little things I'd missed. Things as small as the dirty shovel in his garage or the mud on his shoes the day I'd taken the ring to his house. Small things that meant nothing, until you understood them in the context of his pristine home. Then the bigger things. The fact that Eric had been the one to pick up Reece's helmet, making sure I received the message carved in it. Eric had been the one to take the foot when none of the rest of us wanted it. That Eric had been quietly planting seeds, tossing out ideas, nudging us in the direction TJ wanted us to go.

He had been the perfect mole. Someone we'd all been too sympathetic of to suspect. He'd followed TJ's instructions to the letter: delivering the notes, sending me e-mail messages, and updating TJ and Billy about our meetings and our plans. But in the end, he hadn't only been a messenger.

After TJ was arrested, Billy was terrified. The only money they had had coming in for the last five years were the funds from a small trust account in TJ's name that paid their rent and food and clothing. But when TJ went to prison, that account became useless to him, and Billy wasn't allowed to draw a dime. After Eric's death, investigators found Eric's savings account bled almost dry. He'd been cashing it out in small increments and making payments to Billy as part of his agreement with TJ. In exchange for the money, Billy did TJ's dirty work. He was the one who lured Emily from her room with the promise of a message from TJ. And once he had her in the trees, he'd killed her. The same way he'd killed Adrienne.

And killing Adrienne had been easy. Billy was her neighbor—a familiar fixture in her own backyard. Close enough to abduct her without drawing attention. Close enough to steal a lighter and a phone, and to plant evidence in Lonny's car and in his trash can without being noticed. Familiar enough that no one would remember his presence as anything out of the ordinary when he crossed Route 1 to buy his beer. He'd planted the corked bottle in the walk-in cooler, and left a pack of cigarettes stuffed with a book of smoldering matches by the rubbing alcohol in Bao's store. No one had thought much of it when he set the popcorn to cook too long to cover the smell and walked out. The same way I'd never thought to look behind me in chemistry class at TJ. The way I never imagined TJ could be behind any of this.

But he had been. He'd followed the rules in Powell Ridge. Earned his small freedoms. He'd sent a letter to his uncle, and included one for Eric with the promise of information about his missing father. They'd video-conferenced a few times a week under the guise of unsupervised GED study sessions,

Eric telling TJ everything—everything we talked about, everything we did. And TJ telling Eric what to do next. What notes to plant, and how much to pay, and what information to pass to Billy, who didn't have a computer of his own. He'd written to Billy in the beginning, warning him not to write or try to visit. Telling him to wait for Eric's call. They'd spent the first installment on a car that wouldn't look too suspicious, with a large enough trunk to move a body.

It had been a gamble on a long game, but in the end, the only one who had anything left to lose was Eric.

I stood over his fresh grave, Reece at my back with his hands on my shoulders and Anh and Jeremy to my right. Lonny knelt at the edge of the dirt. Vince stood beside him, his hands buried deep in the pockets of his slacks.

A cool October breeze tumbled brightly colored leaves across the dying grass, piling them at the foot of Eric's temporary head marker. In the end, he could have taken us all with him. He had the striker in his hand, and he made a choice to save us. I wished he'd made the choice to face his demons and save himself. In the end, maybe he saw too much of himself in TJ and Reggie, believing their demons were too much like his own. Maybe he believed he was beyond saving.

Vince patted Reece on the shoulder and headed toward Emily's grave. He walked with his head down, changed somehow. We all had changed. TJ had taken something from all of us. But I think maybe we had all found something too.

The courage to face the pieces of ourselves that frighten us the most. And the power to realize those demons inside only control us if we let them.

Bad people don't stop doing bad things, TJ had told me. And maybe he was right.

But maybe we weren't all bad. Sometimes, good people just make mistakes. Like Reece and Lonny and Emily. Like Eric and me. But maybe we aren't the sum of our mistakes or our genes or our circumstances or our fears. Maybe, in the end, we're the product of our choices. And maybe it's when we hold someone's life in our hands—the choices we make in those moments—when we get a taste of what we're truly made of.

EPILOGUE

LATER THAT NIGHT, I stood on my pillow, plucking the push-pins from my wall. Los Angeles, Vegas, New Orleans, Jersey City. No sense patching over the holes. The universe and I would always know they'd been there. But no sense dwelling on them either.

The last pin put up a fight, and I lost my balance when it finally let go of the map. Reece reached up to steady me. Then pulled me down beside him on the bed. I curled into him, and laid my head on his chest.

His hand found my hip, then my waist. Climbed up my side and stroked its way down my arm, his fingers trailing lightly over my sleeve.

I held the pins over the side of the bed, opened my hand, and let them fall, one by one into the wastebasket. Reece slid his fingers between mine and laced them together. I wrapped my legs around his and held on to him tight.

My bedroom door was open and I wished I could shut it. Reece would have to leave in a few hours, and I didn't want him to go. But it was Sunday night, and Mona was home, playing Scrabble with Butch, and she never let Reece stay past ten on a school night.

"What are you doing next Saturday?" I sighed, already thinking ahead to the next time we could be together like this.

Reece looked at the ceiling. "I probably have to work."

I bit my lip, trying not to look disappointed. "Doing anything special?"

A thoughtful crinkle appeared between his eyes as he traced my pendant with a finger. "Gena and Alex want me to put a little time in with this girl."

"A girl? What's she like?" I wasn't sure I really wanted to know.

The corner of his mouth twitched, like he was holding back a smile. "She can't seem to stay out of trouble."

"Oh, yeah? What else?"

"She's smart."

"How smart?"

"Crazy smart. I hear she can solve a Rubik's cube in like . . . a minute and twelve seconds." The hard, serious angles of his face melted away, and I shoved him playfully in the gut.

When our eyes met, Reece tenderly brushed the hair back from my face.

"What else?" I asked.

"She's fearless, and beautiful," he said softly. "I can't stop thinking about her."

He dipped his head to mine. I closed my eyes.

A throat cleared in the hallway.

My heart skipped and Reece and I scrambled to sit up. Mona leaned into my room, tapping her long nails on the doorframe.

Butch stood behind her, silently assessing the bed.

"What? The door was open!" I snapped, heat creeping up my chest. I narrowed my eyes at Butch. "We're completely dressed and on top of the blankets!"

I was scared they would ask Reece to go. That our time would be cut short and I'd have to wait until next week to taste that moment again.

They both cracked a smile, and then Butch retreated to the living room, his shoulders bobbing with laughter.

"Butch and I are going out for a while," my mom said, smoothing her hair. She looked beautiful, in a pretty new dress and soft makeup, and her curls pulled back in a twist. "He's taking me to dinner and a movie, and . . ." My mother's voice trailed off as her eyes found the smooth surface of my wall where the pushpins used to be.

"It's okay," I told her. "I want you to have a good time."

When she looked at me, her eyes were misted over with unshed tears. She smiled and blinked them away. "I will."

She turned to go. On her way out, she closed the door.

For a moment, all I could do was stare at the space where she'd stood. So much had changed in the last few months. We used to live by such hard, fast rules, each of us holding on to rigid expectations of each other. All this time, I had thought it was because neither of us trusted the other to make the right choices. Looking back, maybe we had just been too afraid to lose each other. But lately, each time my mother nearly lost me, instead of holding on, she'd loosened her grip. The door she had just closed didn't feel like a barrier between us. Maybe, instead of trusting me less, she believed in me more.

I eased back down into the bed beside Reece. I was quiet for a long time.

"You know that girl you were telling me about?" I asked.

He wrapped himself around me, dotting kisses behind my ear. "You mean the smart, sexy one that completely rocks my world?"

"What if she isn't as fearless as you think?"

Reece stopped kissing. "What do you mean?"

"What if . . ." I pulled myself up on my elbow to look at him. "What if all this time, when you thought she didn't trust you, she was really just scared?"

"Of what?"

"Losing you."

Reece folded me into his arms and pressed his forehead to mine. "Then I'd tell her she's got nothing to worry about. Never did."

When he kissed me, I tasted everything we were inside— all our bitter insecurities and the lingering bite of past mistakes. But surrounding it all, there was something more. Something sweet and hopeful. Something courageous and confident. It was the overpowering promise of everything we could be.

Acknowledgments

Writing is a solitary endeavor, but the creation of a book is a collaborative one. I am eternally thankful for the hands, hearts, and minds of those who helped me along the way.

For my agent, Sarah Davies, who is both my compass and my anchor. I would be lost without her wisdom, her guidance, and her passionate support.

For my editor, Kathy Dawson, who knows Nearly and Reece as well as I do, and continues to love them in spite of their flaws. Continued thanks to Claire, Lindsay, Regina, Nancy, and Vanessa. I am so grateful to the entire Penguin team for bringing my books to life.

For my devoted critique partners, Megan Miranda and Ashley Elston, who make me laugh even in my darkest hours and keep me grounded in the heart of my stories.

For the members of Bat Cave 2013, who generously shared ideas and feedback during the plotting and drafting of *Nearly Found*.

For The Lucky 13 and OneFour KidLit author communities, who have shared so much of this journey with me. It's been fun holding hands along the way.

A great deal of research went into the creation of this

Acknowledgments

story. I've taken some liberties in the name of fiction, but this mystery wouldn't be as rich in details, both real and imagined, if not for the following people:

I am grateful to the faculty, staff, and sponsors of the Writers' Police Academy. My experiences at WPA educate me, entertain me, and inspire me every year.

Special thanks to Deputy Rodney Walker of the Guilford County Sheriff's Office for allowing me to ride along and indulging my many questions.

Thanks to John Griffin, Director of the Virginia Department of Forensic Science Northern Lab in Manassas, VA, and Patricia Jackson, for the informative tour and the real-life glimpse of forensic science behind the scenes.

My thanks to Lydia Kang for indulging my dark questions about chemical reactions, Kathleen Murphy-Morales for assisting with Spanish translation, and Holly Bryan for answering my many dubious legal questions.

My heartfelt thanks to the readers and fans. I am eternally grateful for the early support of the following *Nearly Gone* readers, whose endorsements meant so much to me: Megan Miranda, Megan Shepherd, Kimberly Derting, Jill Hathaway, and Kim Harrington.

To the June 2002 Moms who cheered me on from the beginning of this journey, all the way through it, to every "The End."

Nearly Boswell would not exist if it weren't for the encour-

Acknowledgments

agement of my parents, whose support allowed me the time and freedom to find myself and discover my stories.

For my sons, Nicholas and Connor, whose imaginations keep my mind young and my heart full.

Finally, for my husband, Tony. Our adventure is greater than any fiction I could imagine. I'm so, so lucky to share it with you.

About the Author

Elle Cosimano grew up in suburban Washington, DC, the daughter of a maximum security prison warden and an elementary school teacher who rode a Harley. She annually attends the Writers' Police Academy at Guilford Technical Community College, Department of Public Safety, to conduct hands-on research for her books. *Nearly Found* is the sequel to her highly praised debut novel, *Nearly Gone*. She lives with her husband and two sons in Mexico.

Learn more at www.ElleCosimano.com

@ElleCosimano

/ellecosimano